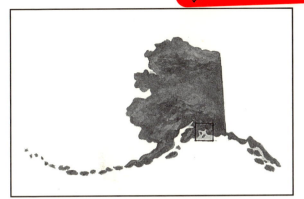

Legend

✳   Shipwreck

●   Cabin

⬤   Town

○   Set net site

〉〉〉   Whale's route

- - -＼⋀   Orca's route to save Sven

————   Orca's intended route to save Sven

▲   Payday Point

··········   Corky's fishing area

KEEP THE ROUND SIDE DOWN

Keep the ROUND Side Down

by TIM JONES

illustrated by SUSAN OGLE

McRoy & Blackburn, Publishers
Ester, Alaska

McRoy & Blackburn, Publishers
P.O. Box 276
Ester, Alaska 99725   98-23

Book and cover design by Paula Elmes,
ImageCraft Publications & Design
Fairbanks, Alaska

ISBN   0-9632596-4-4, paper
            0-9362596-5-2, cloth

Printed in the United States of America
First Printing July 1996

For Barbara

In memory of the Blueberry Queen.

CONTENTS

Acknowledgments, *ix*
Preface, *xi*

1   Spring Arrivals, *1*

2   Sam the Nearsighted Salmon, *13*

3   A Cloud on the Horizon, *19*

4   Sludge at Force Eight, *41*

5   Ciphers and Eagles, *47*

6   Swimming With Lions, *59*

7   Getting Ready, *71*

8   Salmon Runs, *91*

9   Captain Skooks and the Whale, *107*

10   Three for the Blueberry Patch, *113*

11   Prince William and the Blueberry Queen, *139*

12   Gone Fishin', *155*

13   Innocents Ashore, *171*

14   The Legend of Adak Charlie, *193*

15   Smit Tells a Racy Tale, *207*

16   Gainful Employment, *217*

17   The Skookum Alaska Fish Co. and Maternity Ward, *225*

18   The Voyage Home, *235*

19   Legends are Born, *247*

ACKNOWLEDGMENTS

THE FOLLOWING FOLKS had an enormous influence on the stories within:

Sharon Nault, Mike Rentel, Virginia Sacco, Phil Alborn, Janine Corey, Gail Somerville, Patty Friend, Lane Boyer, Vince Kelly, George Fleming, Ray Cesarini, and Jan Kirk.

With special thanks for their technical help to Beverly Coleman and Myra Casey.

PREFACE

To SAY THE SEA WAS ANGRY gives it personality and character it doesn't have. The sea just is; whether glassy smooth or beaten into a froth, the great water suffers from no emotional burdens. All who venture upon it receive exactly the same consideration without regard and those who see the ocean as enemy and, for that matter, those who see it as friend, must accept their treatment equally, no matter what human perceptions they bring with them when they step off the shore.

One might think for an emergency the powers would abate to allow a passage, but the sea greets all travelers impassively. On the day of this passage with perhaps a life itself at stake, that unfeeling sea greeted the voyagers with waves and winds that threatened them even more than what had forced them out in the beginning.

Land disappeared into the driving rain on both sides of Knight Island Passage, leaving their boat in a void of gray. Green, frothing waves marched out of the southwest, lifting the boat to dizzying heights and thrusting it forward like a madman's surfboard, then sweeping under the hull to drop it into the troughs behind, obscured by walls of water all around.

The young skipper fought hard at the wheel trying to take waves on the quarter, angling eastward toward Knight Island, making every effort to avoid the rocks jutting upward from the ocean floor off Crafton Island. Those rocks, standing farther out into the passage than logic would allow, lay covered on the high tide, but just breaking the surface on the low, waiting for the unwary skipper to make a fatal mistake, waiting to tear into the bottom of a boat or knock off some vital piece of machinery. Like the sea, the rocks don't care.

Beside the skipper in the little Cordova bowpicker's cabin his wife sat comforting a newborn child. Riding simply as passengers made them uncomfortable in the pitch and roll of the boat and apprehensive as the waves threatened their only sanctuary in the storm.

Why they might have been in the passage during such a storm can be left only to conjecture. For those who live away from the comforts of what goes for civilization there are a thousand dangers and only the mind to protect one from them. The newborn might have held a clue.

Whatever their reason, the two adults in the boat silently wondered if maybe they shouldn't have waited out the storm. Their trip to town on a calm day took them only three hours, but in the storm, that time doubled and then lengthened again as the skipper had to slow the boat to handle the waves. They'd be six hours or more and that was if they didn't have to seek shelter in one of the bays that cut into the shore everywhere.

The skipper watched each approaching wave over his shoulder, turning the boat slightly to take it on the point of the quarter. Then he turned back away from it and, slowing the engine, let the wave slide underneath the keel.

Land just a mile away on either side of the boat had vanished and with it all of his navigation points. He kept a wary eye on the compass, guarding against the possibility that in the fog they could drive right out into open ocean, or even worse into those rocks off Crafton Island.

The woman lay down on the one bunk, comforting the baby and fighting the nausea growing within her. The baby remained quiet, perhaps content with the motion of the boat. Through her pregnancy she'd worked the boat, so the pitching, rolling world was what was familiar to the child. She smiled weakly at the idea of a human being uncomfortable when the world under him wasn't in motion. She held the baby tightly to prevent him from taking flight, quietly pleased that at least he wasn't fussing.

The storm had blown for three days by the time they ventured out. They'd hoped it had begun to subside, but as they worked their way north in the passage, it seemed only to grow in intensity. Out of the dim, the outline of Crafton appeared off the port bow. The skipper figured they would pass far enough offshore to avoid the rocks, but he cautiously angled farther out to the east whenever the waves allowed. At the same time he prepared himself for what he knew would be the worst of the storm, certain to thrash them even worse as they cleared the north end of Knight Island.

The mountains on the island presented a natural lee in a southeast wind, splitting it so that the wind curled around the southern tip of the island to blow from the southwest in the passage, but with less velocity than it pounded the east side of the island. At the north end the formation broke into several small islands and then faded into the sea. There he knew the boat would receive the full force of the wind. Off the north end of the island he reckoned the waves had forty miles of fetch in which to grow to tremendous size. As the boat entered the open water he also knew he'd have to fight these waves coming from astern, and others coming from the east against the starboard side.

Those waves growing out of the east across that open stretch of water would be bigger yet, and more dangerous.

The bowpicker caught the brunt of that east sea just north of Crafton Island.

Here waves came from two directions. Now the skipper had to watch not only each wave rising under his stern, but sets of waves attempting to roll him sideways. He would take a wave on the stern quarter, then take another, larger, off the bow, each of them trying to gain control of the bobbing cork of the boat. Occasionally the waves ran together to create a foaming V of water but he found, as threatening as that looked, the colliding waves dissipated each other's energy and actually made his battle a little easier for a few seconds. His greatest difficulty came when a set of waves from behind took all his concentration, leaving him to forget for a moment those from the east. Then they would slam the boat before he could turn to meet them.

The roar of the engine rose in pitch each time a wave lifted the propeller out of the water. That fluctuating engine noise, mixed with the background roar of the storm and the snicking of wave tops as they passed, filled the boat's cabin.

Just as they cleared Eleanor Island off the north end of Knight, the skipper fought a particularly severe set of waves against the stern. He'd had to turn the boat three waves in a row toward the mainland off to the west to keep from rolling over sideways, and the waves had taken every bit of his concentration. In the trough behind the third wave he realized he'd lost track of those waves from the east. As he turned to look, his hand inadvertently pulled the wheel along with his eyes and swung the boat beam to a fourth wave in the set from behind that he hadn't anticipated. This tallest of the four caught the boat, lifting it by the stern and driving it straight into the trough. He watched in terror as he saw the bow knife toward the water at the bottom. The long, open deck of the bowpicker, a haven from which he had fished in season, now became his enemy, a giant scoop that would fill and sink him. He turned the wheel slightly to ease out of the slide down the wave, but just as he did, a large wave from the east broke over the bow, filling that scoop and standing the boat on end. From the new altitude in the stern cabin, the skipper stared straight down into the sea. The baby flew from his mother's arms across the cabin and the woman followed. The initial lurch slammed the skipper flat against the windshield where he lay as the boat teetered uncertainly, seeming to question which way to settle. The skipper's fall knocked him against the throttle, pressing it to its extreme. The engine raced out of control while the propeller spun completely out of the water. Then another wave hit the vertical boat from behind, slamming against the exposed bottom. That wave flipped the boat upside down in the water. It floated for a moment bottom up, then air still trapped in the cabin forced a roll that brought it upright but swamped and filling. Everyone and everything in the cabin bounced from overhead to bulkhead to deck until they came right side up again. The combination of uncontrolled racing and the dunking killed the engine.

Now the skipper had no doubt. The boat was sinking. He splashed through the deepening water to the forward deck to cut loose their inflatable raft. The woman rescued her baby from among the debris floating in the cabin and then followed. Frantically the man hacked at the restraining lines with his knife until he freed the raft and flipped it overboard. He took time only to loop its painter line haphazardly around a cleat. He hollered for his wife who had made her way through the water in the cabin to the forward deck. She reached out, handing the baby to him but in doing so, she had to release her own handhold. Just as the man clutched the baby to him, a wave washed across the deck. The force of the water carried the woman overboard. In his rush to save his wife, the man tossed the baby into the raft floating next to the boat. Then he ran across the deck to where the woman had disappeared. He spotted her in the water, yanked his boat pole from its lashing and stretched as far out over the boiling water as he could. He felt her touch the pole, but the numbing cold already had sapped her strength and perhaps her will. She couldn't grab it. He reached farther overboard trying to snag her clothing with the hook at the end of the pole. As he did, another wave rolled under the boat and threw him into the water with her. The waves quickly separated them from the boat and each other as they fought to survive. In its last act, the boat turned bow down, raised the stern cabin skyward for a moment, then slid into the depths of the passage.

In that last slide, the boat released the hastily tied line to the raft, then abandoned the surface to the one survivor, but a survivor whose fate was just as likely to be the same as that of his parents. No boat would come to the rescue in this storm.

Then, as if the sea did have some character, only had needed some sort of sacrifice and now was satiated, the storm began to subside. First, the rain stopped, then holes began to appear in the clouds. Streaks of sunlight fell through the holes, widening them until the sun burned away all of the overcast and began to warm the earth again. The wind gradually fell off and with it the waves. Within an hour or two, the baby floated in his raft on a sea of glass under a hot sun with the islands around him shimmering green again. But, while the sun warmed him, nothing fed him. As the hunger attacked, he began to squirm in his wet blanket and before long he began to cry loudly. No one could hear.

He cried on that sea until his voice turned hoarse. His little voice rasped and his throat hurt, but still he cried. He cried until he exhausted himself and then he relinquished the fight and fell into sleep, warmed by the sun as it drove the moisture out of his blanket. He slept there alone comforted some by the movement he'd come to know as his world. But while the sea has no emotion, no caring, no one is truly alone on the sea either. Forces were moving around the raft, forces that even if he were older he might not have understood.

There came a thump against the raft, hard enough to wake him. He felt another thump and, anticipating a meal, he began to cry to gain attention. A loud "whoosh" right next to the raft startled him and then a mist floated over just as a large black triangle of flesh appeared next to him. Another "whoosh" sounded on the other side of the raft, joined in harmony by another and another. All around him appeared the dorsal fins of killer whales. They surfaced and rubbed against the raft. Then one rose straight up with his head out of the water. An eye almost as big as the baby himself looked into the raft, then slipped back into the water below.

The whales circled the raft for several minutes, the riffles they raised rocking it gently. Then the raft began to move. One whale after another rose to the surface, pushed a black nose against the boat and nudged it forward, always in the same direction, always with purpose. They took their turns, those who had been relieved swimming alongside while another of their number pushed. One whale never took a turn. A male swam out front, his six-foot fin scarred from his many years in the sea, leading the way if that could be possible. Occasionally this leader outdistanced the pod. Each time he returned he made a circle around the raft. As the whale made his survey, the baby could feel vibrations from the pod's clicks and squeaks coming through the thin rubber of the raft's bottom. Those sounds began to reassure the baby as he became familiar with them. Despite his hunger he calmed and at times even responded to the sounds he heard, gurgling happily back to his new friends. Whenever the baby made a noise, one of the whales would rise to look into the raft.

While the motion and the sound served to reassure the child, nothing could take care of his hunger. Eventually he began to fuss and then cry again. This appeared to disturb the whales and they began pushing the raft faster. Whales swam past the boat at the surface, rocking it and sometimes nudging the fabric to make it roll even more. The additional motion eventually rocked the baby back into sleep.

In that manner the procession moved eastward across Prince William Sound, the whales escorting their new charge toward a destination only they could know.

CHAPTER 1

SPRING ARRIVALS

S VEN AND ORCA SUFFERED APRILS. The sun rose ever higher in the sky and stayed longer each day on its journey from the vernal equinox to the summer solstice. Yet with the days tantalizingly longer and warmer, some years snow surrounded them, piled to the eaves of their small cabin while rain fell through the season holding them indoors. The crab season had long since passed and the fishermen who visited them during the winter months had returned to their towns, caught between seasons, putting away the crab gear and preparing for the summer's herring and salmon fisheries. Few boats ventured into Prince William Sound in April and Sven and Orca received no visitors to break the monotony of their weather-imposed prison.

This particular year brought heavy rains even for the season. Spring rains fell day after day, sometimes mixed with snow, washing older snow off the mountainsides in thin, cascading waterfalls that in turn sent rivers of fresh water flowing into the salty waters of the sound where it floated in lenses visible on the surface.

Trapped indoors by the incessant, windless rain, Sven and Orca puttered about their cabin, or read, or fixed things that didn't need fixing, or simply paced, occasionally peeking out the window to see if by some miracle the rain had stopped. Even the view from the window offered little escape. Through the rain they could barely see the mouth of Cabin Bay. About all they saw were the gradually diminishing piles of snow in their yard. Their few ventures out of the cabin were limited to mad dashes to the wood pile or the outhouse and back.

They played cribbage for hours on end, the twelve-year-old Orca giving the old man enough of a game to make it challenging.

When they tired of the game, they returned to their books or cooking or whatever else they could find to keep their minds occupied until at least the promise of sunny May allowed them outdoors. Even their meals became less interesting as they reached toward the bottom of their winter stocks, slowly running out of this and that. Sven with little else on his mind tried to create new and different dishes. Still, salmon was salmon, venison was venison and sourdough was sourdough no matter how many ways he could find to prepare them.

They had read all their books. With no boats visiting, they had little opportunity to replenish their library. Books traveled through the sound, traded from boat to boat, often spending time on Sven and Orca's shelves until they had been read and passed on to the next visitor. By late spring many of the books had received their second and, some, even third readings.

Toward late afternoon on another of their dreary April days, the two had just settled at the table for their fourth Cribbage-Match-of-the-Century that day when a different sound intruded through the din of rain on the metal roof. At first it was so far away, so low and steady they barely noticed. As the sound steadily increased in volume, first Orca sat up listening, then, when Sven stopped shuffling the cards, he heard it, too. Through the constant dripping and pounding of the rain they recognized the high-pitched, steady roar of a big outboard motor growing louder by the minute.

Shoving their chairs back, they raced for the window in time to see the white bow wave of a large skiff as the boat turned at the headland into the mouth of Cabin Bay. As the skiff approached, they could make out two people, one in the bow facing into the rain, and the other in the stern operating the motor. Sven and Orca elbowed each other as they pulled their oilskins from the pegs by the door. They struggled into their rain gear and ran down the beach to greet their first, and unexpected, visitors of the spring.

As they watched, the boat took an erratic course through the bay, casting back and forth in long sweeps.

"Ain't much of a boatman if he can't keep 'er steady in here," Sven said, looking over the calm water. "Don't recognize the boat."

Maybe at his age, Sven's eyesight was fading a little or the rain was too thick for him because Orca saw clearly a red shear stripe along the gunwale.

"I think it's Corky," Orca said, "that red stripe."

"Maybe 'tis Corky," Sven answered, brushing water off his eyelids with both gnarled hands.

The boat changed direction several more times as it meandered across the bay; then the man in the stern appeared to spot the two on the beach and headed straight toward them.

"Wonder why he's not slowin' down none," Sven said as the boat came closer. "Sure is Corky and he should know better'n that."

"Look out !" They both shouted.

The skiff slammed hard into the beach as if it were going to plow right through the island. Sven and Orca jumped out of the way just in time to avoid being hit. The passenger almost pitched over the bow into the water as the boat stopped abruptly in the gravel. Once upright again, the passenger giggled and walked toward Corky in the stern.

"What a nice boat ride," came the lyrical sound of a feminine voice. And, in slow melodic tones: "the birds . . . the water . . . so pretty . . . it should go on forever."

The woman's colors struck Orca first. Where he and Sven lived mostly within the natural browns and grays and muted greens of their surroundings, her clothing contrasted, teal against the gray water, fuschia against the dark green forest, cobalt against the gravel on the beach and loden against the muted yellow popweed at the tide line. Even her face seemed an unnatural white to him with dark curling hair, now wet and plastered to her cheeks, outlining the pale skin and finely defined features. Her dark eyes seemed dull to him, though that may have been more due to her present condition than to a matching personality.

Rain had soaked her clothing, darkening the colors. Sven and Orca could see she had not dressed for the soaking, nor, for that matter, had Corky. The bow of the skiff nudged into the gravel, but the steepness of the bottom left enough water for the boat to float. The two people easily could have stepped off the bow onto solid land, but instead, the woman went over the side into waist-deep water that couldn't have been more than 38 degrees. Corky passed her a duffel bag.

"My bag," she said, stroking the canvas. She slogged through the water to the beach. "I bought it just for the trip. Isn't it smart?" She put it down in the gravel and waded back out to Corky who, by then, was out of the boat and wading toward Sven with another bag.

"You all right?" Sven asked his friend.

"I'm just fine," Corky answered. "Take care of this, old man. There's some stuff for you in there."

He waded back toward the stern of the boat where he and the woman talked in such low tones Sven and Orca couldn't hear what they were saying.

"We got to get them inside quick," Sven told Orca. "I seen this before. They're cold, real cold and they ain't thinkin' right. You tie off the boat. I'll get them in the house.

"You come with me, now," Sven shouted to the two people in the water. "You come in and get dry, get warm."

The woman turned and looked at him. "But I'm not cold. It's okay, really," she said.

"You come with me," Sven insisted and the two waded to the beach and followed him docilely as he climbed toward their cabin.

Orca took a line from Corky's skiff and ran it up the gravel to a huge stump they sometimes used to moor their own boats. He looped the stump and tied a quick bowline knot. He yanked it once to make sure it would hold, then went for the bags still on the beach. They were heavy for the boy, but he lugged and tugged until he had both bags at the doorstep under the eaves out of the rain. Then he went indoors.

Sven had stoked up the stove and the cabin was too hot. He'd managed to get the soaked clothing off the two people and they stood near the stove wrapped in blankets. Sven rummaged through the cabin, tossing out all the blankets and sleeping bags he could find. To Orca, Corky and the woman looked pale with maybe a hint of blue in their complexions. He'd read about this in the book that had been his primer when he was learning to read.

Sven just hadn't had any kind of learning materials for a youngster. The one book he'd had to teach the boy reading was a first aid manual he'd carried for years. So, Orca had received a double education and unlike so many other youngsters, he knew what a tourniquet was before he knew what a cow looked like. And looking at the two people standing in the cabin triggered a memory from that primer.

Exposure.

The woman resisted when Sven wrapped more blankets around her and nudged her as close to the stove as he dared. When she had accepted his ministerings, Sven put big hot coffee mugs in front of each of them. Seeing Corky lift his mug, words from his primer flashed before Orca.

"Don't!" he shouted loudly enough to startle even himself. "Take them away, Sven."

Sven hesitated, "Why?"

"It's not good for them. I read it."

"It's got to be good. We need to warm them up."

"No, it's too fast. Something. I read it. They've got to warm from the outside in. Let me find the book." Orca ran for the shelf. He located his primer and flipped through the pages hurriedly. "Don't bump them around either," he said. "If you hit them too hard you can start the heart fibri . . . fibri . . . well, it looks like you can hurt them.

"Here," he said, "here, read this."

Sven read quickly how when people were chilled, their circulation slowed and the small blood vessels in their arms and hands, legs and feet, closed down, trapping cold blood in them and preserving the warmth of the blood closer to the center of the body. He read how hot liquids would stimulate circulation and the heart would pump warm blood from the inner body to the extremities which opened the capillaries. They in turn released that cold blood they'd been holding and that cold blood shot to the center of the body, cooling the heart and lungs and sometimes killing the victim.

Sven dropped the book and yanked the coffee mug out of Corky's hand, then pulled the other away from the woman. They looked at him dumbly, like disciplined children.

"I want my coffee," the woman said. "It feels good."

"I'm sorry," Sven said, "you can't have it."

"What are you doin' old man?" Corky demanded.

"No coffee," Sven insisted. "You hungry?" Sven looked at Orca, but the boy shook his head.

"Naw, I'm not hungry."

The woman insisted, "I want my . . . oh, never mind. You're all against me, anyway."

Then Corky began to shiver.

"It's a good sign," Sven said, even though the shivering was almost violent. "Means he's comin' back." Soon the woman began to shiver, too, as her body temperature rose in the warmth of the cabin and the blankets. They spoke in soft tones as their limited conversation slowly drifted. After a short time, Sven shoved the bunks nearer to the stove and bundled the two people into them. They fell off immediately to sleep.

When their steady breathing indicated a sound sleep, Sven said, "That woman don't look like she done a thing in her life, but Corky, he shoulda knowed better. Wonder why he didn't bring the *Salmania*."

"Good thing you knew what to do," Orca said.

"You're the one probably saved their fool lives, you and that book."

The boy pulled himself up, pumped full of acceptance. "We did it," he said, his voice filling with pride.

"You done all right," Sven said. "Maybe you ain't just a boy no more. Maybe you're goin' to be a good one yet." He winked at Orca, pausing, and then added, "But don't let it be goin' to your head. Now, hustle and get them bags."

Orca propped the door open and dragged the two bags into the room. Sven opened the duffels and hung the clothes around the cabin to dry. "Looks like a laundry in here," he said when he'd finished. "Wonder what they was doin' here anyway." He looked at the pile of blankets over the sleeping woman. "Wonder what she's all about."

He picked up her bag and found an identification tag. "Miss Priscilla M. Braithewaite, Alaska Department of Social Services, Division of Child Welfare."

Sven felt his own blood run cold, but he recovered before he thought the boy noticed. He rolled up the bag quickly, making sure the tag was inside where Orca wouldn't see it. Then he fell into his chair feeling drained.

"We'll have to take turns stayin' up. Keep the fire burnin' hot," he said, "You ready for that?"

"Sure, I guess so," Orca answered, looking up from the book where he was checking to see if there was anything else they needed to do. "It says here to just let them warm up slow. By rights we should crawl in with them."

"I think they come back past that now. And, I ain't crawlin' in with no old fisherman," Sven said.

"I guess you're right. Tomorrow it says we can give them some warm liquids and soft food. Maybe some bull coffee."

Sven looked at the boy and almost laughed. Bull coffee, indeed. It was a trick the old man had played on the boy one day when he'd tried to drink a mug of Sven's thick coffee: A little bouillon, a little hot water and a word that hinted it was a kind of coffee too strong even for somebody like Sven. "Bull coffee might be just the thing," he said.

Throughout the night they kept the fire going and watched their two sleeping patients carefully. They made sure the breathing was steady and the people stayed warm.

Once when beads of sweat formed on Corky's exposed forehead, Orca took two of the blankets off him.

They took turns, watching for two hours, then waking the other. But Sven sat slumped in his chair awake the whole night. He never let Orca off the hook, though. He always awakened him when it was the boy's turn to watch, but the tag and what it might have meant kept creeping into his mind, blocking all other thoughts and keeping him awake even as he pretended to sleep in his chair.

As he sat he fell into reverie: His mind took him back to the day he'd found Orca and he recalled it as vividly as if it had been the boy and not his friend Corky he'd rescued from the beach just a few hours earlier. He could almost hear the killer whales breathing and splashing in the bay, drawing his attention to the water.

He felt and heard the crunch of gravel as he walked toward the inflatable raft bumping gently against the shore. And then he almost exclaimed out loud expressing again his surprise at finding a baby inside, happily chuckling with the motion of the tiny waves under his cradle. The next years as Orca grew and learned the ways of the sound flashed by in seconds until the cold reality of Priscilla M. Braithewaite shivered him into the present.

"I should have known. Sooner or later they had to find out. Can't keep no secrets, not even out here. I shoulda done somethin' sooner, before they come to me. I shoulda gone to them."

Sven had no idea about Orca's origins, only that he'd shown up on the beach that day, it seemed escorted by a pod of whales. Sven even had gone looking for boat wreckage and asked his friends from town if they'd heard anything, but Orca's appearance remained as much a mystery that day as it had been twelve years earlier.

"Would they take him away? Could they take him away? Or, is she just checkin'. Maybe it's just a school thing. That won't be any problem. He's educated. Did that myself. Was it good enough?

"Where would they take him? Some home somewhere; with neat little rooms they had to clean themselves for inspection and a bathroom down the hall somewheres. Probably some home for problem kids. But, he ain't a problem kid. He'd be with all those city kids, the ones in trouble all the time, in that home because they had problems, and they'd make him one of them. I shoulda done something. What do you do? Where do you go? Who do you ask? Asking might just bring more problems, let them know he's here. Now they know anyway.

"And, what do you tell them? A bunch of whales brought me this kid. Can I keep him?

"How could they take Orca from me, now? He's a good boy. I raised him right. He can read. He can do his ciphers. He can think. Heck, everybody overloads their boats just to bring him books. He learns from them. Today, even, what he learned in books probably saved those two. He eats good. He's took care of.

"Shoulda done somethin'. I got no legal claim. Nothing says he belongs here. Nothing except twelve years. He does belong here.

"Seems like I ain't never been alone on this island. It's like life sorta started when he got here. We been together so long, now, can't remember what it was like without him. They don't know what's good for a boy. Can they teach him where to set for salmon or how to handle a skiff in a skookum chuck? Can they teach him to cook and take care of himself? Can they make him happy, or happier? He'll be gone to some city and they'll teach him all that city stuff, make him live city. Suppose that's all right, at least if he don't go bad. I'll fight them. There's got to be a way. I got some rights, too. I raised him for twelve years. I'll fight . . . You can't fight. They got laws and people and money and if they want him they'll take him. What's one old man got to do with it? If they want him, they'll take him no matter what I do. Got to make him fit the mold. Maybe it'd be all right. I've got to think of the kid, too. He'd meet other kids his age. He sure hasn't had any playmates out here, except once in a while a kid off the boats. He'd learn to get along with other people, not just us scruffy old fishermen around here. The schools'd sure be better than the teachin' I give him. He'd see a lot more, do a lot more. There's a lot to do here, too. Maybe it'd be better. Nah, better off here, I say.

"They don't care about nothin', nothin' but makin' everybody like everybody else. Sure enough they'll try to take the wilderness out of him, make him like everybody else.

"Orca, meet Miss Priscilla M. Braithewaite. She's goin' to take you and teach you about the world. What world? All the world you need's right here. Keep in touch. Miss Braithewaite. Probably wears petticoats and she'll teach him how to keep his fingernails clean. Teach him 'til they take all the toughness out of him, all the natural savvy. Turn him into a lubber of some kind, a land man. Keep your nails clean, kid, I'll see you.

"And what about those whales? They got something to do with him. They was here when I found him. They been around almost everything we do. Whatever it is they got to do with him, they ain't gonna like this. Pretty funny seein' a bunch of killer whales runnin' up a river somewheres tryin' to get to some city school. I can see a headmaster, some stiff bald-headed old guy, 'Mr. Orca, we have rules about bringing pets to school.'

"Why didn't I do something sooner. Fooled yourself, didn't you, old man? Figured nobody'd come lookin'. Less said the better. Well, they did come, they're here and you got yourself in a real fix. My God, what if I do lose him . . . ?"

Orca threw a new log into the fire. Sven started, his head jerked up and he looked at the clock. It was past time for him to take the watch and he looked at the boy. Tired as he must have been, Orca seemed nervous to Sven. Orca checked the blankets on the two sleeping people and came over to Sven's chair.

"Is something bothering you?" he asked.

Sven looked at him. Should he tell him his fears? He decided against it, at least for a while. "Having trouble staying awake?"

"I guess. I'm tired, but I'm not sleepy."

"We only got a little while 'til dawn. Want to hear a story? Might help us stay up."

"Yes."

Sven leaned back into his chair, stared up at the ceiling and then he started. Despite the way Sven normally spoke, a school-teacher somewhere deep in his past must have drummed into him the proper way to speak English. When he came to telling a story, he had a way of dropping his accent and his slang. To others in the room, when Sven began relating a tale, it sounded stilted, but Orca heard it differently. Sven always had encouraged him to speak more correctly than he did and though they lived so closely and away from others, their speech patterns grew differently. As Sven began, he fell into his more formal syntax.

Chapter 2

Sam the Nearsighted Salmon

Sam Salmon was the laugh of the lot. He'd always been the runt of this and the brunt of that and when he turned up nearsighted it was about all the young salmon could stand. He swam away from the school. He watched the other salmon from a distance. He'd watch them and then he'd try to do what they did but in his near-sightedness he kept swimming into things he couldn't see until it was too late. Embarrassed by his blunderings and suffering the insults of the rest of the fish, Sam became a loner. His only friends were the lowly hermit crabs who seemed to understand his exile. Sam even took a liking to one crazy sea gull who did barrel rolls and postulated on existence, another outcast from the flock. But Sam wasn't a true loner. He hated his solitude. He wanted to be part of the school. So he practiced. As he practiced his dreams saw him beyond simply joining the group, but becoming a leader, a star in some great drama, an adventure he felt growing within him. He practiced swimming through shallow riffles with his back showing and splashing as much as he could. He practiced holding steady in a strong current. He practiced turning red. But, most of all, Sam practiced his jumps. In his fantasies, Sam saw himself making the most spectacular jump the school had ever seen.

With thoughts of glory swimming in his head, Sam would dive as deep as he could go, and then with powerful thrusts of his tail he would blast toward the surface with all his might until he broke through the water into the air flying free. Then he'd twist his body so he'd land on his side with as loud a "thwack" as was possible for a fish. His jumpings and his landings always caught the attention of the rest of the fish in the school, but Sam could never see if they approved. It didn't matter. They would see him when his jump would be most valued and then he'd be a part of it all.

As fall of the year approached, Sam and the rest of the school followed their age-old routes toward the freshwater stream where they'd been born. Sam swam with them even if occasionally he bumped into one of his traveling companions.

When they reached their river Sam stayed with them all the way upstream. When they went through the riffles, Sam always got his back farther out of the water than any of the others. His tail always made louder splashes. When they rested in the current, Sam was the only one who could remain perfectly still, and he could stay like that longer than any of the other fish. That he occasionally blundered into the others in his near-sightedness didn't bother him anymore. They'd brush him aside with their tails but everyone was so intent on making it upstream, the others paid him little heed, except when he did one of the things he'd practiced so long and so hard. Then the other fish took notice.

There was this particularly cute Chinook who took to swimming near him, who watched him in his steadiness, who tried to splash as much as he did in the riffles. Since she swam so close, Sam blundered into her often, only she didn't brush him away, but nudged him back a little. The farther up the stream they went, and the closer the Chinook Cutie came to him, the more Sam did to impress her. He found when he occasionally swam into a rock, he hoped she wasn't looking. Once in the riffles he went completely out of the water. And once, resting steadily, she rested next to him and they touched pectoral fins. It sent a thrill through Sam like he'd never felt before even when he flew free in the air on one of his jumps.

In time he realized they were traveling together. When his skin turned red in the fresh water, even though he had practiced it, he was absolutely sure it was from blushing at the Chinook Cutie's attentions. Once he noticed the others turning red as well, it didn't bother him so much. He wondered if they were blushing, too, embarrassed at feeling the same things he was feeling.

The day came when his school caught up with another one. All the fish were milling around in the water, their migration stopped by some force invisible to Sam. He went ahead to see about the hold up. Bumping his way through both schools, he came to a dam, a big concrete thing that had most of the salmon stumped. Sam looked it over as best he could through his nearsighted eyes and decided this dam could be jumped even though the top of it was just a blur to him. This would be his moment, but he'd need a running start.

He forcefully bumped his way back through the gathered fish, clearing a way for himself to charge the dam. When he reached the Chinook Cutie, he nudged her to watch. Everything he had lived for, had practiced so hard for had been aimed at this moment. Sam would jump the dam, not only doing it, but showing the way for the rest of the fish, and he would do it with style. He began circling, gathering momentum. Of course he bumped into another fish and had to start over, but the others were beginning to catch on to Sam's intentions and left him room. He began circling again, building up speed. He circled faster and faster and then he came off the last of his sweeps and powered himself toward the dam. Others watched in awe. The Chinook Cutie followed slowly in his wake. He drove faster and faster for the dam until he was on his final approach. Then he dove, brushed the bottom with his belly and sped toward the surface, breaking water into the clear, joyous freedom of the air. And there, free of all the encumbrances, with thousands watching, Sam absolutely panicked. All he could see in front of him was gray concrete and he had no way of stopping. Sam, at his moment of glory, slammed into the dam. He slammed into the dam and fell back into the water, not with the acclamatory "thwack" he'd practiced, but with a disappointing "kerplunk." He had failed at his very moment in history.

Sam swam alone into an eddy, skulking. He wished everyone else were as nearsighted as he was. But he knew they'd seen. The Chinook Cutie joined him, nudged him. What was this? She nudged him back toward the mainstream, toward the other salmon, who were still milling about aimlessly, still stalled by the dam. She wanted Sam to try again, but how much humiliation could one salmon stand? Sam decided he had nothing more to lose. At least now he knew how high the dam was, that he'd have to leap higher than he'd ever leaped before. After all, wasn't that what practice was for, to learn and prepare for the true test, the test in which you exceeded all you had done before?

He made a practice circle, judging the distance to the dam and the distance from the bottom of the stream to the top of the dam. After one pass, he decided in a rush to try again. He circled, built his speed and then dove deep straight toward the dam. This time his belly didn't touch bottom to slow him for the final jump. He drove for the surface with more might than he thought he had and again broke water into the crazy, heady freedom of the air. In midflight, he looked out and panicked all over again. He couldn't see anything. No concrete. No water. Only sky, air. Suspended almost in midair, he couldn't see the dam. It was then he realized he'd cleared it. He was over. He twisted onto his side and the water came up to meet him with the happy, heroic "THWACK" he wanted. Sam the Nearsighted Salmon had jumped over the dam.

His landing drove him deep into the water behind the dam and as he swam back toward the surface, he felt another splash beside him. Almost immediately the Chinook Cutie sluiced up next to him. They touched again and then turned upstream. Behind them, salmon after salmon, silver flash after silver flash flew over the dam following the lead of the nearsighted hero.

And Sam felt all the joy of his accomplishment even if the Chinook Cutie did have to nudge him now and again to keep him from blundering into rocks in the stream.

"Tell the rhyme, Sven," Orca said when Sven had finished.

"It's not a rhyme, it's just a bunch of morals. Every story has to have a moral."

"Come on, say it," Orca insisted.

"Oh, all right," Sven said, "here goes: A nearsighted Sam is no good as a ham;

"A nearsighted Sam shouldn't jump dams,

"A nearsighted Sam is a sham as a ham.

"There's this old song:

"And he swam, and he swam, right into the dam."

Orca laughed as if he had heard the story for the first time. "I thought she left him. When he hit the dam she just swam off."

"Doesn't seem like we ever tell the story the same way twice," Sven said "I thought it'd be nicer with a happy ending."

While Sven was telling his story, the two had forgotten their patients. When they looked, they could see stirrings in the blankets. Outside the day was brightening.

"They're burning daylight," Sven said.

As the two people became more restless, Sven watched Orca stoke the fire and then start a pot of bull coffee. The boy took his mug and sat at the table, waiting for the pot to boil.

The rustling in the bunks brought Sven back to his fears of reality and he said, "Goin' outside." The rain had stopped during the night and Sven walked unencumbered to the water's edge. He looked out over the placid bay for solace but found none. This was their fight and powers maybe stronger than those in the nature they knew were at work.

CHAPTER 3

A CLOUD ON THE HORIZON

S VEN SAT ON A ROCK watching little but the incoming
tide. In the predawn, nothing stirred, the water lay flat calm
and the normal symphony of their surroundings waited hushed as
if a conductor only had to tap a baton to raise the instruments.
Then an oystercatcher peeped its way across the bay, red spike of
a beak parting the air for the fat little body flapping furiously to
remain airborne. The conductor had tapped his baton and the
orchestra awakened. Two gulls shrieked their protest at some petty
infraction. Kittiwakes responded in gentler but still insistent tones.
Something out in the water splashed. On the beach across the
bay, two eagles fought over some piece of carrion the tide had left
until one, defeated, flew to a shoreside tree and croaked his out-
rage for the world to hear. As he listened, Sven missed the terns.
No chattering screech joined the other instruments. He would have
loved to see an Arctic tern hover close to the bay surface, its
sharply pointed wings beating in a blur to hold it in place until it
dove for the fish it had spotted. Sven saw the terns as the perfect
birds, sleek and efficient, capable of flying 20,000 miles a year in
migration and flawed only by a rasping call that offended the
beauty of the bird. They'd be along in a month or so. He wondered what else he missed. The tide reached Sven's boots and
with the symphony well into its first movement, he stood.

As he walked back up the beach, with the rising sun glowing dimly, fighting its way through the haze on the horizon, Sven wondered how much disruption the day might bring.

Inside the cabin Orca sat at the table sipping at a mug of bull coffee and leafing through his first-aid book.

While Corky slept on, ignoring the growing activity in the cabin, Miss Priscilla M. Braithewaite's movements indicated a serious attempt to awaken. Contemplating her, Sven wondered how his friend, their friend, could have brought this woman to them.

With blankets pulled tightly to her chin, Miss Braithewaite opened her eyes, taking her first real look at their home. Whether she was shaking off the effects of sleep or didn't like what she saw, Sven couldn't tell, but he detected a note of disapproval in her expression.

"Good morning," she said with a hint of embarrassment.

"How you feelin'?"

She thought for a moment. "Weak, I guess, and dull."

"You got pretty wet . . . and cold."

"It was hypothermia, wasn't it? I didn't even know it was happening."

"That's what it was, I guess," Sven said and looked at Orca, who gave him a wide-eyed shrug. They'd never heard the word before and never tried to sound it out from the book. They knew what they needed to know without the fancy name.

Her gaze had followed Sven's to the boy, who set his mug down on the table.

"Mmmm. That looks good," she said. "What are you drinking?"

Sven jumped to interrupt, but Orca got the word "coffee" out before he could stop him.

"Coffee?" She directed the question toward Sven along with a look of mild shock. "This boy drinks coffee?"

"Bull coffee, ma'am," Orca said and that opened her eyes even more. "Sven says it's too strong for him, but I like it fine," he said proudly.

"It's too strong for a man, but you give it to a boy?"

"Yup, bull coffee," Sven said, "Give her a cup."

"Oh, no thank you. I'm afraid I'm not ready for bull coffee, yet," she said emphasizing the word "bull."

"You'll take a cup," Sven said with a sternness that surprised even Orca. "Give 'er a cup."

Orca poured and offered the mug to the woman who propped herself on one elbow, carefully clutching the blankets, to take it.

She sipped cautiously. "But, this isn't . . . "

"Things ain't always what they seem, miss," Sven interrupted her. "Look, Miss Braithewaite, you had a tough time yesterday. I don't think you know just how close you came to real trouble. I seen it before. You're gonna be under the weather for a couple more days and maybe you ain't gonna be right for a couple of weeks."

Miss Braithewaite looked puzzled. "You know my name?"

"The tag on your duffel. And, I think I know why you're here." He turned to Orca. "Whyn't you go catch us a nice snapper for breakfast? Out to the point."

Orca looked at Sven, puzzled. The old man had never chased him out of the room before, even when the fishermen were telling their stories around the table. But now something was going on and he was being sent from the room. He started to protest, but Sven shot him a look that said "go" so Orca dropped his objection and went.

After Orca had taken his fishing pole and started hiking across the island toward the mouth of the bay, Sven turned to the woman.

"Like I said, Miss Priscilla M. Braithewaite, I think I know why you're here and I think we ought to talk private before you go makin' any judgments. I think you better take it easy, too, try to get better and maybe look around and listen real careful before you go upsettin' that boy."

She peered at him over the mug of bull coffee, those round dark eyes that had stared so blankly at him the day before now flashing and narrow, but she chose not to speak.

Corky rolled under his blankets and started to snore loudly, lightening the atmosphere.

Sven laughed. "If that don't beat it. My friend brings you out here, half killing the both of you, turns my place into a laundry and now he's goin' to make it sound like a sawmill to boot."

Still chuckling, Sven went to the kitchen corner and started mixing dough for biscuits and some breading for the fish. He refilled Orca's coffee pot and started one of his own.

Miss Braithewaite sat up on the bunk, the blankets clutched tightly around her and watched him work. "You make the breading before you see the fish?"

"That kid don't miss," Sven said, "If he goes to catch a fish, he catches a fish. He'll be back with one soon enough. Ever had fresh snapper?"

"I guess not that fresh," she said.

"Best eatin' fish there is."

Sven looked out the window toward the point where Orca sat with his line in the water. "Well, will you look at that?" Sven said mostly to himself. The woman, wrestling with the blankets to remain covered, came to the window. She could see Orca silhouetted, sitting on top of a rocky bluff, his pole out over the water and his line descending into the deep, seeking the red rockfish they called snapper. Just a few feet out from the rocks a killer whale had risen, his head out of the water, exposing the white of his chin and looking at the boy.

"Can it get him?"

Sven laughed. "You got a lot to learn. That whale ain't goin' to hurt that boy," he said, "They know each other."

On the rock, Orca watched the whale slip back into the water. He always felt better when he saw one of the whales and right then he needed to feel better. When the whale disappeared he looked back toward the cabin and wondered why he'd had to leave. They had food for breakfast. They didn't really need a fish. But Sven had sent him fishing. What was going on? Just then he felt a nudge on the line pulling his thoughts back to the task at hand. Instinctively he pulled the rod tip up, sinking the hook. He reeled up a red snapper just breakfast size for the four of them.

While Orca walked back to the cabin with his fish, Miss Braithewaite said to Sven, "That was some story you told this morning."

"You was awake, then."

"Not for all of it, but I heard the end."

"There's a lot of stories out here," he said.

"And all of them true, I'm sure," she said.

"All of 'em, just as true as that one."

"I'd like to hear more sometime."

"Oh, with Corky here and Orca, I'm sure you'll hear a story or two before you go."

Corky chose that moment to sit up on the bed, his bare, white legs exposed beneath his blanket. His feet barely reached the floor. A stump of a man, Corky sat almost as tall as he stood, his body as wide and thick as its length, the tightly cropped hair adding to the impression he'd somehow been cut off at maturity. He cradled his head in his hands and scratched through his hair. He shook his head roughly. "Man, I feel awful," he said, "What happened?"

He raised his head to take in the room. Sven stood in the kitchen corner working on breakfast. The woman sat wrapped in blankets on Sven's big chair watching out the window where she could see Orca making his way back to the cabin.

"What happened was, you almost ate the big rock, Corky. You durn near killed yourself and her, too," Sven chastised his friend. "Whatever made you come all the way out here in a skiff on a day like that?"

"Well, the *Salmania's* on the beach gettin' some work done and she just had to come out here right away. Everybody sent her to me. It was clear when we left town, sun was out. The mist come up on us kind of slow-like and then the rain and before we knowed it, we was soaked. Didn't seem worth gettin' out the rain gear then 'cause we was so close."

"You wasn't close enough," Sven said handing Corky a cup of real coffee. "You know who saved your fool hides, don't you?"

Corky's eyes came full open as he took his first pull on the coffee. He glanced around the room. "Where is he anyway?" His question unanswered, Corky sipped his coffee again, looking over the rim of the mug until he spied the open book on the table. He looked at Sven and winked. "Him and that book, huh?"

"Yup, him and that book," Sven said. "I tried to kill you with a cup of coffee, but him and that book stopped me and saved your sorry behinds."

"What book?" Miss Braithewaite asked from the bundle of blankets in the chair.

"That book on the table, ma'am," Corky said, "Orca's first-aid book."

"It's all I had to teach him his readin'," Sven said almost apologetically.

The woman stood up, gathering her blankets tighter around her, looking suspiciously at the two men. She walked to the table, sat down and stretched one thin hand out from the blankets to pick up the book. She flipped through the pages, then looked up at Sven.

"He reads this?" she asked.

"Sure does, ma'am," Corky piped in, "been readin' in it since he's about six or seven." He, too, was proud of his role in rearing Orca. "Reads it good. Many's the stormy night me and my crew sat at this very table and listened to Orca read from that book and, I'll tell you a story . . . " His sentence trailed off under a hardening glance from Sven. But, it took more than a stern look to stop Corky. Ignoring the old man, he plunged into his story:

"Short version," he said, "We had a guy get hurt pretty bad crabbin'. We went to fix him up and guys kept remembering things Orca'd read to them at the table. He likes to show off his readin' and the guys used to listen. Anyway, when we started to patch this guy up, old Mel it was, this and that come to mind from what they'd heard here. When we finally got Mel to town the doctor said it was the best shape he'd ever seen an injured man come off a fishing boat."

"And he reads a lot?" Miss Braithewaite asked.

"Everything he can. They're always bringing him books," Sven nodded to Corky.

"And he understands it all?"

"Enough to save you folks yesterday," Sven answered.

"I'd like to hear him read . . . "

The door slammed open and Orca walked in with his two red snapper filets. He handed the white meat to Sven. "Did you see the whale out there?"

"Sure did," Sven answered, remembering the woman's fear.

"Do you need anything else?" Orca wondered if he would be chased out again.

"No," Sven said, "we'll have breakfast soon as I get these cooked."

"Boy, will you look at him," Corky said. "You musta growed a foot since last fall. You have to duck your head to come through the door?"

"Not yet," Orca beamed.

"Skinny though. Sven, you feeding him enough?"

Sven laughed. "He ain't skinny for lack of food. We're gonna have to put in twice as much this year just to keep him in groceries. Sometimes I call him Seagull. Seems like all he does is eat, poop and squawk."

"He's gettin' big, Sven. Maybe it's comin' time to take him fishin'."

Sven ignored Corky's hint, turning instead to his frying pan.

Orca asked the woman in the chair, "Are you all right, ma'am? How are you feeling?"

"A little weak, but I suppose I'm going to be all right," she said. The spring had returned to her hair and it lay in tight little rings against her head. "I guess I ought to thank you, too."

"Orca, this here's Miss Priscilla M. Braithewaite," Sven called from the stove. "You call her Miss Braithewaite."

"It's nice to meet you, Miss Braithewaite," Orca said. "What brings you here?"

The woman turned to look at Sven as if for direction, but the old man's blank expression gave her no indication.

"Well," she said, "I came to see you."

Now Orca took his turn looking at Sven, but all the old man gave him was the flick of one bushy eyebrow.

"Why'd you come to see me?" Orca asked, surprised anyone he didn't know would make such a trip.

"I came because . . . "

Sven interrupted: "Time to eat. C'mon, Corky."

In two trips Sven brought four plates heaped with sourdough biscuits and breaded red snapper to put on the table. He opened their last jar of blueberry jam.

Corky, still wrapped in blankets like the woman, hobbled over to the table, pushing hanging laundry out of the way as he moved.

"Like I said before, maybe we ought to talk later," Sven said to Miss Braithewaite. Orca ate quietly, wondering. There it was again, this something he didn't understand. He knew he'd be chased out later.

Miss Braithewaite nodded agreement with Sven and turned to her food. Corky didn't say anything. He bent over his breakfast. They ate mostly in silence until the plates were clean and then Orca cleared the table. Corky looked around the array of clothes hanging in the cabin and located his pants and shirt.

"Think I'll get dressed and go see what I did to the skiff. Want to come, buddy?" he asked Orca. Wrestling with the blankets, Corky managed to put his clothes on without exposing any more skin than necessary, practiced as were most Alaskans at the art of dressing in mixed company in a one-room cabin. Then he and Orca went out the door. Sven walked out with them.

"Thought I'd give her a little privacy, time to dress and such," he said. He stayed under the eaves while Corky and Orca walked toward the skiff. Overhead the sun had gained, wearing away the overcast and sailor's pants showed through in places.

Sven watched the two look over Corky's skiff while he finished his pipe, then he went back inside. He went to work cleaning the breakfast dishes, handing the now-clothed woman a fresh cup of coffee. "All right, just why are you here?" he asked.

She sipped from her mug, then offered, "You obviously know something about why I'm here. Let me ask you how you know what you do."

"Well, ma'am, a woman, 'specially one looks and dresses like you, don't just venture out into the sound for your health. 'Tween lookin' at you and seein' the name tag on your bag give me a pretty good clue."

"Fair enough," she said, and then she began: "For almost as long as I've worked in this district, there have been stories circulating about a boy living out here. Just rumors, you understand. Like in any small town, eventually everyone hears the rumors and they came to my office. I'd hear something now and then and there were enough of them that I started to think there was some foundation for them. The stories I heard made me a little suspicious. Sometimes children get lost from the system, don't get their education, aren't cared for properly. It is my job to make sure children are cared for properly. There are other families out here in a couple of places and at first I believed he probably belonged to one of them. But, as I investigated, I found no child who wasn't accounted for who fit the descriptions in the stories I was hearing. No schooling records, no medical records, not even a birth record. Nothing on paper showed the boy, if he really existed, was getting what he needed. As I said, making sure children are all right is my responsibility in this district.

"I began asking questions of people who spend time in the sound. Mostly what I heard were a lot of vague answers. You're a tight-lipped group of people. Eventually the vague answers led to Mr. Netsworth out there, your friend Corky. I found him and talked with him, but his answers were just as vague as everyone else's.

Just the attempt to hide something told me I was going in the right direction. I knew they were hiding something and my suspicion was, there was a boy here and there was some reason why people didn't want to admit it. My suspicions proved correct, didn't they? I'm afraid I tricked Mr. Netsworth into telling me the truth. I will tell you it was like prying blood out of a stone."

Sven looked out the window at Corky and Orca as they bent over the skiff where the had pulled it up so the tide would leave it grounded. His mind raced.

"I'm afraid I also threatened him with a legal charge if he didn't cooperate and bring me out here to see for myself," she said.

"You don't need to cover for Corky," Sven said. "He's our friend, no matter what. I didn't expect he exactly volunteered for this. So, what happens now?"

"I have to make an evaluation from my observations and a home study report about his life and schooling," she said, "and right now I'm afraid it doesn't look very good."

"You're afraid," Sven said, looking straight into her eyes. "You keep saying 'I'm afraid.' What are you afraid of? You come out here and you're afraid you'll have to do this and that, but where's your fear?" Sven felt himself losing control. "You got all the law on your side and I guess what that law can do is take the boy away and you're probably afraid you'll have to do that, too. What're you afraid of? I'm the one could lose, and the boy."

"Is he your son?"

Sven glared at her. Maybe he could tell a story, make something up. Just as quickly, he thought better of it.

"No, he ain't."

"In that case, I'm afraid . . . " she checked herself in midsentence, staring straight back into the old man's eyes with just the hint of skepticism.

"You think maybe I'm going to tell you some story, make something up," Sven said. "It would be real easy to lie to you. I could tell you how the boy was born here and how his mother died early on and how I raised him from there. I could tell you how a fire destroyed all the paperwork. I could get a hundred fishermen to swear to the fact and tell you a thousand stories about how wonderful a woman his mother was. You wouldn't believe how we can stick together when we need to."

"I know how hard it was just to find out the boy was here," she said.

"But," Sven continued, ignoring her comment, "that ain't the way it was, you see, and I ain't goin' to lie. There ain't no lies out here, only hard, cold truth. A man don't survive in the sound with lies because what he does eventually is end up lyin' to himself and when you start foolin' yourself where the natural elements is concerned, you end up dead. No, ma'am there ain't no lies out here. That's the way I live and that's the way the boy lives, so no matter what you're afraid is goin' to happen, you'll hear nothin' but the truth from us."

"I appreciate that, Mr. Kaartoonsen, but your shouting will get you nowhere. I won't be bullied, but I will listen."

"Good enough, Miss Braithewaite," Sven said and then he began telling Miss Priscilla M. Braithewaite, Alaska Department of Social Services, Division of Child Welfare, about how Orca came to live on the island. While the woman wrote hurriedly in a notebook, Sven told what to him was the most important story he'd ever told in his life.

Sven told Miss Braithewaite first about the day he'd found Orca in the raft bumping against the shore, the killer whales swimming around the bay. He told her how he'd searched over the years for anyone who might have known anything about where the boy might have come from, and how he'd never learned anything.

"I lived alone on this island for a long time," he said. "I had life all set up. It was organized just like a ship, everything in place. I went north to Unakwik in the summer to fish for salmon and come back south for the winter. I put up all my own food, bought what little I need from the money I made fishin'. It's a good life for a guy like me. No bothers, just living with the basics. I guess I don't have to tell you how much I wanted a baby around.

"But things happen in life, sometimes little things, and when they're over your life's changed forever, went off in a new direction. A storm at sea can do that. Orca did it here. All of a sudden I had a baby to take care of. Just takin' care of myself was pretty much of a full-time job and now there's this baby with all the stuff they need. But, like I said, sometimes your life takes a unexpected turn.

"So, I took him in. I made him a cradle from one of them Petaluma Egg boxes. I tore up all my old flannel shirts for diapers. When they run out, I used the sphagnum moss, just like the Eskimo women used to. I made him a bottle out of a spice jar and the finger from a rubber glove. For a while there, I was makin' everything, but then when the boys found out he was here, they started bringin' stuff. Wives even made clothes for him. I don't mind tellin' you he was a bother at first. I think mostly I was tryin' to find out where he come from, so's I could give him back.

"I took him fishin' with me up to Unakwik that first year. I got a set net site up there. Had to bolt the cradle into the skiff, so's I could get any work done. Seems like he was always happiest when he was in motion, in a boat; I had to rock him in his cradle all the time. Musta made him comfortable like he was in that raft when I found him. It musta been quite a sight. Here's this rough tough old fisherman out there, pickin' fish from the net and then turnin' a baby over to change his shorts.

"Then when he got bigger, I had to make a little backpack out of some old netting and leather and I worked a couple of seasons with him on my back. 'Course he could walk by the end of that, but there's a lot of ways a little one could get hurt around here and I thought when I was workin' and maybe not payin' so much attention, it'd be better if he couldn't get around so good. He got away from me a time or two anyway. One time I found him playin' in the water. On his hands and knees, water up to his belly, splashin' and laughin' like he belonged there. Funny, them whales was cruisin' around in the bay that day, too. That's why I give him that name, you know, Orca. 'Cause it seemed like the whales got him here somehow. Sometimes I get the idea they're watchin' over him, too. Nothin' you could put your finger on, but it's like they're there and he's there and they got somethin' between 'em. Hard to figure.

"He got me talkin', too. You live alone, it's pretty quiet. Nobody to talk to so you don't talk. Some guys talk to themselves a lot. Not me. So I started naming everything for him. Took a while, but he picked it up. First word was 'whale' of all things.

"He got bigger and got to be more of a help to me. Time he was four or five he could pick fish from the net. Some of them big as he was. Funny watchin' a little kid wrestle a salmon; reminds you of that Captain Skooks."

"Who?" Miss Braithewaite asked.

"Oh, just a guy in a story. Salmon harpooner, back when salmon was really big."

"Any relation to Sam?"

"Anyway, time came I knew he had to do some book learnin'. Books are important to boat people, you know. You'll find people with time on their hands and no place to go take to readin' anything they can get their hands on. See that shelf by the door? That's books we already read. When a boat comes we trade with them, they get new ones, we get new ones. Some books been travelin' the sound for years. But, the kind of books a lot of guys read, you might not want to use to teach a kid. So, I got down with him and that first aid book. Then guys started bringing some out more suitable for somebody his age. They brought learnin' books, too, history and the like. He reads everything. Even can labels. I taught him his numbers. He can do his multiplication, division, addition and subtraction and get it all right. He can do all that." Sven talked for more than an hour, telling Miss Braithewaite about their life in Prince William Sound, Orca growing up, their adventures and the joys they found in their remote life.

"For all the bother he's been over the years, I think it would be a whole lot worse if he wasn't here," Sven finished.

The woman wrote more into her notebook and then looked up at Sven. He had to turn and walk away to the window with his back to her, hiding the mist that had formed in his weathered eyes.

"I got to go outside," he mumbled, "All I can do now is let you see for yourself." With that he went through the doorway and down the beach to where Orca and Corky worked on the skiff.

Miss Braithewaite sat for a long time in silence, the notebook open in her lap, absorbing what she had just heard. She stood and poured herself another cup of coffee, then walked to the doorway from where she could see the three of them working, repairing the damage from Corky's collision with the beach the day before.

When they finished, they stood back to admire their work. Miss Braithewaite heard Sven say, "Look here, it's almost lunch. We got some soup all ready to heat. What say we run up and have some?"

She turned quickly and grabbed her notebook, sliding it into her blankets. By the time they reached the cabin she was taking down the rest of her clothing that had been hanging around the room.

"How about some soup, Miss Braithewaite?" Orca asked as Sven hoisted a two-handled pot onto the stove. "Take a little while to heat."

"That sounds good," she said. "I seem to be hungry all the time today. What kind is it?"

"We call it relentless soup," Orca said.

"Hard to say just what kind it is," Sven added. "Good you're hungry. Means your strength wants to come back."

"Relentless soup?" she asked.

"Yeah, it keeps goin' on and on," Corky said. "I been eatin' it for five or six years now. Same soup, it just changes a little day to day."

Miss Braithewaite walked to the stove and leaned over the pot. "Relentless soup," she said, sniffing.

"We just keep adding a little to it every day after dinner. Leftovers, you know," Sven said, "Can't waste nothin' out here if we can help it."

Shortly they sat down at the table again and Sven filled bowls with relentless soup. Miss Braithewaite picked at hers for a time until the hunger overcame her reluctance and she dug into it just like the rest of them.

When they'd finished, Sven said to Orca. "Tell you what. Tide's almost out and we've got a real low one today. Whyn't you take Miss Braithewaite and show her the beach. Take her over there to Outside Bay and see what you can find." He turned to the woman. "You feel up to a little hike?"

"I guess so," she said.

"Good," Sven said and turned back to Orca. "Take a bucket. See what you can find maybe we could eat for dinner. You got some rubber boots?" he asked Miss Braithewaite.

She looked to Corky. "I got some for you," he said, "maybe a little big."

"Wear some extra socks," Sven told her, and the two men began outfitting the woman as best they could for a hike along the island's beaches. When she had her outfit, Sven pulled her over into the kitchen, she tromping along behind him in her too-big boots.

"One thing," he said quietly with a tone of warning, "Ask him all the questions you want. He's a good kid and he'll answer you best he can. But, don't do no tellin'.' If he asks you, let him know something about why you're here, but please, don't tell him what could happen. If it comes to that, then I'm the one should tell him. I'm trustin' you enough to let you go off alone with him. After all, we are lookin' out for what's best for the boy, aren't we? Please, like I told you this mornin', don't go upsettin' that boy."

She looked up at him and agreed with her eyes.

Orca came back with his bucket. "Ready?" he asked.

"Sure," she said and galumphed out the door after him. Sven and Corky laughed at her efforts to walk in the man-sized boots.

"Bet they don't get too far like that," Corky chuckled.

Orca and Miss Braithewaite headed along a path worn through the snow to the creek where the Cabin Bay dwellers lifted their water. The rains already had melted away much of the snow and the boy found easier going than he'd expected when they reached a meadow higher on the hill behind the cabin. He'd been worried they might have had to go back for snowshoes. The sun had burned off the rest of the overcast and they walked under a clear, blue sky.

Sven hollered after them, "Should be some new fiddleheads. Bring a bunch back."

"What are fiddleheads?" Miss Braithewaite asked Orca.

"They're ferns, ma'am. When they first come up they're curled over like the top of a violin. Later they uncoil and they're not so good, but when they're coiled they make real good greens."

"Where do you find them?"

"They won't be out here in the meadow," he said. "They grow in the trees where there's less sunlight. Over there where the path goes into the woods. It's pretty early for them yet. Might be some, though."

She followed the boy toward the tree line, moving slower in the unfamiliar boots over unfamiliar ground. Orca, who'd never walked on an even surface in his life, for even the floor in their old cabin had its peaks and valleys, had to stop occasionally and wait for her to catch him. They ducked into the tunnel the trees made of the path and walked through deep woods for about half a mile. Orca pointed out the fiddleheads poking through the ground along the path. "We'll get them on the way back," he said. They emerged from the trees into another meadow, this one brown, all the snow gone from the slope exposed to the southwest. The meadow overlooked a bay so placid reflections on the water exactly mirrored the trees along the shore. They walked across the meadow, through some deeper grass, then dropped down a short, steep tidal bank. Orca scrambled across sharp rocks to the gravel beach while Miss Braithewaite felt her way through the rocks more carefully.

By the time she reached Orca, he was hunched over on a gravel bar that the tide eventually would cover to make an island of the tree-covered rock in front of him. She was glad for the chance to stop and rest.

"What did you find?" she asked.

"Just some old bones," he said. "Look." He showed her two vertebrae and a thin rib bone.

"What do you think they're from?" she asked.

"I don't know. Maybe a seal or an otter."

"Look. There's more," she said. They looked down the short gravel bar and saw white spots all along it, the color of the bleached bones they held in their hands.

"Here's some more vertebrae," Miss Braithewaite said and she picked up four more bones, brushing sand away. "They're part of the backbone."

Orca found three more and they laid them out in order of size. "Let's see if we can put it together," he said, and the two of them began digging along the beach, collecting bones as they went, bringing them to a growing pile next to the line of vertebrae.

Before long they had picked the short beach clean of all the bones they could find. Then they sat down next to the pile and began piecing together the skeleton.

"These all have to be ribs," she said, separating bones from the pile. She laid them out in the gravel according to size next to the backbone. "This one's a scapula," she said.

"A shoulder blade, right?" Orca asked. They put the flat bone near the upper end of the line of ribs and vertebrae.

"These smaller, fine bones must be part of the feet or flippers or whatever," she said as they tried to organize the myriad of tiny bones into some sort of order. "Look, here's the pelvis. Now maybe we can find the hind legs."

"I wish we had the skull," Orca said, "then maybe we could figure out what it was. It looks too big for an otter." He walked over to the water's edge. "Look," he called, "there's some more bones out in the water." He took off his boots and socks, rolled up his pants and waded into the bay. Miss Braithewaite shivered at the memory it raised. Orca reached down into the water and pulled up bones until his hands were full. He waded back and gave them to her. "There's a few more. Wait a minute." He waded back. He spotted a rounded piece of bone, covered mostly by the fine gravel and mud of the bottom. He dug away the covering. "I found the skull," he shouted. "It's got to be a seal." He dug deeper looking for the lower jawbone but it wasn't there.

Orca sloshed out of the water and the two took their pile of new bones with the special prize up the beach to where they had been working. They set them down and began fitting in the new pieces.

"I used to love doing jigsaw puzzles when I was a girl," Miss Braithewaite said.

"What's a jigsaw puzzle?"

"Hmm. It's a little like this only the pieces fit together better. They take a picture and put it on a board. They cut it into pieces with crazy shapes. The idea is you take all the pieces and put the picture back together."

"I've never seen one," Orca said.

"When I get back I'll send you a couple. It might be something for you and Sven to do when you're cooped up in the cabin."

Then she turned back to the pile of bones. "Let's see, the skull has to go here, but some of these other bones don't seem to go where we had them." Orca and Miss Braithewaite bent over their task, piecing together the rest of the seal skeleton where they could. In their concentration they lost track of time, concerned only with connecting the right bones to reform the seal that nature in some way had dismantled. They chatted while they worked but took no notice of the surroundings until the tide crept to their boots. The flood strained to cover the skeleton they'd built.

Miss Braithewaite stood and looked at it. "I'm afraid we're about to lose our jigsaw puzzle."

Orca took a stick and drew the outline of a seal around the skeleton in the gravel. "We finished it, anyway," he said. "What do you do with puzzles when you're done with them?"

"I'm going to take the skull," Miss Braithewaite said. "I have a friend in town who's an artist. She uses skulls to help her with the shapes of heads on the animals she paints." She picked up the bone and put it into the pocket of her jacket. Orca grabbed the bucket and looked toward the sun, which was dipping toward the southwestern mountain ridges. "We'd better get going, I think."

When they reached the tunnel in the woods, they quickly filled the bucket with fiddleheads and then walked across the meadow back to the cabin.

"Well, the explorers are back," Sven said as they opened the door. "Welcome home."

"Hi, Sven," Orca greeted him.

"How was your walk?" Sven asked, searching both their faces for some hint of what might have happened.

"We had a good time," Miss Braithewaite told him, offering no answer to his unspoken question.

"We put together a jigsaw puzzle, Sven," Orca said.

Sven looked at Miss Braithewaite. "Where'd you find a jigsaw puzzle out there?"

"We found a group of bones on the beach," she said.

"It was a seal skeleton and we put it together," Orca added.

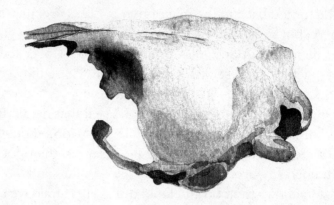

Corky laughed and winked at Sven. "If that don't beat all. Here us fishermen do everything we can to get rid of seals 'cause they rip up nets and rip up fish, and you two go puttin' one back together."

Sven joined the mirth. "Did he swim off when you was done?"

Orca ignored him. "We got a bucket of fiddleheads."

"Great," Sven said. "We got a real surprise for you. Me'n Corky went out and pulled a crab pot while you was gone and we got a couple of nice king crabs."

"Top of that," Corky added, "we got a fair-sized halibut on the ground line. We're gonna feast."

"Can I help with anything?" Miss Braithewaite asked.

"No thanks," Sven said. "We got 'er under control. Maybe you could use a little rest. Like I said, it takes a while before you're full over the kind of chill you got yesterday."

"I'm not really tired. Maybe I could talk Orca into reading me something."

Sven hesitated. He wasn't sure he wanted to see Orca tested by this woman.

Before he could speak, Corky said, "I've got just the thing." He started rummaging in his duffel. "You remember that Jones, used to be around?"

"Yeah, drove those tour boats."

"We call them puker boats," Orca chimed.

"That's the one. I was looking for stuff to bring and thumbed through this magazine and what do you know there's this article that Jones wrote."

Corky pulled a copy of Under Sail Magazine from among the clothes and other duffel he'd stuffed back into his bag.

Miss Braithewaite said, "That would be good," knowing Orca couldn't possibly have read the magazine before that moment.

"All right," Sven agreed, "Let's hear him read."

Corky thumbed through the magazine until he found the article. "There's a picture of him and everything. It's him all right. Kind of a funny story. Here."

He handed the opened magazine to Orca.

The boy scanned the pages for a moment and then began to read:

CHAPTER 4

SLUDGE AT FORCE EIGHT

Hove to in a gale. The wind gusted to 45 and 50. Waves organized into mountain ranges marched by, their blue slopes topped with foaming snowcaps. A storm jib sail stood rigid, resisting the wind aft where we'd hanked the sail up the backstay. The wheel was tied hard over and together the sail and the rudder drove the bow into the waves at their tops and let the boat roll sickeningly broadside in the troughs.

We'd been hove to since the evening before. The storm wasn't so bad we couldn't have gone on, but it came straight at us from the direction we were trying to go which was to be expected since we were bucking the prevailing weather on a straight shot from Cape Flattery off Seattle to Honolulu. As winds blew us off course, at first we joked about going to Japan or Shemya in the Aleutian Islands instead of balmy Hawaii. But, after a day, the jokes weren't funny any more. We couldn't even listen to Jimmy Buffett tell us how beautiful it was because every time the boat heeled too far to starboard, the player ejected the tape.

All the ports to the dorades had been closed because every once in a while parts of a wave decided to tap dance across the deck, slopping sea water into those little ventilators and dripping it into the cabin. Five of us in the crew wavered between motion sickness and hunger. The air was too stuffy below decks and too wet in the cockpit. We were going nowhere at best, backwards at worst. Position approximate: 31 degrees something north, 140 something west and losing ground by the hour.

After more than a day, the hunger became more important than the chance of illness. But what to make? The cookbooks. Like any yacht, this one had a library of them and I searched for a section titled "Bland." Where were the recipes for those days when everybody's almost sick and all they need is a lump of something in their stomachs from which to draw energy and stave off the other lumps higher in the throat? None of the cookbooks have a section called "Bland." Instead there are thousands of ways to cook thousands of things in a fully stocked kitchen using every spice and condiment that's ever traveled this very same route in the hold of some square-rigged ship. Spices were out. We didn't have the full stock from the gourmet shop down the block and even if we did, the jars probably would have been broken and spilling their smelly contents into some exotic bilge water soup. Didn't any of these sea cooks ever go to sea? We needed something solid, unpretentious, inoffensive that could be cooked in one pot on a swinging stove while the cook on his knees prayed to Neptune that he hadn't invented a new wallpaper color. The dockside chefs who wrote cookbooks were no help.

I went to the galley to look for inspiration. I recalled the morning before, when I was at the helm and on an unexpected lurch of the boat saw Illahee Mike's omelet fly across the companionway, hit the bulkhead and drip to the cabin sole. Mike followed the omelet and slammed into the bulkhead like he'd been stood up by a linebacker. I strapped myself to the safety bar, chained into the galley like some dissatisfied woman yearning for liberation.

I flipped open the refrigerator, which now more than halfway through the trip was not even much of a cooler, and dug until I found a package of hamburger, still partially frozen. Just before the lid slammed down on my hand, I pulled out the brownish red package and dropped it, paper and all, into the biggest pot I could find.

In the dry stores locker I watched a package of macaroni slide by until it was out of sight. Inspiration! Sludge, slumgullion, goulash. Bland, at least if you left out the spices which we didn't have anyway. One pot. Go for it. I grabbed the macaroni after it rounded the mark and slid along the windward leg. The canned goods in the next locker rearranged themselves according to the roll of the boat. They'd all stack up on one side of the cabinet, then with the pitch, they'd roll across the shelf and pile up on the other side. I watched the waves pass before me until a couple of cans of tomato sauce surfaced at the top of a breaker and I grabbed them. Now I had the major ingredients and not one among them would make anybody sick but it still would be filling.

I didn't even bother with boiling the macaroni. Once the hamburger was brown (I did take the paper off) I dumped the sauce and macaroni in with it. The pasta would soften sooner or later. I could hang in there, stirring, chained to the stove until it finished. So I thought.

Another Mike, this one prone to vegetarianism, decided this would be the perfect time for him to produce a side dish. Before I could even know what he was doing, he'd reached behind me and lighted another burner and put a pan on it, filled with butter and sliced onions. He mumbled something about pouring it over rice and then ran for a bunk. I'd been blindsided. I looked at this pan full of onions and butter and inched away toward the sink as far as the safety strap would allow, trapped in the stuffy cabin, chained to the very implement that even now was heating this alien pan and its contents. Worse, I had to hold the pan to keep it from following Illahee Mike's omelet.

As the butter warmed and melted and transferred its heat to the onions, I leaned as far over the sink to my left as I could. I chewed on a piece of bread and stared with growing horror at this bubbling yellow mess growing on my stove as it swung with the roll of the boat. So far, so good. I kept stirring my sludge, taking care to keep my nose as far as possible from the other pan, but to no avail. The third Mike in our crew found something in a magazine he wanted to show me. Leaning back against the strap, I inched to my right toward the far side of the galley where I could lean over the refrigerator to see what he'd found so fascinating.

That worked all right until I turned to go back. The boat lurched on a wave, I reached and bent to steady myself and there I was, hunched over, full faced, staring into an open frying pan of bubbling butter and browning, translucent onions. I caught my breath but I don't think there was any oxygen in it, just those onions complemented by the rich smoke from the butter. "Mike!" I screamed, "Mike!" That was the easy part. With three Mikes on board you could always get a response. Illahee Mike ran over while I struggled with the snap on my safety strap. My sinuses were full of onion and butter all the way down to my intestines. It was serious panic time.

"What's the matter?" Illahee Mike asked.

"Unhook me quick," I almost choked in his ear.

"Why?" he asked as he bent over to unhook the devil snap. Then he found out. In leaning, he came too close to the vicious pan on the stove.

"Oh, no," was all he could say as he covered his nose and mouth with his hand. The strap fell free. We fought each other out of the tiny galley, through the short companionway and up the ladder, bursting into the cockpit, almost scaring Captain Vince overboard.

"What's going on, now?" The skipper we'd come to call Captain InVinceable asked. Over the course of the voyage he'd come to be the diplomat serving to settle the petty disputes that inevitably develop when five people are confined within a 44-foot boat. I'm sure he thought something had boiled over into physical confrontation.

We ignored him. The only fight was our gasping for air. Each of us stood clinging to the lifelines, taking in big gulps of onionless air. A horizon, my inner ear was screaming for a horizon to gain equilibrium. But in the dusk the only horizons were the waves' tops and you had to look up to see uneven crests. In time the clean air drove out the onion and butter and we could sit down, still queasy but regaining.

"Close," Mike said.

"Yeah."

"What's going on?" Captain InVinceable asked again.

"Vegetables," Mike said.

"You wouldn't believe it anyway," I said, not wanting to bring up one of those petty disputes that this time had boiled over.

Recomposed, I knew what I had to do. I kept waiting for Mike to do it, but he must have been stalling, hoping I would.

I stood at the top of the ladder long enough to take a deep breath and dove below, plunging into the galley and grabbing the offending pan. Still holding my breath and trying to keep my eyes pinched as tightly closed as I could and still see, I took that pan with a death grip on the handle and ran back up to the cockpit.

I braced my feet against the roll of the boat and flung the onions and butter and, unfortunately, the pan as far out over the water to leeward as I could. I hadn't really meant to fling the pan, too, but it slipped and now that it was gone, it didn't seem to have been such a bad idea.

Behind us the pan and onions floated for a time. An albatross who'd been following for days landed near the debris. He poked around in it for a moment, then picked up what looked like a string of onion. The bird shook his head violently, letting go the onion. With what only could be disgust coming from a bird, the albatross started his run down the trough to take off and fly as far from the boat as he could get. I don't think we ever saw that one again.

With the odiferous mess gone, the air in the cabin slowly cleared and I went below again to stir the forgotten sludge. The macaroni had softened and the stuff in the pot at least had a texture that felt edible. I put on my rain gear and filled two bowls, telling the others it was there.

In the cockpit I handed one to InVinceable and we sat there eating in silence.

He finished his bowl and looked at the cook.

"The goulash is good," he said. But, he said it in that sort of over-polite diplomatic tone he used when he was settling some difference among the crew. I must have reacted with an expression.

"No, I mean it. It's good."

"It'll get us by, I guess," I said.

From below, bits of conversation drifted up into the cockpit.

"Did you taste that?" somebody asked in a voice not sounding all that appreciative.

InVinceable looked apologetic.

"I didn't see anybody else try to cook," I said in defense. What did they expect? Something from one of those cookbooks probably.

"Onion," InVinceable, ever the moderator, said with a sympathetic smile. "Maybe it needed a little onion."

Whether he felt guilty about the comment from below echoing his own thoughts or maybe defending my sensibilities, I don't know. Maybe he was still being polite. He did go below and fill his bowl again.

FORCE EIGHT SLUDGE, A RECIPE

Ingredients:

Hamburger
Macaroni
Tomato sauce
Onion (optional)

Take a pot big enough so you don't have to fill it more than halfway. Cook hamburger until it's brown. Pour off the grease if you can do it without hurting anybody or redecorating the cabin. Dump in the tomato sauce and then the macaroni and cook over low heat until the macaroni is soft. If you're not being thrashed all over the place you can boil the macaroni first in a separate pot. All kinds of pizza and spaghetti spices work here and for a real treat, melt mozzarella cheese over the top when it's nearly done. Keep in mind, melted cheese is difficult to scrape off bulkheads.

CHAPTER 5

CIPHERS AND EAGLES

O RCA FINISHED THE STORY and passed the magazine
to Sven to look at the pictures.

"Sounds like some of the meals we made," Corky said.

"Yeah," Sven said, chuckling, "even the ones on solid land.
Not this one, though." He began putting plates on the table along
with the bowl of crab legs, slabs of halibut and a big dish of
steamed fiddlehead ferns. "This is one of our best."

"You read very well," Miss Braithewaite said to Orca, but looking at Sven.

"Course that Jones never uses no big words," Sven said. "Let's
eat. "

They all moved to the table and conversation all but stopped
as they enjoyed their natural feast. About halfway through, Miss
Braithewaite looked up from her plate and said, "This is marvel-
ous. Do you always eat like this?"

"This ain't so special, ma'am," Sven said.

"Oh?"

"What'd be real special out here would be one of them ham-
burg sandwiches. Right, kid?"

"Yeah," said Orca, "and ice cream." He looked accusingly at
Corky. "You didn't bring any ice cream."

"There wasn't enough time for everything," Corky apologized, glancing toward Miss Braithewaite.

"Next time, maybe," Sven interrupted. "How about you clearing the dishes."

Orca began his chore and Sven took Miss Braithewaite outside.

Once they were out of earshot, he asked, "What happened out there today? Kid don't look none the worse for it."

"To be honest, it was all so interesting, I forgot. And he never asked," she said, "He's an impressive boy."

"That he is, ma'am. That he is."

They stood in silence for a few minutes until Sven finished his pipe and then they went back indoors.

"How about doin' the accounts when you're done there," he asked Orca.

"All right, Sven," Orca said, wiping a dish.

"Accounts?" Miss Braithewaite asked.

"Aw, yeah," Sven said. "Even us simple bush folks got to keep some figures now and again. Orca there does most of it now. Fact is, he takes care of all the numbers we got to keep track of any more. I got no idea what we got for money. Have to ask Orca. It's like sometimes I think the kid lets me have an allowance. Not that there's anywhere to spend it. We send an order in with Corky now and then and next trip he brings groceries and the like back."

Orca put the last dish away, dumped the leftovers into the pot of relentless soup and placed it outside to keep cool. Then he took a pencil and pad of paper to the table.

"Okay," Sven said, "let's see how many fish we got to catch this year. How much you figure they're going to pay, Corky?"

Corky shook his head. "Just like always. The fishermen is expectin' 53 cents for reds and the processors are sayin' 43. Price'll probably be in the middle somewheres. Probably on the low side, too."

Sven told Orca, "Put down 47. And, let's see, figure them fish average about seven pounds apiece. You got that?"

Orca nodded.

"Okay. Now I figure we need about two thousand dollars to get through the year, so how many fish we got to catch, over and above what we have to keep for ourselves? Course that's going to be a lot with you eatin' so much."

He winked at Corky and the woman. "That ought to keep him busy for a minute or two."

Orca bent over his paper, working determinedly with his pencil.

"Isn't that awfully complicated for a boy his age?" Miss Braithewaite asked.

"Maybe it is," Sven answered, "but I believe he can do it. Like I said, he's doin' most of the accounting around here, now."

Orca concentrated over his figures. He rose once, took a knife and sharpened his pencil and then returned. Miss Braithewaite doodled in her notebook.

At last Orca looked up. "We need 820.6 fish, Sven, 821," he said.

"Good job," Sven said. "That what you got, Corky?"

"Sure," came the response, "he's always right." Neither one of them had actually figured the problem. But it sounded about right to them, so Orca's answer would serve.

Miss Braithewaite looked a little concerned. "I don't want to be critical," she said, "but I got a different answer. I came out with 607.8, 608."

Both men looked at Orca. He looked a little embarrassed. Then Sven turned to Miss Braithewaite smiling in realization.

"Did you figure in what it costs us to fish, net repairs and fuel and the like?"

"No, just how many fish it would take to make $2,000."

"How much you put in for costs, Orca?" Sven asked.

"I figured about $700," he said. "We need a lot of twine, and fuel for the motor. Some other things."

Sven smiled triumphantly at Miss Braithewaite. "Why don't you figure in another $700 and see what you come up with."

She began writing quickly. Then she looked up, "He's right, 821 fish. Red salmon? Forty-seven cents? You won't believe what we have to pay for it in the store."

"We know good and well," Corky said. "We do all the work, somebody else makes all the money."

"Well," she said, "That was good."

"Nice job, Orca," Sven said.

"Yeah," Corky echoed. "Sure hope you get 47 cents a pound for them fish so you don't have to go through all that again."

"I wish we had some ice cream," Orca said.

"I'm sorry, kid," Corky said.

"Why all the fuss about ice cream?" Miss Braithewaite asked.

Orca answered, "We can't keep it frozen, even in winter. We only get it when somebody brings it out and then we have to eat it right away."

Corky laughed, "And he means right away. I seen him go through half a gallon in what seemed like two minutes."

Sven said, "Next time. It's getting kind of late. You folks might need a good rest, yet." He walked to the window. "It's stayin' clear. You ought to be able to get back tomorrow. Maybe we all ought to turn in."

Miss Braithewaite looked at Sven, contemplating something. "I heard you tell a story this morning to stay awake. Do you tell bedtime stories, too?"

Orca brightened.

Sven said, "Sometimes we do. Course Orca's heard all of mine, and more than once, most of 'em."

"You mentioned that Captain Skooks today. You said he was a story in himself," she asked.

"Corky knows him better'n anybody," Sven said, "You even knew his real name, didn't you?"

"Yes," Corky responded. "He didn't like anybody knowin'."

"What was it?" Orca asked.

"Well, I learned it from one of his relatives, lived on one of them islands in Southeast. Gregory Finchholder."

"I can see why," said Sven Kaartoonsen. "Maybe you could tell that one about the time with the eagle."

"Gregory Finchholder, Captain Skooks, an eagle?" Miss Braithewaite asked.

"Yeah, seemed like the simplest things turned into an adventure with that guy," Corky said. "Course he was older when I met him. I heard most of the stories second hand. He told me one or two, but by that time I get the idea he added a little to them."

"Let's hear it," Orca said.

"All right," Corky said, leaning forward and putting his elbows on the table. "Now the way he told it to me, he was an old man and he sort of told two adventures at the same time. See, he'd hurt himself and he was goin' to get help and while he was on his way he got to recallin' a similar incident from back when he harpooned salmon for a living."

Captain Skooks and the Bald Eagle

The knuckles on Gregory Finchholder's gnarled hands turned white each time he pulled at the oars as he rowed across Elfin Cove. He winced with every stroke as he put pressure against his injured ankle and cursed the eagle and his own foolishness for chasing it across a rocky beach. The voyage in the little dory was long for an 80-year-old man, even for one who'd been the strongest of the salmon harpooners in the days when men were men and salmon were so big only two at a time fit in a creek and you didn't catch them in these sissy nets people used today, but you stood in the bow of your boat and you harpooned them one at a time. That was when he'd been Captain Skooks, the toughest of the tough.

As he rowed against the tide and the pain, Gregory recalled the other time he'd hurt an ankle. He'd harpooned a big king salmon and as the line played out when the salmon made its run, Gregory's leg got tangled in the bight. When the line came tight, it grabbed his ankle and threw him against the side of the boat. It snapped his leg right below the knee clean as an ocean run salmon. It took some help, but Gregory set that leg, set it good.

The rest of the crew had hauled him to a beach and tied him to a tree. Then they tied another line from the fishing boat to his ankle. Then they hauled on the line with the boat and young Captain Skooks proved so strong they almost pulled the boat ashore before he'd hollered "enough," and the leg was set.

But it wasn't going to work this time. He was alone for one thing, and for another, it was his ankle with all those little bones in there and maybe even more than one was broken. He cursed the eagle again. If he hadn't been fool enough to chase the cache robber down the rocky beach and twist his ankle he wouldn't be in this fix, rowing from his cabin across Elfin Cove to town.

Now, Gregory wasn't used to being weak. Even in his old age he prided himself on his toughness and to be this way, hurting with every pull on the oars, didn't fit with the way he thought about himself. The stories that followed Gregory Finchholder through his life weren't about an infirm old man, they were about this strong, young salmon harpooner. Gregory, himself, wasn't much of a bragger but some stories circulate about his Captain Skooks period that needed telling even if they weren't true. There were so many, it was hard to tell which really happened and which didn't. He was one of those men about whom legends grow, and Gregory never stopped them as they went through all the retellings. Of course they were expanded and embellished until even Gregory couldn't tell where the fact stopped and the fiction began. The lines between truth and fantasy became indistinct and in time even Gregory came to believe that he actually may have done some of the outlandish things credited to his memory. That was just as good, at least as far as story telling goes. One such story tells of the time Gregory, or Captain Skooks, chased another eagle. Eagles, contrary to all their literature, can be bothersome, they're pretty much scavengers, you know, and it was just such an eagle that Captain Skooks chased one day, or, if you believe it, Captain Skooks caught that eagle and that's the real story.

It seems in the old days around the fish canneries, the waste from cleaning all those fish was just pitched out the back door. After a while each season, the eagles would get brave and chase all the gulls away from these piles of fish guts and fly in for a meal. As the season wore on, the eagles lost more and more of their fear of men and began to realize the fish was better going into the cannery by the front door than it was all chopped up coming out the back.

Then they started hanging around the front door on the dock side of the building instead of out back. After all, they probably reasoned, garbage was for gulls, something so majestic as a bald eagle ought to be eating at the head table. Some days they'd line the roofs of the cannery just waiting for a boat to come in and drop a fish during the unloading. Some of the braver ones would even swoop down and grab a nice fat salmon out of the boat's fish hold when the fishermen weren't watching.

Well, on this particular day, Captain Skooks came in to the dock with his boat after one of his worst times at sea. Of course the boat was full of salmon; he wouldn't have returned otherwise, but the crew had had trouble finding fish and the schools had been small and they'd had to stay out much longer than they'd planned. As a result they had run out of food and for the previous five days they'd been eating salmon out of their own fish hold. Now, salmon is the finest meat in the world. Ask any fisherman. The steaks and fillets taken from a fresh-caught sockeye can't be beaten anywhere, but a man has his limits and five days of salmon for breakfast, lunch and dinner were that limit, and Skooks was at his.

As soon as the crew tied up the boat, he hopped onto the dock and headed for the nearest cafe where he ordered the biggest steak they could find, beefsteak, not salmon steak. He barely gave them time to cook it and when they gave it to him, he slapped it between two huge slices of sourdough bread and ran back to supervise the unloading of his boat. He sat on the transom of the boat watching the nets haul fish out of the hold, now and then taking a bite out of that sandwich like he was biting into a little bit of heaven. Suddenly, as he watched, the net full of fish swung out of control, almost dumping its load into the water. Captain Skooks jumped to help his men grab the lines and bring it back under control before they lost their fish. He left his sandwich on the deck. As quickly as they regained the net, Skooks turned back to his sandwich, but only in time to see an eagle grab it in his talons and fly off.

Well, Skooks wasn't going to have any of that and he took off running and hollering after that eagle. The eagle flew low along the dock trying to gain altitude but the size of that steak held him back and he never did get higher than a man's head. Skooks started gaining on that burdened eagle, grabbing and cursing as he ran. He was so intent on catching that bird that he didn't see the end of the dock and he ran right off into the air. Now it looked like two big birds were flapping and squawking and trying to fly, only one of them didn't have wings. In his panic Skooks grabbed the closest thing around which turned out to be that sandwich, which in turn was still attached to the eagle. Now you have to give that eagle some credit. For a minute there he held the sandwich and Captain Skooks airborne. You also have to give a little credit to the strength of that Alaska sourdough bread because it held Skooks. As a matter of fact, it held better than the eagle did because after a few seconds of trying to hold them all aloft, the eagle gave up and man and bird and sandwich took a dive for some twenty or thirty feet into the mud, the tide being out. And there was a sight. The eagle stood up all muddy and a little confused. He took one look at Skooks and then a quick peck at the sandwich, then he shook himself all over, squawked once and walked off up the beach. Skooks for his part sat there covered with gray tidal mud, and eating that sandwich, flicking a speck of mud off it every once in a while.

Skooks' crew and the cannery people stood there on the dock watching the man eat his sandwich while the bird walked off in disgust, and they laughed until it hurt. None of them had ever seen a man catch an eagle by hand before and there were enough of them that the story circulated in a hurry and yet another episode was added to the legend of Captain Skooks, the itinerant salmon harpooner.

When Gregory bumped the shore he was almost laughing. The thump surprised him, he'd been so lost in his story. A couple of fisherman picked him up and carried him to the small village clinic. They asked what happened, but all Gregory told them was, "Watch out for them eagles."

Lost in his story, Corky hadn't watched his audience very carefully. Of course he noticed movements, but when he focused on the people in the cabin again, all three of them had fallen into their bunks sound asleep. This disappointed him, not because he thought they might have missed his story, but because when a bunch of people fall asleep in a small room, it's always best to be the first so the others' snoring didn't keep you awake. He'd be last this time and lose more sleep because of the noise from his bunkmates.

Morning found them on the beach next to Corky's floating skiff. This time, despite the promise of sunshine, Corky and Miss Braithewaite wore warm clothing and put their rain gear where they could grab it in a hurry. Clear skies gave them little to worry about.

Orca talked with Corky for a minute while Sven and Miss Braithewaite walked a little way down the beach. "He really needs a new jacket. The sleeve fell off the old one the other day," Orca said.

"Looks like it has more patch than jacket anyway," Corky answered. "I'll see what I can do."

Farther up the beach Miss Braithewaite was speaking to Sven. "Before you start, you should know, we're not in the business of taking children away from their families. It's usually the best place for them. But, it's the child who's important and the child's well-being is what we want to protect. I don't mind telling you, Mr. Kaartoonsen, that I'm more than a little impressed. You did a good job showing him off and I don't even think you knew you were doing it."

"Maybe not," Sven responded, a hint of mirth in his eye.

"I came expecting the worst, you know. You wouldn't believe some of the children I see, the conditions they live in. It's shameful. To some of them, you folks live in a palace."

Sven looked up toward their small log cabin. One of its corners had sunk slightly, the logs old, and worn. This is a palace?

"I have to write a report. The system has to know he's here. He's going to have to have some formal schooling. There will even be some testing to see where he is, his education, I mean. I think your biggest problem is going to be about his family. Where are they? Where did he come from?"

Sven shrugged.

"Your whale story isn't going to impress anyone. Nobody's going to buy it."

"It's the way it happened."

"If you say so, but I'd keep quiet about it anyway when it comes up. From what I've experienced, if his parents or other family can't be found, you might qualify to adopt the boy, but it's not a foregone conclusion. You don't have a legal claim, do you?"

"Nothing on paper. Don't our years together count for something?"

"Maybe, maybe not. Sometimes it all depends on what one judge thinks."

"So what happens now?"

Miss Braithewaite thought for a minute. "I'll have to do some research. There has to be some record of him, a birth certificate, some trace somewhere. You say he was an infant, didn't you?"

"Still had some marks from birthin'. Few days old, maybe."

"Well, if he was that young, maybe there wasn't a record yet. I'll have to look for that. If we can find any family he might have to go with them. If not, legally, he's a ward of the state."

Sven shivered, "Sounds like he'd be some kind of criminal."

"There might be foster homes."

The fear knifed through Sven again. He pictured the boy living with strangers, town people who didn't understand what Orca knew. For a moment he stared at the woman, thinking: Why did you have to come here, start all of this?

"What I will do for you," she said, "is I'll get all the paperwork together for you to file as his guardian. You can at least get that going. I'll talk with the Department of Education and I'll get the correspondence schooling materials for you, too. As I said, he'll have to take a test. We'll need to know his grade level. I'll send that out, too."

"We'll be going up to Unakwik in a little more'n a month. Corky always knows about where we are," Sven told her.

"I want you to know, I don't have a problem with the boy's living conditions, or for that matter, his education. But you have to know, I'm afraid I'm locked into a path of action by law. Sometimes these things don't go the way I'd wish them. Personally, I think you've done an admirable job raising the boy."

"Well, thank you for that," Sven said.

"There's one other thing. We will have to do a check on your background. It will be pretty thorough, too."

"Uh, oh," Corky had overheard the last comment. Sven grimaced at him.

"Let's go while we got the weather," Corky shouted from the skiff.

Sven walked Miss Braithewaite back to the boat and helped her over the gunwale.

"You'll be hearing from me as quickly as possible. Sometimes these things move awfully slowly," she said to Sven.

"What things?" Orca asked.

Sven ignored him. "We'll hope for the best, Miss Braithewaite. But, don't keep us waitin' too long. Waitin's probably the hardest part of anything like this."

Orca started to ask his question again, but didn't.

"I'll work just as fast as I can," she said.

"You got the shopping list and the money?" Sven called back to Corky.

"Sure do. Orca took care of it. I won't forget the ice cream this time, or anything else for that matter." He winked at Orca. "See you in a few weeks, Sven, Orca." He turned to start the motor.

"Well, goodbye, Miss Braithewaite," Sven said.

Orca called his goodbyes.

"Good-bye, Orca," she said. "and goodbye, Mr. Kaartoonsen." Then a look of mild humor crossed her face, twisting her thin mouth into a sly smile. "Is that your real name?"

Sven laughed. "'Fraid it is, ma'am. 'Fraid it is."

CHAPTER 6

SWIMMING WITH LIONS

IMMEDIATELY AFTER THE SKIFF DISAPPEARED past the headland guarding the bay, Orca began to notice a difference in Sven. As they moved into the period of intense activity preparing for the summer fishing season, Sven seemed distant. He didn't talk as much and didn't seem to show much interest in the work they had to do. Even the anticipation of spring herring failed to brighten his spirits. The first of their spring chores had them bring out the herring gillnet for the few days they might be able to fish. Sven practically lived for the herring season. It had always seemed to Orca that Sven liked the herring better than anything else they caught. Yet, as they worked on their net, Sven plodded methodically and expressed little interest in fishing and even less in his favorite addition to their menu.

At first Orca didn't think about it very much, coming to realize Sven's mood gradually. But when it came time to take the net out to catch herring and Sven suggested Orca do it alone, he knew something serious was bothering the old man. By that time Sven had grown distant enough that Orca was glad to get away from him for a while. He asked but didn't insist that Sven go with him.

Orca left in their dory for the short run to the north into Liljegren Passage between their Naked Island and Storey just across the pass. When he'd reached his fishing spot, he stopped and drifted, waiting.

As he floated in the passage, his gillnet stretched out behind the dory, the rising sun sent sparkles of light dancing off the tips of minute riffles. Orca could hear no sound at all, the world absolutely still as the sun gradually lighted the steep sides of the islands lining the passage, turning the black trees to vivid green and the water from slate gray to blue to deep, clear green. The peace of the day and the slight motion of the boat lulled the boy into long, motionless periods, the world so quiet that he might have been a permanent part of the landscape, a rock rising from the bottom to form a small island on the otherwise unblemished ocean. Maybe a mile away, he saw an occasional flash of light and in time realized it was coming from the tall fin of a killer whale as it turned and caught the sun's rays. For all Orca could tell, nature had stopped except for himself and the whale.

Nature, though, is anything but inanimate; no matter how still the world seems, movement exists, the flow of life continues and Orca knew somewhere, everywhere within his circle of sight, something, probably everything, was moving. The whale exhaled lightly, pastel colors of rainbow forming in the misty breath. As Orca watched, his thoughts drifted with his mood across the water to the landscape beyond and the apparent stillness. Something had to be moving. He wondered how fast a tree grew. If it was growing, it was moving. Could you see the movement if you concentrated? He focused on the nearest tree, trying to detect the slightest motion against the background. Nothing. Not even a little breeze to make its branches wave. What about the shifts the ground made during the earthquakes that rattled their cabin? He wondered if the earth shifted constantly with movement as slow as the growth of trees. Everything around him was alive, the whale, the trees on the shore, the world just beneath the surface of the water. Was the earth alive, too, and the very water that floated him? Could he see the tide move? He could see where it had been or where it was going. Sometimes he could see current or at least a tide rip. But if he watched closely, could he actually see the energy that drove it to creep up the shoreline?

Movement existed in his becalmed world, he knew. Somewhere in the underbrush on shore small animals scurried about the business of gathering food just as he floated on the water in the same pursuit. Beneath him in the depths, fish swam and crabs crawled across the bottom. Somewhere amid the rocks and brush, hundreds of birds flitted and fluttered, gathering twigs and grass or pushing stones around to build their nests.

As if to confirm the direction of Orca's thoughts, a gull appeared and flew along the shoreline just below treetop level. The sun's early rays tinted the bird's white feathers pink as it flew almost lazily to the northwest.

Orca's gaze followed the gull until it had flown almost out of sight, then he turned to look across the surface to the cork line supporting his net stretched behind the boat, trying to spot the telltale riffles the herring would make. The riffles would tell him the little fish were near, as would the silver flashes they reflected as they rose into the sun-lighted water near the surface. The herring would be there; they always came. They arrived almost like the tide. Maybe he was a day early, or two, or maybe the herring would be late this year. Maybe they wouldn't come at all. He and Sven always had brought up that possibility, but the herring always came.

He hoped the herring would improve Sven's spirits. What was bothering him anyway? Orca guessed it had something to do with Miss Braithewaite's visit. Or it could have been just cabin fever. After all, they had been trapped indoors longer than usual this spring. He couldn't be sure, but he thought the visit had been the turning point. She had seemed nice enough. Pretty, too. Maybe that was it. Could Sven . . . ? These kinds of thoughts were new to the twelve-year-old who lived away from most of society's influences. But he wondered just the same.

Off to the northeast the whale lay still on the surface between Orca and the sun. A halo of light lined the high dorsal fin as the

animal drifted with the slightest of currents. Was he fishing, too? Orca wondered. Were they both lying in wait to ambush the herring? He remembered the words from a book Corky had brought him, "hunters of opportunity, preying on whatever they happened to encounter in their endless wanderings." Orca wondered about that. There was a whale not wandering, not hunting, but in the right place at approximately the right time, like the boy, waiting for the opportunity to come to him.

As the sun rose higher in the sky it slowly overwhelmed the spring chill, warming the land and the sea, sending shimmers of heat mirage into the air and distorting the images of the trees on the islands and even the whale's dorsal fin. The warmth drew over Orca like a blanket and, combined with the ever so gentle rocking of the dory, slowly lulled him off to sleep.

While the boy dozed in his boat, the gull, which had appeared from a distance to fly so lazily, actually hurried toward a gathering he could sense, but Orca and the whale could not. Just two miles to the northwest around a point and out of sight of the two hunters, the otherwise quiet sea churned in frenzy. A flock of gulls, screeching and squabbling, dove violently at the water. Again and again they'd fold their wings and crash to disappear beneath the surface. When they emerged, they'd shake their heads with necks outstretched, swallowing. Others in the flock attacked the successful fishermen to steal the catch if they could. Nearby, other birds, puffins and surf scoters, guillemots and murres swam and dove into the silvery mass just beneath the surface. When the gull Orca had seen joined the hovering swarm of white birds it dove, returning to the surface with a herring in its beak. Two others flew at him to steal the fish, but he was quick enough swallowing to prevent the mugging. The marauding gulls drove the school of herring deeper into the water and the sea flattened into calm. The swarm settled, swimming peacefully while the herring swam deeper to escape the predators on the surface. A few scouts flew ever-widening circles, watching for the herring to return within reach.

Other hunters had been watching. Two sea lions observed the frenzy on the surface and when it calmed, they rose higher in the water, curled into a dive and disappeared with a splash of their flippers. For several minutes the water remained calm while the two mammals hunted deep beneath the gulls. Their foray into the depths eventually drove the herring back toward the surface where the scouts saw them and raised the squawk. The rest of the flock attacked again. First one, then the other sea lion rose and exhaled loudly, and it looked like the gulls were attacking the big brown doglike heads. The sea lions waited patiently until the gulls had forced the herring deep again and then they returned to their submerged hunt. As the gulls and sea lions took their turns feasting on herring, the school slowly drew them into Liljegren Passage where two more hunters lay in wait.

The raucous turmoil raised by the gulls awakened Orca where he lay in the skiff oblivious to anything but sky. He didn't rise at first, instead listened, amazed at all the different sounds a single species of bird could make. They screeched and chattered, cried in the most plaintive calls imaginable and sometimes even seemed to laugh. The realization of why they were there came slowly to the boy. The whole mass of birds and fish and sea lions had almost reached the dory before he roused himself into action. Just as he rose to peer over the gunwale to see what was happening, one of the sea lions surfaced right next to the boat, blowing its fish breath almost in his face as the boy came eye to eye with the monstrous head. They saw each other at the same instant and the sea lion jumped away while Orca fell backward inside the dory.

He regained himself quickly and leaped to his net. He knew now the herring were close and despite the fright from the sea lion, he jumped to business. The sea lion surfaced a hundred feet away and rose out of the water, his eyes straining curiously toward Orca and the dory. Then the corks bobbed under water for a second and Orca knew the fish had hit the net. He hoped that was all that had hit. Gulls screamed overhead. He quickly started the outboard motor and circled toward the buoy at the far end of the net. He was using a gillnet which entangled the fish, but he'd learned from Sven if he made a round haul, closing the ends around a school, whatever fish hadn't hit the net yet might still be caught.

He reached over the side and pulled the buoy into the boat. The closure brought a flurry of action from the fish and the gulls began diving inside the cork circle. When the fish dove to escape, they hit the net and dragged the corks under water with them. Even the dory dipped slightly. This Orca liked because he thought the diving gulls would scare the herring and scatter them and more would catch in the mesh of the net. He hoped he had only fish inside the net. He looked in the direction he'd last seen the sea lion. To his relief it still swam on the surface, but it was moving toward him. The boy knew the animal might try to steal from him and in the process destroy his net. When the sea lion came closer than Orca felt comfortable about it, the boy picked up one of the rocks he'd been carrying for just such a purpose and hurled it at the animal's head.

"Out of here, you old monster," he cried as he hurled a second rock. "There's plenty for everybody. Leave these for Sven."

The sea lion sank and Orca thought his rocks had done their job. But a couple of rocks splashing in the water weren't enough to scare a fifteen-hundred-pound animal. Something else had unnerved the sea lion.

The frenzy of gulls and silver flashes in the water had attracted more than a few birds and a couple of sea lions to Orca's boat. As he began to retrieve the cork line, pulling the net into the boat, Orca hadn't seen the whale begin to move, slipping silently through

the water toward the activity. Nor had he seen the two whales who'd joined the first. From about four hundred yards away they slashed through the water toward the massive school of herring, only a small portion of which had been caught inside Orca's net. Their approach, not the boy's rocks, had frightened the sea lion and it had left the country. Not so his partner.

Orca and the second sea lion came aware of each other and the approaching whales at the same time. The whales didn't worry him, but the sea lion did when it rose inside the circle of corks where it had been feeding unnoticed within the chaos all around it. When the animal sensed the attacking whales, it rose looking frantically for escape. It splashed and dove toward the net, looking for a way out from what just moments before had been a luxurious private feeding ground. The sea lion threw its entire weight against the mesh, dragging the stern of the boat almost under water. Again and again, the sea lion attacked the barrier to his freedom. Orca watched, panicked. If the net held, the sea lion might just sink the boat. If it didn't, he could lose the net and the catch with it.

He threw the buoy back into the water. This released one end of the net and exposed an opening. He ran the boat away from the buoy slowly, widening the gap in the hopes the sea lion would find it and swim out. At least he might keep the fish already tangled.

The whales found the opening first and dove after the herring, in turn driving the frantic sea lion farther inside the enclosure.

Now, in desperation, the sea lion headed for the only refuge from the whales he could see, Orca's skiff. Faster than Orca could believe such a large clumsy-looking animal could move, the sea lion swam straight at the dory, at the last minute launching itself out of the water and halfway over the gunwale. Orca ran to the bow as far away from the frightened beast as he could. His weight at least partially offset that of the sea lion as it tried to claw the rest of its way into the skiff with its front flippers. The dory tipped crazily, standing almost on end by the stern as it fought to remain afloat under the mass of animal in the stern. Orca flung one of his rocks at the snarling mouth. The rock bounced off the sea lion's skull and served only to intensify its frenzied attempt to escape certain death in the water. Orca threw another rock and it hit the animal square on the nose. The sea lion growled in protest, its beady eyes drawing down on Orca with animal hatred.

That look more than anything raised fear swelling through his body and Orca at last realized he was in serious trouble. He hadn't thought much to that point, just reacted as the situation demanded. Now the fear of life and death struggle grabbed him. If the animal managed to crawl all the way into the dory, Orca would have to jump into the cold water. If it didn't, the boat more than likely would tip and throw him overboard anyway. Either way he'd be in the cold water with the whales and the sea lion and the herring. The fear raised his awareness to every minute element of his situation. He felt sure the whales wouldn't hurt him on purpose, but in the rush of feeding would they distinguish him from a mass of fish or a sea lion? So far the whales had paid little attention to the matter of the boat as they fed in the school of herring. Then, in the midst of their feast, one surfaced, spy-hopped with her head out of the water, one eye cocked toward Orca's boat where he fought with the sea lion. She slipped beneath the surface and with a powerful push of her tail, propelled herself toward the dory. The sea lion sensed her approach and wriggled all the harder to pull its mass over the gunwale. The whale came up out of the water, her mouth gaping open. Her teeth sliced into the sea lion's hind flippers, using that purchase to drag it backward into the water.

The sea lion let out a bawl of pain as it slipped over the side, clawing at the gunwale in a last futile attempt to save itself. That was enough to flip the boat as the whale dragged the sea lion free through a foam of bubbles and down into the depths of the passage.

The icy cold water hit Orca like a club. For all his time around water, he'd spent very little time in it and he wasn't prepared for the enveloping cold of immersion, nor was he prepared to swim. Sven had always told him boat people spent their whole lives trying to stay out of the water and to concentrate on that. So Orca never had learned to swim. He knew he had to regain the boat even though it had overturned, its flat bottom floating just inches above the water. At first he tried to swim to it as he'd seen the whales do, by moving his tail flukes, in this case, his feet.

Immediately he found out he wasn't built, or powered, as well as a whale. He began thrashing with his arms. What had he heard? Reach out and grab a handful of water, and then another, and kick. The dory wasn't that far away, only a few handfuls of water, but the cold was numbing. He found he could push himself by kicking even after water filled his boots adding to their weight, and in a few short strokes he touched the sanctuary of the dory bottom.

He scrambled out of the water and sprawled there, gasping, spitting out water and absorbing warmth from the sun. He thought he probably hadn't been in the water long enough for hypothermia to give him much trouble and his wool clothing, though soaked, retained some warmth. Still if he stayed wet and exposed, he wasn't sure what could happen. He didn't want to end up like Corky and Miss Braithewaite. Then he felt a tug; the dory jerked slightly and he realized he still had a net full of herring attached to the boat.

He'd heard about boats where fish started dying in a net and dragged net and boat underwater with them when they sank. He rejected the idea. How could little fish like herring sink a boat? He could cut the net loose. Then he thought about Sven and how much the old man loved the spring herring and he thought, too, how much money it would take to replace the net. He fingered the knife attached to his belt and decided to save cutting as a last resort. He wondered if he should swim to shore, but land lay almost a mile off and he now realized how bad a swimmer he really was. He wondered if he could right the boat somehow.

Then he realized his mind might be making bad decisions. In his panic, his frantic recovery of the boat, his hopes of rescuing himself, he'd let his mind race and now was the time to slow down, analyze carefully, take stock and consider all his options before he did something stupid. One of the whales rose next to the boat. "What am I supposed to do now?" he asked it. The whale seemed to regard him for a moment, then it slipped beneath the surface and disappeared. Sven would miss him after a while and come looking. But how long would that be? Probably not until tonight.

At the cabin Sven had dragged their salmon net out of its shed and examined it for damage. Getting ready took more time than fishing. It seemed fishermen always were getting ready. Sven worked under a cloud, despite the sunny day. He hadn't been able to shake the thoughts of Miss Braithewaite since she'd left. He knew he'd been distracted. He knew he might have taken some of it out on Orca and that bothered him even more. He recalled being glad to see the boy leave that morning. He wanted the boy to develop some independence, do things on his own, but he knew he'd also just wanted to get rid of him for a while.

He thought about Orca out there in the dory waiting for the herring run just as he had done for years past. He remembered the days when spring southeasterly storms blew and drove rain into his face while he sat miserably waiting for the herring run and envied Orca this day of sunshine and warmth. As he made his knots repairing the net, Sven's disposition improved with the height of the sun.

Toward midday, he reached for his coffee cup. He found the mug empty and flung the dregs out on the ground. He stood to walk back to the cabin for another when he noticed a whale swimming in the bay. He watched the whale for a moment, then turned toward the cabin. Inside while he poured a new cup, he thought about Orca again. He knew the boy had taken a lunch with him, but he got the idea it might make it up to him a little if he took him something hot.

So, Sven made a pot of bull coffee and heated the relentless soup, put them in containers and went down to the beach. He pulled the outboard in their skiff to life and drove out of the bay. The whale had disappeared.

Sven headed north and then turned northeast into Liljegren Pass. Ahead of him, Orca turned when he heard the sound of the outboard. He stood up on the overturned dory and waved his arms at the approaching skiff.

Sven didn't realize anything was wrong until almost too late. He came up on the dory faster than he should have so when he did see the problem, he couldn't slow the skiff quickly enough. He sent a wave from his wake washing across the overturned boat, soaking Orca's feet again, but the dory remained afloat.

"Hi, Sven," Orca said. "Got a little problem here."

"I guess you do," Sven said, looking over the dory and the boy. "Don't you know you're supposed to run them boats with the round side down?"

Orca wasn't ready for a joke. His sheepishness turned to a frown. "It's not funny, Sven."

"Nope, I guess it ain't. What happened? You all right?"

Orca, still standing on the overturned dory, began an explanation, but just as he started, the herring in the net gave another tug that pulled the boat so hard he lost his balance and almost fell into the water again. "Tell you later," he said when he regained his footing. "We got a little work to do right now."

"Guess we do." Sven brought the skiff next to the dory and they tied the two boats together. Then Orca and Sven started pulling the net over the skiff's bow. For about twenty minutes they worked, pulling the net and picking herring from it, while Orca told Sven all that had happened.

When the net finally lay in a pile on the bottom of the skiff, they righted the dory and Orca jumped in with a coffee can to bail the water out.

"We better get right to that motor, " Sven said, "or the salt water ain't goin' to leave us nothin' but a bunch of scrap."

By then, Orca had finished his story. Sven shook his head: "Real lucky," he said, "real lucky. Coulda been a whole lot worse." He handed Orca the containers of soup and bull coffee and the boy ate while Sven looked over the piles of net and fish in the skiff, the dory and the dripping outboard motor.

Farther down the pass, gulls and whales fed in the school of herring. "Real lucky," Sven said.

They attached a line to the dory and Sven began towing it back toward Cabin Bay.

CHAPTER 7

GETTING READY

REPAIRING THEIR OUTBOARD MOTOR added one more task to the confusion of preparations they had to make before their trip to the summer set-net site in Unakwik Inlet. Then they had to salt the herring Orca caught. When they finally reached the point of getting ready, the work progressed slowly, mostly because Sven seemed to spend more time looking off into nothing than he did repairing the nets. Orca caught him several times sitting on a stump, torn netting draped over his knees and a shuttle in his hand unmoving while the old man stared into the trees or out over the water.

Despite the slight hopes Miss Braithewaite might have raised, Sven felt anything but confident and the longer he went without hearing anything, the worse he felt and the more distracted he became. He forgot to do things and misplaced tools. When they began packing for the move, several times Orca had to remind him to take this or that item Sven had overlooked. Sometimes Sven took to sitting on a beach rock gazing blankly toward the bay. Even the meals of fresh herring failed to liven Sven.

At other times, for brief periods, Sven returned to himself. As their time to leave came closer, almost daily they'd hear the engines of fishing boats passing outside their bay on the way to the grounds.

"'Spect you'll be goin' on one of them boats one of these years," Sven said as they heard the heavy throbbing of a diesel-powered fishing vessel pass one morning. "Hard work, but the pay's good, at least in a good year."

At words from Sven, Orca brightened. "I think I'd like to try it," Orca said. "But if I went, what would you do?"

Funny, Sven thought, that's just what I been thinking about all this time. Aloud he said, "Oh, I think I'd get by. Seems like I did all right before you got here, as I recall."

"I don't know," Orca answered, "We got a lot of salmon to put up."

"That's a fact," Sven said, "and you ain't eatin' no less, that's for sure, Seagull."

Orca laughed. He sounded like the old Sven.

Another boat rumbled near the mouth of the bay. As the sound grew louder rather than fading, they looked up.

"It's the *Salmania*," Orca shouted. "He finally made it." Corky's familiar forty-eight-foot seine boat pushed bay water out of its way as it came toward them. The boat slowed to a stop about two hundred yards from shore. They heard the clank and rattle of chain going overboard as Corky dropped his anchor. Sven and Orca could tell he didn't plan to stay long because he didn't bother to back down on the chain to set the anchor. Crew on the deck began loading boxes into the seine skiff.

"Groceries," Sven said, "We eat tonight."

"I hope the ice cream made it," Orca added.

Sven laughed, "Yeah, ice cream. Ain't a grocery load without ice cream."

What appeared to be the last box went over the side into the skiff and Corky ran it toward shore.

"Halloo," Sven called, "Come on up for coffee."

"Got your groceries," Corky hollered back.

"I see that," Sven answered, "saved our lives again."

"Ain't like I don't owe you one," Corky said. "Good coffee?" Corky knew Sven might be out of real coffee and he wondered if

he was heading for the sour, spruce-bark brew Sven sometimes
made after the real coffee expired.

"Yeah, we got good coffee left. That's about all, though."

Corky slowed the skiff and it nudged into the beach. They
each grabbed a box and headed for the cabin.

On their return for another load, Sven stood for a moment
looking at the *Salmania* and the crewmen standing on deck watching them.

"Who you got with you?" he asked Corky. They each picked
up another box and began walking inland.

"Usual guys," Corky said. "One new one. That kid, Hal, been
comin' with us the last four-five years, he graduated high school
and he's goin' off to college. I had to look around for somebody
new."

"Don't imagine you had any trouble findin' somebody to go in
your crew," Sven said, knowing the good fishermen had more of
a problem with too many people wanting to crew with them.

"You'd be surprised," Corky said. "By the time he told me,
most of the good guys already had a berth."

They reached the cabin, took the boxes inside and set them in
the kitchen corner.

On the way back to the skiff, Corky said, "It got so bad I
thought a comin' out here and seein' if you wanted to let Orca go.
He's old enough, you know."

At least Corky had waited until Orca had run far enough ahead
of them so he couldn't hear, Sven thought. Was Corky going to
ask?

"Finally found somebody. Kid name of Georgie Fagshark,"
Corky said to Sven's relief. He didn't need two threats in the same
summer.

"Not one a that Fagshark bunch from down Southeast?" Sven
asked.

"Yeah, the youngest one, I think. He seems all right. Serious
kid, though. I ain't had no trouble with him and he knows his way
around boats. He'll be all right, I think. When the season gets

goin' full, I'll keep 'em so tired they don't have no energy to get in any trouble, anyway. Wasn't nobody else around."

They reached the cabin with another load of boxes, set them on the floor and Sven poured cups of coffee for himself and Corky. Orca began opening boxes.

"How's the season look?" Sven asked the fisherman.

"I don't know," Corky answered. "Them biologists, they say it might be a bad year. Somethin' about escapement when this year's crop was spawned. Seems they say we caught too many fish that year and there wasn't enough left to get into the streams to spawn."

"They always find some way to blame the fishermen," Sven said.

"Oh, yeah. But it's like always. The good fishermen'll do all right and the others'll complain. The price is good, anyway," Corky turned to Orca.

The boy looked at him with a disappointed smile. "There's a lot of stuff here," he said.

"Might still be another box or two in the skiff," Corky said with a sideways wink at Sven.

Orca brightened. "I guess I'd better go haul them up," he said and raced out of the cabin.

As soon as he was gone, Sven asked, "You hear anything from that Miss Braithewaite?"

"I tell you, Sven, I tried to avoid her all I could. She caught me on the boat day before we left. Got this package for you." Corky reached inside his shirt, pulled out a thick, manila envelope and handed it to Sven.

The old man took the envelope and walked to the window. Orca had almost reached the cabin with the last two boxes, so Sven tossed it onto his bunk.

Orca kicked the door open and shuffled inside burdened with two more boxes. A beam of happiness lighted his face.

"I guess you found it," Corky said. "Better eat it 'fore it melts. Believe I'll have some myself. How about you, Sven?"

Sven shook his head No. He went to the stove and poured coffee and bull coffee while Orca filled two bowls with ice cream.

Sven left them at the table and sat on his bunk, his back hunched, blocking their view of his reading while they ate their ice cream. He would have waited, but the uncertainty had been too much for him, and besides, an answer might be demanded.

He opened the envelope as quietly as he could, pulled out the letter and read:

"Dear Mr. Kaartoonsen:

"I have done some careful analysis of your situation on Naked Island with the boy, Orca, according to the guidelines established by this department. I also have studied regulations pertaining to cases similar to yours and to previous case histories.

"It seems there are regulations and precedents both for placing the boy in a proper facility and also for allowing him to remain under your guardianship.

"In addition, I have ordered a records search to locate any clue to his background. Enclosed is an application for a birth certificate. Please complete and return it. To do this, you will need to provide some confirmation of how the boy arrived at the island. I realize, according to your story, this may be difficult, but please make the attempt.

"From my own observations, I found the boy well cared for and in no need of outside intervention. However, regulation and law may find differently, pending the results of the investigations and any court proceedings that might be required. This will include a thorough check of your own background including your own family and upbringing. Any materials you can provide will aid this investigation.

"As the process continues, actions you can take may mitigate any negative findings. While I found the state of the boy's education acceptable, considering the circumstances, it is my opinion and state law that more formal instruction should begin. To that end, I have enclosed an evaluation examination. At your earliest convenience, please administer this test and send the results to me at the above address.

"In the meantime, I will continue the investigation and I will be forwarding you various legal forms that you will have to complete and return. Among these will be a formal request for adoption. While we are not at that stage yet, it would be best to complete the paperwork so the process can move along smoothly once other portions have been completed.

"In addition, it will be required that the department make at least two evaluation visits each year to monitor the boy's progress.

"I hope this letter finds you both in good health."

"Sincerely,

"Miss Priscilla M. Braithewaite"

After her signature, Miss Braithewaite had added a post script. "I think blueberry season and crab season would be fine for the evaluation visits," she had written.

A smile crossed Sven's face on reading the note at the end of the letter. He leafed through the following pages of the test. The letter sounded to him like they'd won her over, but that might not be enough. He knew for some time a cloud would hang over their lives while forces he had no control over decided their fate, people who didn't know them but simply looked at paper would make the final decision, based not on anything they knew about himself or Orca, but according to rules designed to fit the way the judges lived.

"What is it?" Orca asked.

Sven realized he'd been quiet too long.

"Just a letter from that Braithewaite woman," Sven said. "I'll tell you about it later. You guys leave any ice cream?" He slipped the envelope and its contents under his blanket, stood and walked to the table. Orca handed him the ice cream container and a spoon. Sven looked into the box. They'd left him about three spoonfuls.

"Seagull," was all he said as he reached deep into the box with his spoon.

Corky asked Orca, "Did you find the other thing you ordered?"

Orca looked back at him blankly for a moment, then smiled and ran to the boxes.

"Should be in the same box," Corky said.

A triumphant Orca pulled Sven's new jacket out for display.

"What's this?" the old man asked.

"You needed it," Corky said. "Put it on."

Sven tried to join them in their attempt at revelry. He donned the jacket and sashayed around the table, exposing the fleece lining, touching the fancy copper rivet buttons, fondling the outer material of heavy wool plaid.

Corky and Orca clapped their hands at Sven's flaunting.

"That ought to keep you warm." Corky said, then he rose. "I'd best be going. Like to get somewhere before dark. I imagine the crew's gettin' a little tired of sittin' out there."

"Well, thanks, Corky," Sven said. "You put in a good season."

"I'll see you sometime before the summer's out. How soon you goin' up to Unakwik?"

"Couple of weeks yet."

Sven and Orca walked to the beach and watched Corky make his way back to the *Salmania*. The chain rattled again, coming aboard this time, and the boat left them to themselves once more.

Corky's visit inspired greater activity in the two people working in Cabin Bay. There was nothing like seeing another fisherman on his way to the grounds to motivate those still getting ready.

In the next two weeks Sven and Orca intensified their efforts to prepare their gear for the trip north. Sven's mood improved only slightly after Corky left and Orca still found himself having to pick up after him. When at last the bulk of their preparations had been completed and they'd packed the dory, they spent what they thought would be their last night of the spring in Cabin Bay, too restless to sleep.

Then the weather failed them. After what seemed like weeks of beautiful sunny days, they woke to find a storm howling over the island. Outside the bay they could see the ocean churned to a froth. Rain didn't fall, it flowed, almost horizontally. They took one look outside and they knew they'd have to stay in Cabin Bay at least another day. But now they had nothing to do. They'd already just about closed the cabin for the summer. All their gear lay packed in the dory, even their cribbage board. As they sat over what they'd thought would be their last breakfast both fell silent, knowing they had been trapped.

"Tell you what. Now might be a good time," Sven said.

"What?"

"That Miss Braithewaite sent you a test."

"A test? What for?"

"Just to see how you're doin', I guess. You could do it now," Sven said as he rummaged through a bag of the papers they planned to take with them. He found the test and handed the paper to Orca. "Just answer the questions best you can. You'll do fine." Sven hoped he did more than fine. He wanted Orca to remove any doubts about it. But he wasn't going to pressure the boy.

Orca took a pencil and bent over the test. Sven began rummaging through the cabin looking through long forgotten boxes for records of himself. Over his lifetime, he'd kept every tool, every scrap of wood he'd ever found, but the paper trail that follows most people he had ignored, casting this or that document into a box never to be seen again. Now he had to find those papers to help in his battle to save their life. Against the wall deep in a corner under his bunk he found the box he sought. He sat at the table while Orca did his test, sorting through the few documents of his lifetime, separating the ones he thought would be important. They made a very small pile. When he finished, he borrowed one of the books from the library he had planned to take with him for the summer, the library Corky had replenished recently, and read for the remainder of the day.

By the following morning the storm had passed. They boarded up the cabin, went to the dory and began their trip north to their fishing grounds.

As they proceeded out of Cabin Bay, Orca hoped the anticipation and activity of fishing would bring Sven out of whatever was bothering him. Just moving started the process. They were off to a new season, new adventures, escaping the confines of spring, moving on into summer.

"Kind of like this new jacket," Sven hollered to Orca over the whine of the outboard after they had cleared Cabin Bay and turned north. "Can't feel any wind through it. Course, there ain't much wind blowin'."

For the next two hours they rode to the northwest across calm water, each lost in his own thoughts. Sven fell to wondering how Orca might have done on his test. They had it with them all finished and addressed to Miss Braithewaite. They'd have to wait until someone came along who could take it to town for them. Thoughts of the test led Sven to others as his mind again became entwined with Miss Braithewaite's.

"Watch out!" Orca shouted suddenly.

Sven spotted the log and swerved just in time to miss it. He looked a little sheepishly at Orca. "Got to pay attention all the time," he said, vowing to do just that.

As they neared the first small barrier islands that protected the mainland where Unakwik Inlet cut deep into the surrounding mountains, Orca pointed to his left and shouted, "Hey, look over there!"

Toward Olson Island that stood directly in the mouth of the inlet, the ocean had come alive with splashing.

Sven looked behind him at the sun and then said, "We got time. Let's go take a look."

Sven turned the dory in the direction of the splashes. Distances on the ocean deceive. What looks so close can take hours to reach. By the time they reached the place where they'd seen the activity, the water's surface lay as smooth as it had been everywhere else. Not a riffle indicated the whales had been there.

"We can wait a little while," Sven said. "They got to come up somewhere."

Then, as they scanned the glassy surface, froth erupted in the water and from the middle of it, a bright, silvery salmon flew skyward, reaching much higher than a fish could jump by itself. Just before the fish reached the top of its arc, a killer whale followed it into the air, catching the salmon in its mouth and crashing back into the sea.

Before the waves from the first jump had leveled, a second whale surfaced, rolled on its side and made a shallow dive, once, twice, a third time, then disappeared. Next to the widening circles the last dive made, a third whale broke the surface and turned, his huge dorsal fin flopping as he circled on his side, rolled and dove again. Another whale broke water and began slapping his tail. Then it arched its back and slowly sank beneath the riffles, rising head first shortly after with a salmon's tail just disappearing into its mouth.

While Sven and Orca watched, two whales swam one behind the other in an ever-tightening circle right at the surface, once in a while slapping their tail flukes, until so quickly it surprised the watchers, a third whale slashed through the center of the salmon school trapped by the whales. One salmon, frightened into a frantic escape, cleared the water and slammed into the side of the dory. The loud thump startled Sven and Orca. Stunned, the salmon fell back into the water and swam away sluggishly.

"'Bout took the breath out of me," Sven said.

"Me too." Orca responded, "You think that might have been Sam?"

Sven laughed. "They sure can work a school of salmon. Sometimes I wish we could fish that good. We'd make a lot more money."

Orca looked out over the water.

"Course usually you got to give them fish to the buyers whole. If they got your teeth marks all over 'em or they come in little chawed up pieces, them buyers ain't goin' to give much for them."

Orca giggled.

"A little guy like you don't take the mouthful them whales do," Sven said.

Another slap drew their attention as the whales started circling again, only this time another whale rose from deeper water up through the center of the circle, chewing, gulping and swallowing as his head rose three or four feet above the surface. When his momentum faded, the whale fell back into the water and disappeared.

Orca and Sven sat in the dory for more than an hour, becalmed except when waves from the whales' actions rocked them. Sven finally said, "Well, maybe we better get to our own fishin'. If those whales are feedin' this close, they must be runnin' up to Miners Bay. If they left us any."

"I think we should use nets," Orca said.

"Yeah," Sven chuckled his amusement. "Let's use nets."

He turned the dory north and ran the outboard up to speed. Each again fell into his own reverie. They skimmed across the water, passing Payday Point, named by the successful men who fished there. Then they entered Unakwik Inlet itself and the land closed around them. No more than half a mile wide, the inlet sides consisted of low hills at the south end rising into a mountain range with 10,000-foot peaks to the north. The ridge on the east side of the inlet blocked the sun, leaving the trees in deep shadow, a mysterious forbidding green. On the west side, facing the sun, more shades of green than an artist could manage on a palette formed lines and patches up the hillsides. Neon-bright green of the scurvy grass at the tide line contrasted with the dark spruce, while devil's club, ferns, grasses and alder filled the spectrum between the extremes. Sunlight reflecting off the trees colored the water a shiny green. Farther north the white-capped mountains turned it blue and almost white.

Lines of snow descended through the forest vertically from the hilltops, marking ravines on the shadowed sides of the slopes. All along they saw the silver flashes as salmon jumped, following the same route Sven and Orca took toward the spawning streams. They passed half a dozen sea lions diving into the returning schools and here and there a solitary seal, its round brown eyes right at the surface watching them go by. The inlet cut into the mountains for about twenty miles and the farther north they went, the narrower the passage became.

About halfway up the inlet, Sven slowed the outboard and stopped. "Maybe you ought to take 'er in," he said.

They changed places and Orca took the tiller. Sven stayed in the stern with him and together they checked off the points they used to navigate to their set net site. As riffles showed across the inlet just north of Jonah Bay, Orca edged the boat to the east. The change in the water marked a shoal that lay underwater all the way across the fjord. The shoal was a terminal moraine left by Meares Glacier when it scoured the bay centuries earlier. As the glacier had advanced, it had pushed rock and dirt along in front of it. Then when it began to retreat, it left a hill of the debris behind. Tidal currents upwelling from deeper water on both sides of the moraine boiled across it, building difficult eddies, and at times of low water exposing dangerous rocks. Orca guided the boat to the east side where they took their ranges off shoreline rocks and followed a channel across the shoal. Once across and in deeper water again, they saw what might have been a hundred sea otters, floating on their backs in the sun or diving onto the shoal where they hunted for the crabs that lived along its underwater slopes.

In less than half an hour they turned east into Miners Bay and spotted their summer home, nothing really more than a shack Sven had thrown up for shelter during the short fishing season. Still, it was stout enough to survive the heavy winter snows; nothing like their palace on Naked Island, though.

As Orca ran the boat closer, Sven hollered out, "Looks pretty much like we left it, at least from here. You know, I seen enough fish comin' in, maybe we ought to put the net out tonight on the tide and take care of loadin' the stuff up to the cabin in the morning."

Orca was anxious to begin fishing, too, but he said, "Why don't we wait? I just want to get the stuff up. Take our time and do it right." But, he knew whatever it was that drove Sven to fish coursed as strongly as the instincts that drew salmon to the streams. Sven would go fishing.

"Why don't we try to do both. You can haul the gear up and I'll make a set while you organize the cabin best you can. Wish we

hadn't took all that time watching them whales, now. Won't be long 'til it's dark, least as dark as it's gonna get. I really want to make a set tonight."

Orca smiled. "All right, Sven. Let's do it that way, then," he said. He nosed the dory into the beach.

"Tide's just startin' to turn. I want to catch 'em on the flood if I can," Sven said, "So we better hurry."

They rushed to unload the dory, tossing boxes and bags as far up the beach as they could to give Orca time before the incoming tide caught up with him and soaked their gear. As soon as they had everything out of the boat except the net, Sven pulled away to make his set.

Orca began lugging their supplies up to the shack. He took the bags of clothing first and threw them up onto a landing at the top of the steps to the front door. The bags thumped when they landed, but Orca thought he heard more thump than he should have, an extra noise, somehow out of place. He passed it off as imagination and went back for another load. He brought their bedding from the beach and tossed it next to the clothing bags. The softer bedding made little noise when it landed but again Orca heard that extra sound. He looked around. The noise could have come from almost anywhere. Sven could have banged something against the boat while he drove around setting his net. A tree could have fallen. Sometimes they even heard the roar when a particularly large piece of ice calved off the glacier at the head of the inlet. His mind took him through all of the logical possibilities, trying to identify what he'd heard. When nothing fit, he began to suspect something was amiss.

Orca picked up a rock and threw it hard against the shack's wall. A snort! This time he knew it wasn't his imagination. Then he heard a crash and he was sure it came from inside the house. Cautiously Orca circled around to the side and approached a window. Sven had built the cabin on pilings to protect the floor and base logs from the damp soil. As a result, the windows stood higher off the ground than Orca could reach. In order to see through the window, Orca had to prop two pieces of firewood against the logs and then climb up onto this wobbly perch to look inside. He had to claw at the windowsill with his fingertips to chin himself to a height where he could see inside. With his chin on the sill and his nose barely over the wood frame, Orca stared through the thin glass straight into the nose of a black bear, its beady eyes staring right back at him.

The eye-to-nose confrontation startled them both. Orca fell off the wobbly kindling, landing in the soft muskeg on his back. The bear lurched around inside, knocking over the chimney pipe to the wood stove and raising a cloud of black soot.

Orca regained his feet and scrambled down the beach. He called out to Sven, but the old man had his back to the shore and the outboard motor drowned out Orca's shouts. He rooted through their pile of gear until he uncovered Sven's shotgun. Finding the shells took longer, but when he did he loaded the gun and headed determinedly but cautiously back toward the shack.

This time he gave it a safety margin, scrambling to the uphill side where he hoped he could see inside without approaching too closely. He threw another rock at the wall and heard the bear rumble inside. Then the bear appeared, filling the window it had broken to gain entry. Quicker than Orca could react, the bear came through the window, launched itself to the ground and began lumbering uphill toward the trees. Orca raised the shotgun and fired a blast above its head to hurry the bear on its way. The kick of the gun knocked him back a step but he maintained his footing. The noise spurred the bear into a run and the last Orca saw of it, the bear's hind end looked like it was trying to run over its front end. Then it disappeared into the darkness of the forest.

Orca listened for a moment. When he couldn't hear the bear crashing through the brush, he fired another shot into the air, he hoped to put a fear into it that would discourage a return. He knew once a bear had found food, it wouldn't forget. He sat on a stump, shaking. While he tried to calm himself, he loaded two more shells into the shotgun. He looked out toward Sven, who was setting the anchors and buoys that would hold the net in place. Then his gaze fell on their pile of supplies where he'd left it on the beach. The tide had flooded almost to the first box where it threatened to soak everything they had for the summer.

Orca raced to haul the rest of their gear at least above the highest tide line. Then he began taking it piece by piece to the landing. Once the pile had been transferred to the shack, he went inside to inspect the damage.

The damage he found was considerable. The bear must have been in there for a long time or it might even have made more than one tour. Besides the recently dismantled stove pipe, which had left a dusting of black soot throughout the room, every can in the place at least had been bitten into and at worst ripped open with its contents spread as far as they could reach. Mattresses lay shredded, bits of cloth mixed with flour and oatmeal and green beans. Sven always left what food he had in the cabin, covered and protected so the smell wouldn't attract animals, but that hadn't deterred this bear. It looked like he'd even bitten into the moth balls Sven left by the windows to disguise any other scents that might hang about the shack. In one corner a can of outboard motor oil leaked its contents onto the floor through tooth holes in its side.

There wasn't much Orca could do before he cleaned the mess, so he jumped right to it. First he reassembled the stove pipe and started a fire to warm the place. Despite the height of the evening

June sun, the shack felt cool and damp inside. Next he located the one kerosene lamp that had survived the bear's invasion and lighted it. With light and a broom he went to work mucking out the room, always with the shotgun nearby and his eyes and ears alert for the bear's return.

Out on the water, Sven hadn't heard a thing. Not even two shotgun blasts had diverted his attention from setting the net. Between that and the constant splashes he heard as salmon jumped around him, he had no interest in anything but fishing. He never heard any of the commotion on shore over the sound of the idling outboard motor on the dory.

After he had anchored the net to shore, he climbed into the boat and made sure the webbing would pay out evenly, then he prepared to make his set. He turned the dory out into the bay letting the net, anchored to the beach, slowly slip through his hands off the stern. To keep it from fouling the propeller, the net went off the opposite side from the offset outboard motor. Round white corks popped through his hands to float on the water holding the net upright while Sven ran the motor ahead, watching the pile unwind from the bottom of the boat. As the net went over the transom, Sven slowly turned the throttle on the outboard, giving himself more and more speed. He'd done this thousands of times in his life and the work became so automatic his mind wandered from what he was doing.

The net and corks flew by faster and faster, but Sven was arguing with judges and courts and Miss Braithewaite and worrying about losing Orca. He wondered again what he could do to stop the world from intruding into their lives and separating them. He wondered if they could run, go deeper into a wilderness and hide somewhere. All the while the net raced through his hands and the boat skimmed out into the bay. Suppose he went to town and hired a lawyer or somebody else to find out just what he could do to protect them. He'd have to catch a lot more fish to pay for that. He wondered how many more fish.

Then his arm jerked almost out of its socket. The jolt ripped him from his seat and dragged him across the boat. He slammed against the transom but his center of gravity was too high and he pitched off the stern, trying desperately to grab it as whatever was pulling him yanked him into the water quicker than he could react. He hit the cold water still not knowing what had dragged him overboard. The boat continued on its way, speeding across the bay laying out net as if Sven still sat at the helm.

In the water, Sven tried to swim but he couldn't. Every time he lifted his arm the net came with it. He felt along that arm with his other hand until he touched the webbing. The tough net material had caught on one of the copper rivets on the sleeve of his new jacket. He'd been pulled out of the boat by the net. He clawed at the button where the net held him until he tore it free. Then he heard a loud bang from the boat.

The dory had reached the end of the net. Sven heard the rattle of metal against wood as the chain he used to hold the offshore end of the net to the buoy he'd anchored out in the bay, slipped overboard. Free of the encumbering drag, the boat's speed increased and it turned into a graceful arc curving toward the beach.

Sven clutched the cork line and pulled himself along it, partly swimming, sometimes floating. His hands cramped in the cold water. His new jacket and the rest of his clothes grew heavier and heavier as they soaked through, threatening to weigh him under. The buoy was closer than shore and he made for it, slowly, hand over hand along the cork line. In one agonizing last rush he reached the can and slung his arm through the line tied around it, supported at last by something with more buoyancy than his own. He knew his own couldn't have lasted much longer. He relaxed once he reached the buoy, still realizing he had to do something to stay alert, to keep his senses in the numbing water and save himself. The line of white corks stretched away from him into the twilight toward shore. He wondered if he could make it. Off to his left he could see the light from the warm shack, sanctuary, where Orca busily cleaned after the bear, unaware of the old man's predicament.

Over the sounds of his sweeping, Orca could hear the roar of the outboard as the dory sped toward the beach. He felt better knowing Sven was heading back. He hadn't been particularly happy alone in the cabin as the evening darkened and that bear probably wandered in the woods nearby. He didn't expect the bear to return now that a fire burned in the stove and the light was on and human scent had reclaimed the shack. Still, the sound of Sven returning reassured him. He also looked forward to someone helping him clean what remained of the mess, although by that time he had it at least under control enough so that he had begun a search for something to cover the broken window. The fire had warmed the cabin somewhat, but much of the heat was escaping through the opening.

It took some time for the idea that the outboard had been running way too long to intrude into Orca's thoughts. It only occurred to him when he went toward the porch to bring the rest of their gear inside. On the landing he scanned the bay until he saw the dory trying to climb the beach where it had come to a halt in the gravel. The motor still ran almost at full throttle, kicking up a fountain of water and pebbles and mud behind it, trying to push the boat up onto the beach. Orca ran to the boat, shut down the motor and looked inside. No Sven. He called across the bay but heard no response, or did he? Had he heard another of those noises that could be almost anything? Sven was out there somewhere. A bolt of cold shot through his body.

Frantically he shoved the dory back into the water until it floated free. He jumped in and started the motor again, hoping the rocks hadn't damaged the propeller so badly it wouldn't push the boat. He pulled the shift lever gingerly and the motor chunked into gear. The boat began moving. Orca followed the shore until he reached the cork line. He turned and followed the corks out into the bay slowly, hoping he could hear Sven calling over the sound of the idling motor. He shouted once more and thought he heard an answer. He worked his way along the net hoping he wouldn't find a dip in the cork line where it might have been pulled under water by a heavy weight. He scanned the water near the net for disturbance, but saw none.

Hanging onto the buoy, Sven watched the boat approach. He'd been about ready to try to pull himself to shore along the cork line when he'd seen Orca guide the boat away from the beach. His arm had numbed where the line around the can cut into his circulation and his muscles cramped in the cold. He shouted.

Orca heard him, but Sven floated low in the dark water next to the buoy and Orca couldn't see him yet. Then Sven slapped his free hand on the water and Orca spotted the splash. He raced to the end of the net and pulled up next to the can and Sven.

"You all right?" he called, relieved to have found him.

"No. I ain't all right. I'm in the water and I'm hangin' on this durn buoy. Git me outta here."

"I'm coming, Sven, hang on."

Orca eased the dory closer to Sven until the old man could grab the gunwale with one hand and slip his other from underneath the rope on the buoy. Orca helped him over the side and Sven flopped soggily into the bottom of the boat, much like the salmon did when they were picked from the net. "Let's get home," he said.

Orca powered for the beach as fast as the dory with its bent, curled propeller would move the boat. He hit the rocks almost as hard as the dory had hit earlier. Sven went over the side and sloshed up the beach, water dripping from him, squishing out of his boots with every step. He dropped his clothes outdoors and Orca unpacked blankets to cover him. Sven sat by the stove while Orca took another blanket and nailed it over the broken window. Sven watched him cover the opening and looked around the room as what remained of the bear's mess came into focus.

"What happened in here?" he asked.

"Bear," Orca said. "While you were out there swimming I had to chase a bear out of the cabin. It looked a lot worse than this when I started."

"I imagine it did," Sven said. "He was in here when you come up?"

"He was inside."

"Whew. What'd you do?"

"He pretty much ran when he saw me. I fired a shot over his head to keep him going." He handed Sven a cup of coffee.

Sven looked at the cup in his hand. "You sure this is all right? You ain't tryin' to kill me?"

"You're not that cold," Orca said, smiling.

"Aren't we a couple of yahoos," Sven said. "Here it's been I don't know how many years and we both go swimmin' in the same month. Far as I'm concerned, that's enough. Course, maybe it's just me. I'm the one sent you off fishin' herring by yourself. Then I go leavin' you to fight off a bear and in the process I almost go and leave you all together. Maybe we ought to make a deal here, we do things together. No more of this castin' all over the place in different directions, at least until we got things under control. Don't know what was so all-fired important about a couple of fish anyway. Guess I just needed to get doin' something. How about a deal like that? Okay?"

Orca sat down on a box next to Sven. "You said something on the way over today," he said. "You said, 'you got to pay attention all the time.'"

"That I did," Sven answered. "You startin' to give me lessons, now?"

CHAPTER 8

SALMON RUNS

THE FOLLOWING MORNING, Sven lay in his bunk, his muscles stiff after the dunking he'd taken the night before. He watched Orca making coffee and bull coffee.

"Sure hated to leave that net out all night," he said. "There's sure to be fish in it and them seals'll get 'em all. What we'll get is a ripped-up net, if we got any net left at all." He shook his head. "That's what you get for bein' in a hurry. I shoulda waited. Great way to start the season, huh?"

Orca handed him a cup of coffee.

"Maybe it's not ripped too bad," the boy said. "We sure did a lot of work on that net just to see it all ruined. I'd hate to have to start all over again."

"Me, too," Sven agreed. "We just got the house tore up and took care of and now we probably got to fix that net again. Speakin' of tearin' things up, gimme that jacket."

Orca found the garment and gave it to Sven. The old man located his knife and began cutting all the rivets off the jacket, except for the few down the front he'd need to hold it closed. Orca worried he might cut the whole jacket to shreds, but after a few surgical slices, Sven held it up for examination, then said, "That ought to take care of that. Now, let's get going."

After Sven had dressed they took their mugs and walked down the beach to where Sven had anchored the net to shore.

"Don't look good," Sven said as they walked. "Look at them." He pointed toward the bay where the heads of more than half a dozen seals showed just above the surface of the water. Some swam near the net, others farther out toward the creek at the head of the bay.

"If there was a fish in that net, it's gone now. Maybe the net, too. Can't tell from here. At least the corks're still there." He lifted the line and gave it a tug but not enough showed for him to tell anything about the state of the net. "We can't tell anything 'til we get out there in the boat."

They walked to the dory and Sven tilted the outboard to examine the propeller. He felt the rough, chewed edges of the blades where they had ground into the gravel beach the night before. "Might as well start at the beginning," he said. "We did bring another prop, didn't we?"

"I packed it," Orca replied, "I'll go find it." He knew they'd brought a spare because it was one of the things he'd had to pack while he tried to cover for Sven's distractions. He ran back to the cabin and rummaged through boxes while Sven took the damaged propeller off the motor.

"We might be able to save this one with a file," Sven told Orca when the boy returned with the new propeller. "Ain't goin' to be good for much but a gettin'-home prop, though."

They slipped the new propeller onto the shaft and tightened the locking nut. Sven stepped toward the bow of the boat. "Time you did more than sit," he said. "You best be gettin' more experience runnin' the skiff."

Orca smiled broadly and went to the motor. He pulled the starter rope and the motor roared into life. Sven pushed the bow of the dory out and hopped aboard. Orca slid the shift lever into forward and they eased away from shore into the bay.

"Run along the net slow," Sven said and Orca guided the boat toward the cork line. As they ran along it, Sven shouted, " Can't see nothin' from here. Take 'er out to the buoy."

Orca steered the dory toward the blue can where it floated at the end of the line of corks. The boat's movement and noise scattered the seals. He slowed the boat when he reached the end of the net where it floated free and Sven reached over to grab it. He pulled the first section of net into the boat. "Let's haul 'er all the way and spread it out on the beach, see what we got."

While Orca ran the motor as slowly as it would go, Sven began pulling the net into the boat over the bow. As he had feared, the few fish left in the net had been mangled by the seals. He cursed every time he saw a head or half a fish entwined in the webbing and he pitched the remains overboard. He cursed even louder every time he ran across a hole where there had been a fish and a seal had torn it out, usually taking some of the net with it. After one particularly large tear, Sven let out a string of complaints that made Orca laugh.

"Ain't funny, bud," Sven said. "This gives us at least a full day's work. That's if we can save the net at all. At best we lost a whole day's fishin'."

Orca's expression turned serious.

"'Course it's my own blasted fault. I'll tell you what. If it wasn't my own fault, I'd really be mad."

"I've never seen you madder than this," Orca said.

"Oh, I been madder," Sven said. "It was my own fault then, too. Let's keep goin'."

Sven kept up a steady undercurrent of grousing until they'd pulled the entire net into the boat and Orca nosed the dory against shore. Once on land, they began hauling the net out of the boat and stretching it along the beach. Seeing the whole of it, or what was left, did nothing for Sven's humor.

"Looks like they fought a world war in there," he said, picking up a section of the net and then throwing it down disgustedly. Orca skidded up the beach to the shack where he collected their spools of net material and shuttles. He returned to find Sven marking the holes they'd need to repair. They bent over their work reluctantly, dreading a full day on the beach with the attendant sore backs and scraped knees. At first Sven worked almost

violently, jerking and yanking the web and the shuttle, occasionally slamming the tool to the ground in frustration. When he
dropped a tool or slipped on a rock, he'd let out another bellow,
then compose himself and start over. Orca worked quietly at one
end of the net as far from Sven as he could. To help calm the old
man he made extra trips to the cabin for coffee and at lunch he
made a fresh, hot meal, but nothing seemed to improve Sven's
mood.

In between his fits of anger with the net and the reluctant
tools, Sven would finish a section and look out toward the water
where the seals still swam lazily. He'd holler curses at them and
once he even ran down to the water's edge to hurl a rock at one of
his real or imagined villains when it ventured too close to shore.
The seals always slid beneath the surface, easily avoiding the rocks
long before they came anywhere near them, and that seemed to
make Sven all the angrier. Orca wondered if it was just the seals
and the net that were bothering Sven.

By midafternoon, working from opposite ends of the net they
had almost reached the middle. Much of Sven's anger had been
reduced to muttering and except for that they worked without
talking, slowly threading the net back into one piece. Working
toward the middle, they came closer together and the closer Orca
came to Sven, the more his mood began to affect the boy. The
length of the task had done nothing to slow Sven physically and
he worked his shuttle furiously. Working in that proximity, eventually they bumped into each other. Sven's shuttle flew from his
hands and he let out a howl. He started to stand up, but his feet
flew out from under him on the slippery rocks. He fell into a
sitting position, cursing the net and the seals, the beach and fish
and fishing.

"You're awfully mad over just a torn net," Orca said, stopping
his work. "Is that all that's bothering you?"

"Maybe I am," Sven said, but he wasn't about to tell Orca what
it was. He ducked the question and rolled to his knees. He crawled
back to where he'd dropped his tool and bent over in silence, at

least for a time. Before long Sven began muttering again. They stitched for about half an hour until they bumped again. This time Orca dropped his shuttle and mumbled something under his breath. Sven heard one of his own words, not a particularly pretty one. Sven reached over and cuffed Orca on the shoulder, the only part of the boy he could reach. He hit the youngster hard enough to knock him over from where he stood hunkered, but not hard enough to hurt. Still, the boy sprawled backwards onto the stones.

"You might get away with your bull coffee, but you ain't gettin' away with talkin' like that. No, sir, you ain't talkin' like that."

Stunned, the boy fought tears.

Then Sven realized what he'd done, how far his mood had taken him. The anger flushed from him, exhaled almost audibly like the breath of a whale. He reached over and helped the youngster gain his feet. He pulled Orca to him and wrapped his thick arms around the boy and held him there while he looked out over the water to the mountains beyond. Mist rose in his eyes and he squeezed until Orca almost had trouble breathing. "I'm sorry," he whispered, "real sorry."

Sven released his grip and slid his hands up to the boy's shoulders, holding him at arm's length and looking into his eyes. "I shouldn't of done that." Orca smiled up at him, nervously, still fighting his feelings. Sven had caught him by surprise. He never knew what to expect anymore. One minute they talked and kidded just like old times, the next Sven's mind wandered off into space, or worse, he grew angry. This time Orca had been hit.

"It's all right, Sven, really."

"No, it ain't all right," Sven pulled the boy to him again and this time Orca's arms went around the old man's waist and they stood like that for a moment as one on the beach.

"Tell you what, son," Sven broke the silence. "there's really only room enough on that net for one guy to work anymore. Whyn't I go up and make us a good dinner and you finish up. Then we can figure out how we're going to handle this fishing. We might still catch one tide tonight."

"That sounds good to me," Orca said.

They let go of each other and Sven traipsed up the beach slowly with heavy footfalls, turning once to stop and watch the boy bent over the net, knotting the webbing into an integral piece again. He noticed seals swimming out in the bay, but they didn't bother him any more. They were part of the whole. They couldn't be isolated from it. Their gray heads belonged on the clear water that reflected the green of the mountain's slopes and the whites of their tops. Sven saw the continuum. The seals were part of the flow, from the cabin, the stretch of beach and the water filling the sound all the way out to the North Pacific and beyond and back again to the beach where the boy sat working on his net. Somewhere in that flow, the whales hunted in the same waters that lapped against the dock pilings in a town where their future was going to be resolved. He saw himself and Orca part of the flow and decided Miss Priscilla M. Braithewaite was part of it, too. Whatever happened, he and the boy remained together, connected, whether Orca went to school in town or stayed with him in the sound. They would always be connected, Sven thought, if he didn't let his own preoccupations drive the boy away. Right there he decided to retain his perspective, keep their lives as they were, without the mental intrusions Miss Braithewaite caused. He focused on the seals again, those hated net robbers. "They're all part of it," he mumbled. Then he turned toward the shack and dinner.

After dinner, a renewed Sven returned to the beach with Orca. They carefully fed their repaired net through Sven's makeshift bow roller into a neat pile in the dory. As he passed the net through his hands into the boat, Sven examined the work the boy had done that day, looking over the knots Orca had sewed.

"You done a fine job here," he told the boy, "real fine. Can't really tell which you did and which I did."

Orca beamed. "Thanks, Sven. I guess you taught me right."

"Guess I did at that."

Once the last of the net went into the dory, they attached one end to the shore anchor. Orca ran the outboard, backing away from shore while Sven fed the net, this time over the bow and more carefully and slowly than he had the night before. As they worked, Sven explained the process: "You got to learn to watch and experiment to find where the fish go. Here we got a good eddy and when the tide starts goin' out, the fish kind of jam up in the current and start milling around right where we set. You go to a new place and you got to learn the currents and the tides. Sometimes you can set just a hundred feet away from another guy and catch every fish and the guy next to you won't catch nothin' just because you know the currents."

Of course, Orca had heard it all before. Every time they set the net, every year they came to Unakwik, Sven explained his theories of fishing and guided the boy through the process. Orca could have written it on paper verbatim. But he never said a word, just listened politely as if it were the first time.

"Here we catch 'em comin' both ways," Sven went on. "They come in on the flood real close in to shore and we get some of 'em then. When the tide changes, they start that millin' around in the creek mouth. On the ebb they end up in this eddy and then we got 'em comin' and goin'."

Orca guided the boat slowly as the net slipped over the bow into the water, always watching behind him to see that he was making for the buoy. When they came to the end, Sven attached the net to the anchored buoy that had held him the night before.

"Some guys'll leave the net now, but I prefer stickin' around. You seen what happened the other night. You can pick fish all the time or just wait. I'd rather wait. You can tell when you got fish in the net. The corks start bobbin'. Best, I think to stick around with them seals and all. We got a lot of 'em here. They can go a long way under water, and fast. You see 'em way over there and the next thing you know, they're right here rippin' fish out of the net. Lot of guys shoot 'em or drop little bombs in the water to scare 'em off. I don't abide by that, partly 'cause them bombs scare the fish away, too. I just like to hang out and run down the net now and again, scare 'em off that way."

Orca let the boat drift once they released the net.

"Some places you can just wait for the tide to go out. Where they got long tide flats, it leaves the fish and the net high and dry and you just walk along it and pick fish. Real muddy work. Too deep here, so we do it the way we do."

"Ain't too many fish just yet," Sven said, "Just as well. After last night looks like we need the practice. I think we can put in a good summer. Both of us workin' and standin' watches we can fish maybe twenty-four hours."

They drifted watching the net until Sven told Orca to drive the boat out of the bay into the inlet. "If we're gonna have fish, we better get some ice," he said.

They ran toward the north end of Unakwik until they reached a raft of icebergs floating seaward from where they'd fallen from the face of Meares Glacier. Using a dip net, they captured ice pieces of a size they could lift from the water and filled the bottom of the dory. When they had all the ice they could carry, Orca drove them back toward Miners Bay.

They turned into Miners to find the *Salmania* riding at anchor just off the shack. "Wonder what he's doin' here," Sven hollered to Orca. "Season's goin'. He should be fishin'."

They went over to the bigger boat and when they maneuvered close, Corky came out on deck. "Hey!" he shouted.

"Hey, Corky. What's the deal? You takin' a vacation?"

"Naw. They shut it down for a couple of days. Got a visitor. She come out on a tender. Just had to see you."

Miss Priscilla M. Braithewaite emerged from the *Salmania's* cabin. "Hello," she said.

Sven and Orca nodded their hellos. "You comin' to shore?"

Corky looked at the mound of ice in the dory. "Think I'll bring my own skiff."

By the time he and Miss Braithewaite had followed Sven and Orca to the beach, the two had begun lugging their catch to Sven's ice house up the hill behind the shack.

Corky picked a small chunk and followed them up the hill, Miss Braithewaite tagging along behind.

They found Sven handing ice to Orca who was inside the house. Corky said, "See, Sven dug this hole in the hill, and then he built the logs around it. They haul ice up here to keep it cool and this is where they keep their fish until the tender comes in to buy it. See that pipe there?" Miss Braithewaite's eyes followed the pipe where it ran downhill toward their shack. "That pipe carries the melt water down to the cabin. It drips into a drum and they got less water to haul. Nothin's wasted."

"Clever," she said. "Do they keep their food cold there, too?"

Sven said, "Best refrigerator there is."

When he'd handed the last chunk to Orca, he turned to Miss Braithewaite. "Good to see you again. What brings you out? Is anything happening?"

"I wanted to see your summer home," she said. "I brought some more forms for you and I haven't received Orca's tests yet."

"Mail's pretty irregular out here," Sven said. "He took the test, though. I got it down to the cabin if you want it."

Orca emerged from the ice house. "How are you?" he asked Miss Braithewaite.

"I'm fine," she answered. "How are you?"

"Just great," Orca smiled, looking at Sven.

"How is your season?" she asked.

"Oh, we're just getting started," Orca said. "We just made our first set a little while ago."

"It's more than a little while, now," Sven said. "Maybe you ought to make the pick."

"How about coffee, first," Corky asked.

"Sure," Sven said. "Orca, whyn't you go get the skiff ready?"

They walked to the shack where Sven poured them each a cup and they took them to the beach.

"We'll watch from here," Sven told Orca. "You go pull the net."

Orca pulled away in the skiff and Sven resumed his lecture. It didn't matter to him who his listeners were. Here he had a new audience anyway. Orca heard him begin and realized for all the times he'd heard Sven describe set-net fishing, he was going to miss hearing the old man's speech.

They watched Orca insert Sven's version of thole pins in the gunwales of the dory. He'd learned the technique from older boat builders who placed vertical pins in pairs to serve as oar locks along the gunwales of the boats they built. Sven had adapted the idea to fishing, placing two pins about an arm span apart on each side of the dory.

"A lot of guys just haul the net over the gunwale, or off the bow or stern," he said. "They pull the boat along and let the net come in over one side and off over the other. These puller pins work a lot better."

Orca pulled a section of net, slipping the mesh over the tops of the pins, letting it hang there while he reached down and lifted more. With each pull, he slipped more netting over the pins until he reached the leadline, the lead-weighted rope sewn into the bottom of the net that made it hang straight in the water. As he hauled, now and then he'd have to stop to disentangle a fish caught by its gills in the web. The first red salmon he held up triumphantly for the audience on shore.

"First fish," Sven said.

Each time Orca reached the leadline, he carefully fed that section over the side again and then moved along the net to the next.

"See," Sven continued his lecture, "we just pull up part of the net at a time and loop the web over those sticks. You can keep right on pickin' all day if you want. And, the rest of the net keeps right on fishin'. This way you're right on top of it. You get the fish fresh and you get 'em before the seals do. Keeps from havin' to pull the whole net, too."

"It looks heavy," Miss Braithewaite said. "Does he always do it by himself?"

"We take our turns." Sven answered, "Sometimes we work together. Depends. It's a chore for a guy his size." He watched Orca struggle with the net. "But he's a strong kid. When the runs start comin' stronger, we'll both work at it, but there ain't much fish, yet."

"It looks like hard work," she said. "How often do you pull the net?"

"Oh, come the height of the run, we'll work 24 hours. Take watches. Sometimes both of us."

Orca reached the shore end of the net and brought the dory to the beach in front of the audience. "Got six," he shouted.

"Slim pickin's for all that work," Sven shouted back. "Give 'em here."

Orca handed the fish to Sven, who laid them on the beach.

He turned to Miss Braithewaite and back to Orca. "Go pull the net in. Don't look like we're gonna get any more work in tonight and no sense takin' another chance."

"What do you mean another chance?" Corky asked.

Sven told him and Miss Braithewaite the story of his swim the previous evening and their day on the beach repairing their net.

"What if you really suffered an injury?" she asked. "What would you do? Where is a doctor?"

Sven smiled toward Corky, then answered, "Don't really go to the doctor. Mostly you got to be careful. Everything you do, you got to stop first, kind of see where the places are you could get hurt and then do things slowly. "

"Were you doing that when you went into the water last night?"

"Well, no," Sven answered.

"Has Orca ever seen a doctor?" she asked.

"They got a public health nurse over to the Native village," Sven said. "We been there a couple of times. Got his shots. Don't really need a doctor. Boy never gets sick."

"He should be getting proper health care," she said.

There it was again. Here he hadn't received any answers to all his old questions and she raised a new one. Health care now. That made schooling, guardianship, parents, home life and health care. He wondered what she'd demand next. "I better clean these fish," he said pulling a knife from his belt. "You hungry? We could make one real quick. These reds are the best there is."

"I got some other stuff in the boat. I'll go get it," Corky said and left in his skiff.

Miss Braithewaite stood quietly, alternately watching Sven clean the fish and Orca pull the net into the boat. When both had finished, Sven took the fish, all but one, to the ice house while Orca brought the dory to the beach.

She walked to the house with Orca. "Did your friend like the seal skull?" he asked.

"Oh, yes. She was already painting from it when I left," Miss Braithewaite said. "How did you like that test I sent?"

"It was all right," Orca responded.

"Could you do it?"

"Oh, sure, it was pretty easy."

They met Sven at the shack. Inside, Sven cut fillets from the salmon, added his own little touches and put them in the oven.

He'd given Miss Braithewaite the envelope containing Orca's test and she sat quietly reading it, not with a pencil making corrections, but casually, to give herself an idea of how well he had done.

The sound of Corky's skiff returning sent Orca scurrying out the door.

As soon as the door closed, Sven asked, "How'd he do?"

"It looks like he did very well. Of course I'm not grading it, but from what I've seen, he's only missed a couple. There are kids in formal school who don't do this well."

"He's a smart kid," Sven said. "Is there any other news?"

"I'm afraid not much," she said. "So far nothing has been found regarding his background. The investigators are just about to give up on that. I have some forms here for you. It's an application for adoption. If you complete that and it's approved, that will solve everything."

"What else is there?"

"Well, there's the birth certificate. You won't be able to complete the adoption until that's resolved. Have you been able to find anything that confirms how he came to you?"

"All I found was a calendar I marked the day he showed up. Don't supposed that's anything legal."

"I doubt it."

"There is something else, maybe."

"What?"

"You know, I heard a boat's log book is considered a legal document."

"Is that right? But what does that matter?"

"Well, I was thinking, you know, maybe somebody come to visit around that time, maybe made a note in his log. That might at least give a idea when he come."

"Maybe. Would Corky have something like that?"

"He'd be the most likely."

"We'll try him. Now, what about your own background? They couldn't find much on you, either."

"I found my citizenship. Some other old papers. I put them in the envelope with his test and that birth certificate."

"Have you ever been in trouble with the law?"

"Not so's it matters," Sven said. "I ain't lived a life it's easy to track on paper. Been to sea or out here since I's a boy. Not good places for the paper pushers to catch you. I don't even have a driver's license, never made enough money to pay taxes."

"I'm amazed that people can live without records, but they do."

"So, if I can adopt him, no one could take him after that?"

"No."

"Then what about schooling?"

"Well, I'll take this test back. They'll make an evaluation. You should be getting some correspondence materials from the school district. There are lots of students in Alaska who go through their whole public education at home. It will take a lot of work on your part. Also, you might want to consider his socialization. He's lived so isolated for so long, it might be good for him to go to a school for a while just so he learns to get along with other people."

"Something to consider, " Sven said, unconvinced. "So, where are we really?"

"Things look very good for you," she said. "I don't want to be too optimistic. Something always can go wrong. A judge can decide this just isn't the proper life. Something might come up in the adoption. If the birth certificate goes through and nothing shows up in your background, and they believe how you came to find him, I think you'll be all right. I would say you're more on the positive side than the negative, but hold your celebration for a while."

"It sounds good," Sven said.

Corky and Orca came through the door to find Sven smiling broadly. Corky knew Miss Braithewaite must have brought good news. Orca saw a happy Sven and that was enough.

"Corky brought ice cream," he shouted.

"These modern boats," Sven said, "They got generators and electricity. Freezers. What I wouldn't do to have some electricity down to Cabin Bay. "

Corky looked at him, "You know how much fuel I'd have to haul for you to keep a generator going out there? You know what it would cost?"

"Never mind," Sven said.

"Got some salad stuff, too," Corky said. "We all ate before, but a little salmon and salad wouldn't be bad."

"We ate, too," Orca said, "but it's the first salmon of the year." He took the bag they'd brought from the *Salmania* and began preparing a salad.

When they placed the plates on the table, Sven asked, "Miss Braithewaite, why don't you tell Orca here about life there in town?" Then, through a lighthearted dinner she told them how she'd come to Alaska and moved to Prince William Sound. She told of her neophyte adventures coming to understand what to her had been almost a foreign country. Corky and Sven added their analyses of why she might have encountered the problems she did. Orca listened and laughed with them, enthralled with her description of the town. When they'd finished, Corky said, "Well, best be gettin' back to the boat. We got to get going early. You got to catch that tender headin' back to town first thing. I 'magine the crew's gettin' a little restless out there, too."

"Haven't we got time for one story?" she asked. Sven and Corky looked at each other. They never told stories on demand. It was what you did when it came up in conversation, something to fill time when you couldn't think of anything else to do.

"Tell the one about Captain Skooks and the whale," Orca said. "I like that one."

"You tell it. You're the one knew the guy," Sven said, "I just heard about it."

"All right," Corky said. "But, the short version. I ain't goin' to take all night."

Miss Braithewaite handed Sven the envelope with the adoption forms. He sat filling in the blanks while Corky fell into his storytelling voice.

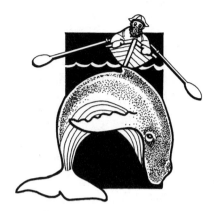

CHAPTER 9

CAPTAIN SKOOKS AND THE WHALE

Gregory Finchholder couldn't have timed his trip home from town any worse than he did. Weakened after his time in the clinic with the broken ankle, he couldn't row as strongly as he usually did and a hefty tide carried him out of the cove into more open water. Gregory accepted his situation and kept pulling against the current even though each time he put pressure against his foot to pull on the oars he felt a needle of pain fly up his leg. He bent to his task with little of his concentration left for anything else. That's why he was so surprised when something gave the skiff a good healthy bump. He turned quickly, thinking he'd thumped into a rock, but nothing stuck up out of the water in front of him.

The second thump wasn't so hard, more just a contact, but it lifted the skiff out of the water. By this time Gregory was beginning to figure out what was happening. He shipped the oars, brought them inside the skiff, and waited. Sure enough, even though he wasn't moving, a third thump lifted the little boat again out of the water, then set it back down. Gregory began to fear he might tip over. He wasn't worried about any danger from what was lifting his boat, just that he might capsize from its overzealousness. He lowered himself off the seat and onto the bottom of the boat so it would be more stable, then he leaned over the gunwale to see if he could see anything.

The whale rose so close to the skiff that the moisture from its blowhole soaked him. Forty feet of humpback whale came out of the water and lay there on the surface, the giant eye right even with Gregory's and staring at him. Gregory laughed a hello. "Halloo you old whale, you," he hollered.

Whales are feared because they're big, but anyone who's been around them for any length of time knows they're friendly, or curious, or at least they go about their own business and don't bother anybody. The only problem was if one got affectionate there was the chance the big animal could bounce a boat as easily as a toothpick in a teacup.

Looking at the whale next to him, Gregory recalled the one in Wrangell harbor that time. She had stayed around town all summer and folks got to recognizing her. Nobody could figure out why she stayed. She became a common sight and people liked having the whale around, but she also became something of a nuisance. It seems even humpback whales like having their backs scratched and this particular whale, whom the fishermen had taken to calling Esmirelda, wanted her back scratched, a lot. The only problem was, there weren't all that many whale-sized backscratchers around. So, Esmirelda didn't have a lot of choices about where she was going to scratch her back.

As a result, many a fisherman returning from a hard time on the grounds got the scare of his life when he was near the harbor and all of a sudden the whole boat would shudder as Esmirelda rose underneath and made use of the barnacle-covered bottom to relieve a whale-sized itch. From shore you'd be watching a fleet of boats near the harbor and all of a sudden one of them would rise a few feet above the others for a couple of seconds, probably sending the crew sprawling all over the deck. A few seconds later with a flip of her giant tail Esmirelda would sound, waving her tail to the fishermen as she dove while they shouted and screamed at the ripples she left on the water.

Several plots were hatched over that summer to try to discourage Esmirelda, but none of them worked. What finally discouraged Esmirelda started out as a simple, harmless practical joke.

Gregory Finchholder, whom you might remember was called Captain Skooks in those days, and was fishing out of Wrangell at the time, had a friend who was a trapper up country from town. The friend's name was Pete LaFeet, at least that was what everybody called him. Nobody knew Pete's real name or if he was really French. What everybody did know was that Pete had a thick accent of some kind and he wore size 18 boots. So he became LaFeet and even he seemed to like the name. Pete at that time was the only trapper along the Stikine River who didn't have to mark his trap line. Anyone seeing a trap with the tracks made by those size 18 boots around it just naturally stayed away.

Well, Pete, spending so much time alone like he did, wasn't afraid of much. As a matter of fact, he only had one real fear and only Captain Skooks knew what it was. Pete LaFeet was afraid of water. As far as he was concerned, water was made to be frozen and walked on, not soft and chilly and wet to fall into. Once the ice turned to liquid, Pete LaFeet avoided it at all costs. He even dreaded going to Wrangell the once a year when he had to sell his furs and pick up new supplies. Wrangell was right on the salt water, almost big ocean and Pete didn't even like a creek very much. Skooks guessed Pete was afraid of water because he figured if Pete ever fell in and those boots filled with water, well, nothing could save him then. So Pete stayed away from water as best he could.

Pete had another little quirk when he came into town. It seems he spent so many nights sleeping on the hard ground or in rough beds while he was up there on his trap line, when he came into town and fell into a nice, soft civilized bed, he went to sleep and had been known to stay asleep for two days at a stretch. There were no tree roots or bugs or rocks to wake him up. The combination of Pete's sleeping and his fear of water was what led to Esmirelda's downfall. Skooks and his friends decided to take advantage of both to pull a great practical joke.

Skooks found two big burls off a spruce tree that someone had left in town when he was traveling through from the north. Skooks nailed those two burls to the bottom of a skiff, then put the skiff into the water at the end of a dark alley. After setting up that end of it, he and his friends went looking for Pete and waited until he went to bed. Once Pete hit the sack they gave him another hour to settle right into a two-day sleep and then they picked up him and the mattress and all and hauled him down the alley and dropped him into the skiff. Pete, all comfortable on that mattress, slept right through the whole trip and went right on sleeping as the skiff drifted out into the harbor.

Pete LaFeet must have slept all night or was too afraid to say anything because those watching never saw him above the gunwales or heard a peep out of him. Nothing was heard at all until midmorning when Esmirelda found that little skiff with the back-scratching knobs attached to the bottom. Once that old whale felt those burls along her itching back, there was no stopping her.

She bounced that little boat around the harbor like a ping-pong ball. She'd lift it clear out of the water on her back, she rolled so her belly could scratch along the knobs, she splashed around in joy leaving the skiff for a moment, then went right back to it.

Pete, for his part, awoke with the first jolt, screamed once, then clutched the bottom of the boat.

Esmirelda would scratch a little, then she'd come along side and roll over, then dive, come up and scratch again. Sometimes she'd float right up next to it on the surface and stay there for a couple of minutes. A terrified Pete LaFeet clung to the boat, his fingernails digging troughs in the wood.

After this had gone on for a couple of hours and they'd had their laughs, Skooks and his friends figured the joke had gone far enough and they took a boat out to rescue the horrified LaFeet. As one of them said, they'd better get going because it looked like "that fool whale's fallen in love."

And for all purposes that's what it did look like. There was the whale rubbing right up next to the skiff, quiet and tender as could be. From the inside of the skiff all that showed above the gunwales were the heels of Pete's big boots as he lay face down on the bottom.

When the rescuers approached the skiff they hollered to Pete. Captain Skooks shouted, trying hard not to laugh, "Pete, you gotta save yourself. That silly whale's in love with you and won't let me get close. You gotta discourage her. Do whatever you have to do so we can pick you up."

This was the first Pete knew anyone was there besides himself and the water and the whale. He peered cautiously over the gunwale. When his head came up and he saw Skooks, he glared. "You got me into this."

Esmirelda went, "WHOOSH."

Pete spent about ten minutes just getting over his terror enough to do something. He finally forced his fright way down deep inside him and afraid as he was of water, he stood up in the skiff. In that thick accent of his he told Esmirelda he was sorry. Then he hauled off and laid one of those size 18 boots right up behind her eye. Afraid of the water as he was, Pete LaFeet kicked forty tons of loving whale. If a humpback whale can look shocked, Esmirelda looked shocked. She swam off a couple of hundred yards thrashing with her huge tail and almost swamping both boats. As soon as she was far enough away, Skooks moved his boat in close to the skiff and the three of them hauled Pete LaFeet out of the skiff and into safety. He was soaking wet from the thrashings of the whale's tail and so mad he couldn't talk or at least didn't want to until he had solid land under those boots again.

Skooks headed for shore. Esmirelda went back to the skiff and gave it a few tentative nudges. Then she came after the bigger boat. The skiff might have been nice for scratching but now it was Pete she wanted. Skooks gave his boat more throttle to go faster. Esmirelda made a couple of rushes at it but evidently it looked too big for her and being basically nonviolent, she finally settled to following at a distance.

When they finally got Pete ashore, he looked at them for a minute like he was going to fight. Then he just tromped away. The last anybody saw of him he was headed back to his trapline a full two months early and from then on he never came near the ocean again. He even trusted another trapper to bring in his furs every year and haul back his grubstake for the next year.

As for Esmirelda, she never went back to scratching her back on fishing boats. For three or four days she swam back and forth along the waterfront, making sounds like a cow with a sore throat. Then one day she disappeared. But for the next few years, every once in a while Skooks would hear about a humpback whale showing up at some waterfront or other, scratching her back on a boat or two and swimming around the harbor making that hoarse cow sound, crying her love for Pete LaFeet, who was hiding somewhere up the Stikine River. Or, at least that's where everybody thought he was. After a while nobody in the coastal towns heard from him any more.

But that was years ago. Whales don't remember that long. Or do they?

Gregory watched this one as it watched him. Could this be Esmirelda? And if it were, would she remember him? After all, he was the one who caused it all. He was sure it couldn't be the same whale, or could it? He looked along the side of the whale next to him but saw nothing familiar.

Then the whale moved and Gregory braced for another thump. The whale slipped below the surface for a moment but there was no thump. She rose on the other side of the boat. Gregory took another close look, this time at the opposite side of the whale. He started at the bumpy head and searched along the whale. Something caught his eye. He stared. There, behind the whale's left eye, barely visible now was a mark, a boot mark, unmistakably a big boot mark—a size 18 boot mark.

"Esmirelda," Gregory shouted as if to an old friend. Then he realized he might have made a mistake. There he was on the ocean alone with a whale that might blame him for her misery.

Esmirelda breathed loudly, as if to sigh, blinked her eye, then simply slipped beneath the surface and disappeared as mysteriously as she'd appeared. The impression she left, Gregory understood: she knew and she was just letting him know she knew, leaving him always to question what he'd done with his practical joke. Gregory rowed for home even less of Captain Skooks than he had been before.

CHAPTER 10

THREE FOR THE BLUEBERRY PATCH

CORKY FINISHED HIS STORY and Sven looked up from his papers.

"Captain Skooks, huh," Miss Braithewaite said. She looked accusingly at Sven.

All he said was, "I got this done. You want to look it over?"

She took the paperwork. "I can look at it later. I'm sure it's fine."

"We got to get going," Corky said as he stood and headed for the door.

"We'd invite you to stay," Sven said to Miss Braithewaite, "but you can see we don't really have the accommodations."

"I thought your other cabin was small," she said.

Sven refused to apologize for it. "We're only here a couple of months. It's fine for that. We're outside most of the time anyway."

"It's perfect," she said. "It's so comfortable and with the scenery . . . "

"Let's go catch your ride," Corky insisted.

They left the cabin. Orca walked to the beach with Miss Braithewaite. Corky and Sven fell back, talking. "Price any good?" Sven asked.

"Looks like it's going to hold about where I said," Corky answered. "You might get 50 cents for your reds."

"How's your crew holding out?" Sven asked.

"They're lookin' pretty good. Course it's early yet, but they're okay, even Fagshark. He's quiet, sticks to himself, but I ain't had no trouble. Speakin' of crew, you know, Sven, you ought to think about lettin' the boy go with me next year. I was watchin' him last night with your net. He's good. I didn't see any wasted motion. Strong, too. How many, what's he, twelve, twelve-year-olds could lift that net the way he did?"

"Why's everybody all of a sudden tryin' to get him away from me?" Sven asked with mock irritation.

"Hey, hey. I was just thinkin'. He'd make a lot of money fishin' with me."

"I know he would. And we might need more money pretty soon. Might be good for him, too. It's just hard to think about lettin' him go."

"I guess I know what you mean," Corky said. "Maybe in time."

"Sure," Sven said.

They caught Orca and Miss Braithewaite at Corky's skiff.

Corky took Orca and began showing him the workings of the seine boat.

"Well, nice to see you again, Miss Braithewaite," Sven said. "Maybe you ought to come out some time when you can stay longer." He'd offered a hesitant invitation. He wasn't sure he wanted to spend a lot of time with her around.

"I've thought about that," she said. "I do have some time coming."

"Later in August, the rain sort of stops and we get lots of blueberries," Sven said.

"I'll see if I can get free," she said.

"Orca, come over here and say good-bye to Miss Braithewaite," Sven shouted. Orca left Corky at the skiff.

"Let's do this," Miss Braithewaite said, "If I'm going to come out for a real visit, invited and everything, please call me Priscilla. You, too," she said turning to Orca.

"All right, Priscilla, then," Sven said. "We'll look forward to seeing you again. And, thank you, too, for all the work you're doing. We appreciate it."

Corky helped her into the skiff.

"Good-bye, Miss . . . Priscilla," Orca said.

"Good-bye."

"Hey, Corky," Sven called, "You put in a good season. You keep the round side down."

"Sounds like better advice for you two," Corky shouted back. "See you."

They watched the skiff return to the *Salmania*, then turned up the beach. "We better get a good night's sleep," Sven said. "Fishin' starts for real tomorrow."

The *Salmania* had left by the time they began their morning's work. That day and through the next few, Sven and Orca worked themselves into the routine of the summer fishery. They made their sets and picks on the schedule of the tides, day and night, eating when time allowed and, in between, working on their cabin, hauling ice to the ice house, fish to the buyer's barge and making the repairs to their equipment that the wear and tear of constant operations made necessary. They prepared the fish smoker where, later on, Sven would preserve most of the fish they planned to keep for the winter. During the early part of the salmon run, they sold almost all of their fish, waiting until the end to save what they'd need in Cabin Bay.

One day Orca came into the shack after picking the net to find Sven stretching a measuring tape along one wall.

"What are you doing?" he asked.

"I figure we better do this," Sven answered. "If a woman's comin' to visit we're goin' to have to do some redecoratin'. Give her a bunk. Some privacy, too."

Among other chores, they turned one corner of the cabin into what they hoped would be a comfortable place for Priscilla when she arrived.

As the run grew stronger they caught more and more fish, forcing them to make more frequent runs to a barge the fish buyer had anchored in a cove just south of Miners Bay. Each day and sometimes twice they'd load their catch into the dory and run to the barge, placing the fish in a bin marked with their names and picking up mail the buyer's tender boat had left for them.

On one of their trips, Sven said, "Hey, the tide's way down. Let's go over to the beach there and see what we can find." He pointed to the east side of the moraine that crossed Unakwik. The receding water had exposed a wide tidal flat. They took a bucket from the boat and began walking the beach.

"Otters have pretty much cleaned out the clams," Sven said pointing to the broken shells that lay scattered along the flat. "Might find a few, though."

They walked to an exposed rock, more of a boulder. From along its sides, Sven scraped limpets into his bucket. They'd steam them with butter later, their cone-shaped shells making a perfect serving dish.

They pulled mussels from their hold on the rocks. Sven scraped the meat from one and offered it to Orca. "Take a little taste. If your lip or mouth feels a little numb, don't eat any more," he said. "It's how you test for red tide. These guys get it first."

Orca had heard this before, too. "Paralytic shellfish poisoning," he said. "The algae gives it to them. Sometimes it turns the water red." He wondered how Sven liked hearing his lectures come back to him.

Then they separated. Orca took a shovel and began digging in the flat, looking for clams. Sven went to the water's edge where he poked around among the rocks. Looking up from his digging once, Orca saw Sven's hand dive into the water. It came back up with a long red tentacle attached to it. Sven tugged until he'd pulled the whole octopus from its lair. The animal immediately began exploring along Sven's arm, grasping and touching everywhere, trying to figure out just what was happening. The old man freed himself, dumping the octopus into his bucket. He continued his exploration, constantly having to shove the tentacles back inside when the octopus tried to escape.

Orca stomped along the beach, then looked where he'd stepped. If a hole appeared, he knew he'd found a clam. He dug furiously behind the hole until he uncovered the shell, then picked it out to drop in his own bucket. Being the otters' favorite food, and the covering tidal water being shallow making them easy prey, Orca didn't find very many clams. After more than an hour's digging, he'd put eleven into his pail. He walked back to Sven where the old man wrestled the octopus back into the bucket yet again.

"How'd you do?" Sven asked.

"Not many left anymore," Orca said. "How about you?"

"Got this octopus and a couple of sea cucumbers." He showed Orca the bulbous cucumber-shaped critters. Later they would cut the five long muscles from them to cook with their other treasures.

"I'll run up and get some of that scurvy grass," Orca said, indicating the bright green plants growing just above the high tide line. "That will give us a great meal." He scrambled up the beach and filled the rest of his bucket with greens.

When he returned, Sven said, "Let's go pull one of our shrimp pots, too."

They took the dory and ran out to an orange buoy just to the north of the moraine shoal. Sven pulled the buoy into the boat and they took turns hauling on the quarter-inch line. In time the black, rectangular pot came into view. They lifted it into the boat and dumped the contents onto the deck. Two dozen of the eight-inch long spot shrimp fell out of the pot. "Now we got a dinner," Sven said. They put a couple of salmon heads into the pot for bait and dropped it overboard again, watching it sink into the depths.

"Aw, will you look at that," Sven said. Orca turned to see the octopus' last tentacle slip over the gunwale into the water. "Never seen a animal could find his way out so fast."

"We lost the octopus, but we gained a bunch of shrimp. I like shrimp better anyway," Orca said.

"No use cryin' over spilt octopus," Sven said. They turned for home and dinner with what remained from their afternoon's hunt.

To their routine, they added a beach hunt when the tide permitted. The salmon run turned into a big one and their constant

attention to their net left little time
for anything else. They fell into
their beds exhausted each day, rising again to meet the next flow of
incoming fish, taking turns at the
net, the runs to the tender barge,
cooking and sleeping.

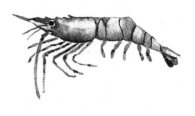

When the rains began in mid-July they barely noticed. Like the
herring and the salmon, rain arrived almost on schedule. Warm
moist air from the ocean crossed the sound until it bumped against
those mountains at the head of Unakwik. Trapped and cooling,
the clouds dumped their load of rain on Sven and Orca and they
spent their days in sweaty oilskins. To their routine they had to
add the time it took to put on, take off, dry and patch their rain
gear. It barely interfered with their all-consuming fishing.

In mid-August when the sun was dipping toward the autumnal
equinox and darker nights cooled the air, rain ceased and they
enjoyed sunny days again. Also in August, the salmon run began
to dwindle, leaving them more time for other activities. Most of
the fish they caught they took to their smoker, preparing it for the
winter meals they'd have at Cabin Bay.

With the fishing less hectic than its earlier pace, Orca took
over tending the net while Sven smoked fish. During the slack
periods, the boy joined the old man at the smoker, cleaning and
filleting salmon. Sven noticed how quick and sure Orca had become with the fillet knife. He could cut three fish to Sven's one
and he left less meat on the bones, wasting very little.

During one of those days, while Sven chipped wood for the
smoking fire and Orca fought his daily battle with the seals, both
of them turned to the sound of an approaching engine. The sound
came through higher pitched than the usual thrum of the fishing
boats' diesels. From their separate tasks, they both looked skyward in time to see a small airplane clear the ridge at the eastern
head of the bay and dip toward the water. The airplane circled
low over their cabin while they watched. Then it turned out over

the bay, headed into the slight breeze and came down to a landing on the water. Orca quickly ran the dory along the net to show the pilot where it was so he wouldn't hit it. Once the airplane had slowed from the landing, the pilot taxied toward the cabin, the floats cutting a double wake across the bay.

Near shore, the pilot cut the engine. When the propeller stopped turning, he stepped out onto one of the floats, hopping off in time to stop the airplane before the floats ground into the beach gravel.

Sven met him and steadied the airplane while Priscilla descended from the tiny cabin and inched her way along the float to step gingerly onto the slippery rocks.

"Hello, Miss Brai . . . Priscilla," Sven said as he took her hand to help her to the beach. "Welcome. Orca's just coming there in the dory."

"Hello, Mr. Kaartoonsen."

"You picked a good day," he said.

"A whole lot better than the first time," she answered.

"Yeah," Sven said, "You won't have to spend all your time recuperatin'."

Priscilla laughed, "Or drying out either. I brought some things." The pilot rolled his eyes, walked back along the float and reached into the back of the airplane.

"Hello, Miss Braithewaite," Orca called as he pulled the dory to shore right next to the airplane.

"Hello, young man, how are you?"

"I'm just fine," Orca assured her. "Glad you could make it back. We've been watching for you. We didn't know how you were coming."

"I'm afraid I took the easy way this time," she said.

Orca scanned the airplane. "I've never been up close to one of these before."

"Here, young fella, give me a hand," the pilot called. He pulled a box from the cargo compartment and handed it to Orca in the skiff who walked it forward and passed it to Sven on the beach. The pilot continued to lift boxes and bags from the airplane, passing them to Orca who handed off to Sven. When the pilot signalled he'd emptied the cargo hold, Sven surveyed the mound of boxes and duffels on the beach. "It's a wonder that thing got off the ground . . . all that weight," he said.

The pilot laughed. "It was nip and tuck at the end of the lake back in town," he said. "Here, kid, you want to take a look?" He helped Orca into the cockpit and began explaining the various gauges and controls.

"Looks like we lost him for a while," Sven said to Priscilla. "How's everything look? How'd he do on that test? I got to tell you, your last visit took some of the worry out of it."

"He tested very well," she said. "He's ahead of his age group in reading and social studies. He's going to need some work in mathematics, though. And I think he needs some work in the arts, too. But, overall, he's ahead of his grade level. Most of those boxes are from the school. They're the correspondence materials. You're going to have to work hard, too, just to keep enough ahead of him. I had a long talk with the school officials and they saw no reason to intervene. There is the socialization factor, though. You ought to consider it."

"What about the other?"

"Well, the investigators finally just threw up their hands. They couldn't find any record of him anywhere. They even sent a request Outside but nobody answered. It seems he just popped out of nowhere. Only one thing came up. There was a couple reported missing about the time you found him. Nobody's around who remembers them. Apparently they just moved out into the sound without telling anybody. They lived alone. The report didn't even have the name of the person who made it. Somebody noticed they were gone from a camp they had and so was their boat. They might have had something to do with him. Most likely not, but it could be."

"Never heard of anybody like that," Sven said. "Course every once in a while some ding-dong thinks he's going to live off the land. They learn pretty quick. Wilderness separates them out. I asked, too. Nobody ever told me about no missing people."

"At any rate, I put your request for adoption in with the court along with the investigators' reports and the school evaluation. We've submitted the application for a birth certificate based on your statement. Your background report is complete, but there's not much to it. You might have to tell your story to the court. Also, I've been gathering references from people who know you. Mr. Netsworth helped me with that," she said. "From there, it's up to the judge."

"That's the second-best news I heard all summer," Sven said. "I really want to thank you, Miss Braithewaite."

"There's no need to thank me, Mr. Kaartoonsen. The way you've raised the boy is what made the whole process work. Sometimes a situation like this can be very difficult. I'm afraid if we'd found any relatives at all, you would have had a bigger problem. And, will you stop calling me Miss Braithewaite? Priscilla, please."

Sven laughed. "I was gettin' a little tired of bein' 'mister' myself."

Orca hopped down from the cockpit and balanced himself along the float. They helped the pilot push the airplane away from shore. "Five days, then," he called.

"We'll be lookin' for you in five days," Sven answered, "give or take the weather."

The pilot waved, stepped up into the cockpit and cranked the engine over. Within minutes he had the airplane speeding down the bay, filling the mountain basin with the engine's roar and leaving behind a heavy white mist from the prop wash. Then the little airplane lifted off the water, cleared the trees on the ridge and disappeared.

When quiet had returned, Sven said, "Best get this stuff up to the cabin."

Sven hoisted one box and said, "This one's heavy. It's a wonder that airplane ever got off the ground."

"There is a load of books," Priscilla answered.

They moved up the beach with their burdens. Sven asked Orca, "You ever wonder, you know, how much time a year we spend just lugging stuff up and down beaches? I bet it's a considerable amount."

"Not to mention the trips back and forth in the boat," Orca responded.

"We'll have a load goin' back this year," Sven said surveying the materials Priscilla had brought. "Might have to make two trips with the fish and all."

"I didn't think of that," Priscilla said. "We probably could have taken it to Cabin Bay later."

"We'll make do," Sven said. "It's all right. I'd rather have it than not."

When they had hauled everything to the cabin, Priscilla looked over the boxes, hunting through them. "There's one in here we should open quickly," she said, "Oh, here it is." She opened a box and reached inside. In a minute she pulled out the requisite package of ice cream. "I wouldn't expect this to last very long in the heat," she said.

"It ain't gonna last too long anyway with that boy around," Sven said. He turned around to say something to Orca but the boy already had disappeared into the cabin. He emerged a minute later with bowls and spoons. Sven and Priscilla laughed. "Don't waste no time, do ya?" Sven said.

"I didn't want it to melt," Orca answered.

"Sure," Sven parried, "I know. You got to eat it to save it, huh?"

Orca dished out the ice cream and they sat down on stumps to eat.

"It's very pretty here," Priscilla said.

"We like it," Orca said.

"Makes a nice change of scenery," Sven said.

"Why don't you just live here year round instead of making the trip every year?" she asked.

Sven looked at her, pondering the question before he answered. "Never really thought about it much," he said, "I started out at Cabin Bay, there, and never thought no different. Course it's a lot colder here in winter and this little bay freezes over sometimes.

That'd make it tough to get in and out if we had to. Get a lot more snow here, too. I guess I like the change of scene, breaks up the year."

"It is beautiful," she said.

"Once we get you settled, we'll show you around a little. Hope you brought something to take blueberries home in. The rain let up a week ago and the sun's makin' them pop out all over the place. Should be sweet, too."

"Oh, I did, don't worry."

When they'd finished their ice cream, Sven stood up and said, "First let's show you your home for the next couple days."

They went inside the shack. Orca ran to a curtain hanging in one corner. They'd made it by weaving what bits of cloth the bear had left through an old section of netting. He pulled it back to reveal a bunk neatly built into the corner. Above it on the wall a row of shelves rose to the rafters. A shelf over the head of the bunk held a kerosene lamp. "We made this just for you," Orca said.

"Figured you might like a little privacy," Sven added. "But, hey, somethin's missin'."

Orca looked puzzled until Sven said, "'Member what we's talkin' about?"

"Oh yeah," the boy said, "'Be right back. 'Scuse me." He disappeared out the door.

While Orca ran his errand, Sven and Priscilla brought the rest of her gear indoors. Near the kitchen stove she unpacked boxes of fresh fruit and vegetables. "I wasn't sure what you'd like, but I guessed you don't see much of this the way you live." She unpacked bananas, oranges and apples and several varieties of vegetables. "I even found some corn on the cob."

"Sure don't," Sven said, "Tough to grow that kind of stuff out here."

"I imagine it is," she laughed.

Then the door slammed open and Orca, almost breathless, came back into the cabin. From behind his back he produced a clump of flowers, mountain iris and forget-me-nots, bluebells and muskeg daisies. "These're for you," he said.

"Well, thank you. You do make me feel welcome."

"They woulda been here when you come if we'd knowed when," Sven said.

"They're beautiful. Is there something to put them in?"

Sven found an empty Mason jar and filled it with water. Priscilla placed the flowers in the jar and put it on the table. "They really brighten up the place, don't they?"

Sven and Orca traded glances. "Didn't really think much about the place needin' brightening," Sven said, "but now that you say it, does look kind of nice." He winked at Orca and the boy turned to hide a giggle. Priscilla did her best to ignore them.

"Well," she said, "You must have work to do. So, why don't you just let me get myself together here."

"I'd better get back to the net," Orca said.

"Fire's probably out in the smoker," Sven said.

"You just go take care of things, then. I'll be right here."

Orca took an orange and headed down the beach to the dory, dropping peelings as he went.

"You just make yourself to home," Sven said. "We'll get things under control so we can spend some time." Then he, too, disappeared out the door.

Orca and Sven stayed busy at their respective chores for the remainder of the after- noon. Orca picked fish from the net and hauled them to Sven who cleaned them and hung the fillets on racks inside the smoker. When he wasn't cutting fish, Sven chipped logs to fuel the fire and keep it smouldering. He told Orca to save one salmon for dinner.

"I'm a little tired of it, myself, but I'll bet she'd really like a piece of fresh salmon. Funny how those people live so close to the water and they never seem to get out into it. Look at fresh salmon like it was a big steak."

Toward the end of the day, they organized their equipment so they could leave it without worrying and then they returned to the shack. They found Priscilla standing at a window with a tape measure in her hands.

"What's this?" Sven asked.

"Oh, nothing," she answered, trying to hide Sven's tape behind her back. Then she thought better of it.

"I saw the cabin last month and I thought maybe you'd like a little color." From her bed she picked up a bolt of brightly colored fabric. "I thought I'd make you some curtains while I'm here . . . if you like, of course."

Sven looked at the cloth she held.

"Does look kind of drab around here, don't it?" he said. "We never thought much about prettyin' up. Never had much time either. Might look nice, kind of."

Priscilla caught the hint of hesitation in his voice. "Please," she said. "I don't want to seem nosy or pushy. If I'm doing something you don't like or I get in the way, please tell me. You always have things, well, so orderly. I'm afraid I'm kind of messy. You should see my desk. I don't want to disrupt anything. I don't want to overstep any bounds, so just tell me. And, if you don't want curtains or anything else, just say so."

"Don't worry about that," Sven told her. "I expect you'll do just fine." He looked at the cloth again and winked toward Orca, but in a way so Priscilla could see him do it. "At least there ain't no flowers on it," he said.

"We brought you a fish for dinner," Orca said, showing her the bright red salmon meat.

In the evening after dinner, they sat around the table and Priscilla began showing Sven and Orca the school materials they would study during the upcoming winter.

"Kind of looks like fun," Sven said, thinking ahead to the winter days when they'd be trapped in Cabin Bay with little to do.

"It can be," she said, "but I assure you it has to be more than fun. Some of the lessons and tests have to be sent back to the school district so they can evaluate his progress. These have to be done on the schedule they sent. That's one of the reasons I asked them to send the materials through me. This way I can keep track of how he's doing. I have to make evaluations along the way, too. It's one of the conditions of granting the adoption. This will help me, and if you do it properly it will help you, too. For one thing you can figure out where he's having difficulties and work harder in those areas."

"What is adoption?" Orca asked.

Priscilla's eyes narrowed toward Sven. "You haven't told him?"

"Told me what?"

"I didn't want to worry him none." Sven mumbled, looking down at the floor.

"He never told you anything about why I'm here? What these books are all about?"

Orca looked at her helplessly.

"I guess it's time," Sven said. Then he and Priscilla explained the purpose of her visit to Cabin Bay, why she'd brought the school materials and told him about the legal machinations going on in the town. As they spoke, Orca began to realize why Sven had been so distracted, why he'd had so many mood swings over the previous few months. In the course of their explanation, Sven admitted as much and apologized to the boy. Throughout, Orca questioned every aspect of the process, feeling first the fear Sven had felt, then the measured relief as he came to understand the situation as it stood then. He also felt a sense of adventure when he contemplated the unfamiliar life in town and going to a real school.

"That's why it's so important for you to do well with the schoolwork," Priscilla concluded.

"I guess we'd better get to it, then," Orca said. Priscilla selected a workbook and text from the materials on the table and the two of them sat reading while she explained how one related to the other.

They studied until bedtime when Priscilla retired to her private room.

In the morning Sven and Orca awoke to the popping and snapping of bacon frying in a pan on the stove. Sven struggled into his clothes under the bed covers, then walked over to where Priscilla stood in the kitchen corner.

"I watched you cook last night," she said. "I saw how you started the fire and I thought I'd get a head start this morning. Coffee's ready, and bull coffee, too," she nodded to Orca still asleep in his bunk.

"Don't look like you need any help from me," Sven said. "Mornin'. I see the boy's burnin' daylight again. Hey, Orca, c'mon, get up."

Orca moved under his covers. His head emerged and he asked, "What's that smell?"

"Bacon," Sven said. "I guess Priscilla here can do more than just paper work," Sven said, sipping from his mug. "Coffee ain't bad either."

She flashed him the barest hint of a scowl and held it just long enough to make sure he saw her. Then she brightened again.

"Breakfast in a minute," she announced.

"Eggs, too." Sven peered over her shoulder. "Ain't had eggs since Corky come out last spring."

After breakfast, Priscilla asked them to show her how they fished the set net. They spent the bulk of the day involved in their chores. They reset the net with Priscilla along in the dory asking questions and trying to help where she could, though with three of them in the boat, she interfered more than she helped. With the salmon run down to only a few occasional fish, their work proceeded easily and they moved at a slower pace to accommodate their guest. Even warm sunshine joined the other elements in relaxing their labors. They laughed and talked and joked through the day's chores as the old man and the boy slowly drew the woman into their routine. The few fish they caught rendered firing up the smoker unnecessary so they cleaned their catch and put the fish in the ice house for the next day.

In the afternoon they took Priscilla up the inlet to gather ice. They also took her to view the face of the Meares Glacier. They worked the dory through the lines of brash ice close to the face of the glacier and watched as huge slabs calved into the inlet, sending rounded waves to lift and lower their boat. Sven pointed out where the glacier, in its mysterious cycle, was advancing along the northern shore, pushing up onto land and into a stand of tall, old spruce trees. "Them trees got to be 200 years old, so the glacier hasn't been this far out in at least that long," he said.

When they returned to the shack, Priscilla went inside while Sven and Orca hauled their ice to the ice house, tended their net and attended to the myriad of other chores it took to keep them functioning in Miners Bay. By the time they finished and went to the shack, Priscilla had begun hanging a curtain in the first window. Sven looked over what she had done.

"Well, look at this," he said. "Curtains." He walked to the window and felt the bright fabric, twisting it between his fingers.

"What do you think?" she asked.

"It does brighten up the place," Sven answered. "Looks kind of frilly, though. Changes the whole room."

"I think it looks good," Orca said.

"Thank you, young man," Priscilla said, still looking to Sven for some hint of approval. "Drapes can really make a difference."

"They sure can," Sven admitted. "It does look nicer in here. We're so used to it, never thought much about window coverin's. Course if somebody sees it they're gonna think we gone soft or somethin'."

"They will help you sleep better, too," she added, "I don't know how you get used to all this daylight. I can't sleep when it's light out. I brought enough material for Cabin Bay, too."

Orca looked at Sven. Twenty hours of daylight didn't bother them. All that light made their work easier at night and they always fell into bed exhausted anyway, no time to think about how they wished it were dark.

"I'll be finished in just a few minutes and then we can eat," she said, "I brought some steaks, too."

"Better be careful. We might start gettin' used to this," Sven said, winking at Orca. "Might want you to stop by every week, or better, we could just keep you. We ain't eaten this good in a long time."

It wasn't until late evening that they finished cooking and eating and then Priscilla sat at the table with Orca again, explaining more of the correspondence school materials. Sven left them to step outside and light his pipe. By this time in summer, the sky had begun to darken noticeably earlier and the evenings and nights were turning cool and crisp as the sun plunged toward its date with the equinox in September.

"Ought to be seein' some termination dust on the mountains one of these mornin's," he said when Orca and Priscilla joined him later.

"Termination dust?" Priscilla asked.

"That's the first dusting of snow on the mountains," Sven said, "Marks the termination of summer. Means you ought to be choppin' wood for winter. In the old days, it meant all the seasonal workers, the fishermen and the miners, took it as a sign to head south for the winter."

"I read, much of the night, and go south in winter," Priscilla quoted.

"What?"

"It's from a poem," she said.

"The Waste Land," Sven added, causing Priscilla to turn her head sharply. Realizing her surprise, he answered simply, "Boat people read."

Unfazed, she continued, "By T.S. Eliot. You might find it in your school books."

"We go south for the winter," Orca said.

Sven and Priscilla laughed. "It's true," Sven said. "Never thought of us as a couple of them outlanders, but we sure do go south for the winter. Course, it's only by twenty miles or so. Those guys went all the way to the Lower 48. Lot of 'em still do."

"I guess it's not quite the same, is it?" Orca asked.

"Not quite," Sven chuckled, "but we might as well admit it; we do go south for the winter." He looked toward the mountains north of the bay. "Now I know it's comin'," he said. "Look there."

Over the white crests of the highest peaks, vertical shafts of light paraded toward them in waves, brightening the night sky. The lights wavered as they marched, fading and brightening, changing from green to yellow and back to green again. The waves of light bent and curled around the stars and reached out of sight toward the Milky Way. The three people limited to the ground sat silently on their tree stumps, bending their necks to watch the auroral display as the lights marched across the heavens above them. Occasionally they'd remark on a particularly bright change and point it out to the others.

"I seen 'em red once," Sven broke in, "Up in the North Atlantic."

"What makes them?" Orca asked.

Priscilla started to open her mouth, but Sven spoke first: "Don't really know. And," he said glancing toward her, "I don't want to know. They just are, or should be. I like 'em and I like seein' them and I like the mystery of 'em. Knowin' what they are would take somethin' away from them somehow. I'm sure there's some scientific explanation. I don't need to know what makes 'em. Just as long as they show up once in a while. Gives a man a feelin' of peace and gives him a little respect for what's around 'im."

Priscilla had swallowed whatever it was she had intended to say. They looked skyward in silence. In front of the shack, made so minute by the display above, they watched the northern lights until the colors gradually dimmed and the waves disappeared behind the mountain range from where they'd come. When the sky faded to dark again, they stood up and walked back into the cabin, still in silence.

Once inside, Sven said, "Ought to be a nice day tomorrow with the sky clear and all. Good day for them blueberries. Whyn't you take Priscilla and go pickin'? I might as well stay here and take care of them fish. Could start gatherin' stuff, too. We'll be headin' south for the winter pretty soon."

As Sven had promised, the next day dawned bright and clear as if the northern lights had washed the sky clear of even the threat of clouds. Orca told Priscilla they would pick berries across the bay where the hillside faced south and where, as Sven said, "the sun just pumps them little berries full of sweetness."

After breakfast Orca pulled Sven through the door, out of Priscilla's hearing. "Do you think I ought to take the shotgun?" he asked.

Sven hesitated. "I dunno. Maybe not. Probably just scare her all the more," he told Orca. "I 'spect them bears is all up at the creek eatin' fish anyway. Whyn't you just leave it here."

"Okay, Sven, but I'd sure hate to have anything happen."

Orca ran down the beach to make sure the dory was ready and Sven went hunting for buckets. When he returned to the shack, Priscilla had just finished dressing for the day in the woods.

"See you got some boots that fit," he said pointing to her feet. "Me'n Corky had a good laugh over you trompin' around in them big boots last time."

"I must have looked pretty ridiculous," she said.

"Sounded even worse. You was a sight to see . . . and hear."

"Ready?" Orca called as he came through the door.

"Let's go," Priscilla answered and they walked down the beach to the boat.

Orca ran them across the little bay quickly and nosed the dory into an almost vertical bank. They climbed out and scratched their way up the steep hillside.

"There's places here where you can just sit down and fill the whole bucket without moving," Orca said. "All you do is bend the branches to you." They scrambled through thick undergrowth into a stand of taller trees. Using exposed roots for handholds, they pulled themselves up the hillside until they broke through the tree line into a sunny meadow. Along the edge just inside the woods, blueberry bushes grew thick and heavy with their summer's fruit.

"It's best to find a rock so you don't get your seat wet," Orca said, indicating the moist muskeg. "This is it."

"They're so thick," Priscilla said, " "I've never seen them like this."

"Sven told me a story once," Orca said, "It was about an evil giant that lived here. One time he captured a beautiful princess and carried her around with him. Sven said she was so sad she cried all the time. The way he told the story, when the sun came out, a blueberry grew everywhere the princess dropped a tear."

"She must have cried an awful lot right here," Priscilla said. "You're right. We won't even have to move to fill the buckets." She found a flat stone, sat down next to a bush and began plunking blueberries into her bucket. Orca walked off a way, found his own bush and sat down to pick. They picked in silence, far enough apart they would have needed to shout to be heard. Slowly but steadily they filled their buckets with the small berries. Now and then they did have to move to a new bush as they thinned one after another of its fruit. Their fingers turned purple from the juices and before long their tongues and lips took on a purple hue as well. Almost as many of the berries went into their mouths as went into their buckets.

Sunshine warmed their backs as they proceeded with their harvest and they shed their jackets. Now and then they stood to stretch, working out the stiffness that constricted their muscles from bending over the bushes. After almost two hours, Orca had nearly filled his bucket and he rose, stretching his arms over his head. He looked across the meadow in time to see brush move on the far side uphill near the next tree line. He watched closely as branches and leaves waved, signaling the progress of whatever moved across the edge of the clearing.

"Looks like we got a visitor," he shouted to Priscilla.

She stood at the sound of his voice. So did the bear, its wet nose twitching as the animal tested the air currents to find what his dim eyesight hadn't yet.

"Hey bear!" Orca shouted, waving his arms. The black head turned toward him and then the bear dropped to all fours and stepped out of the brush into the clearing.

"We'd better get out of here," Priscilla said, her voice wavering.

"Not yet," Orca called back. He took a step toward the bear and waved his arms again. "Hey bear!"

The bear let out a loud "huff" like a cough, turned sideways exposing the shiny black fur of its flanks and took a step. It turned toward Orca, its nose still testing the air. The boy tried again. He made a couple of running steps toward the bear, shouting and waving his arms as he charged. The bear raised its head, watched and then lowered it again when Orca stopped. Instead of running off as the boy had expected, the bear held its ground. Then it started swinging its head from side to side and took two steps toward where Orca stood.

"Let's get out of here," Priscilla insisted, this time with more shrillness in her voice.

"I think you're right," Orca said, taking a couple of slow steps backward. "I don't think he's seen you yet. Take your bucket and walk backwards slowly until you're in the trees."

The bear advanced a body length toward the boy.

Orca retreated two more steps. He bumped into his blueberry bucket and almost knocked it over. He bent to retrieve the bucket, keeping a wary eye on the bear. When he straightened, the bear had started running toward him at a trot.

He wasn't ready to relinquish his blueberries quite yet, but he broke almost into a backward trot, churning his legs for the tree line. The bear quickened its pace. Orca fought the temptation to turn and run.

"Climb one if you have to," he shouted to Priscilla, "only remember, black bears climb trees, too."

"I know, I know," she called back from behind the tree where she'd attempted to hide.

Priscilla's call caught the attention of the bear. It turned toward the sound of her voice and broke into a run straight toward her tree. Orca raced after the bear shouting. The bear closed with Priscilla's tree but before it could find her, Orca flung his bucket of blueberries at its head. The bucket caught it right behind the ear and the bear stopped and grunted. The bucket fell next to it, half its contents spilled on the ground.

While the blueberries distracted the bear, Orca ran into the trees where Priscilla, peeking around the trunk of a thick spruce,

stood almost obscured by the lower branches. When he reached her, he turned to see if the bear had followed, but the bucket of blueberries had proved more interesting. The bear sat on its haunches, its snout in the white bucket lapping up the berries Orca had spent the whole morning picking.

"That stopped him, but not for long," Orca said, "Let's get out of here while he's still in the pail." He grabbed Priscilla's hand and pulled her away from the tree. She followed him deeper into the forest, scrambling, stumbling and falling down the slope through the trees and underbrush. Devil's club tore at them, but even scratched and torn clothing didn't stop them as they crashed down-hill toward the dory. In their mad scramble, Priscilla held on dearly to her blueberry bucket and when they reached the boat she hoisted her berries in first. Then she followed, with Orca right on her bootheels. He pushed the boat away from shore with an oar and hopped in. They drifted away, watching up the hillside for any sign of the bear, but the woods held their silence.

"A guy told me once you could bluff a bear," Orca said once they'd drifted far enough from shore to feel safe. "He said you could huff right back and they'd run off."

"I've never heard that," Priscilla said, "It didn't work either. I can't believe you, you actually charged that bear. Maybe we were in his private blueberry patch."

"It's his now if it wasn't before. Pretty smart bear when you think about it," Orca said.

"Why do you say that?"

"Pretty patient, too. He was probably around there all morning just watching us. He got us to pick the berries for him, didn't he?" Orca said, the excitement wearing away.

"Not only that," Priscilla had started to catch the humor of their adventure. "He waited until we filled the buckets, too."

They both laughed out loud and the levity removed what re-mained of the tension they'd felt escaping the bear.

"We could get another bucket and go find blueberries some-where else. We could go see what Sven's doing," Orca suggested.

"I'd rather face Sven than another bear. I don't know what I'll do with all the berries I've got now."

Orca ran the dory back across the bay where Sven had heard them coming and met them at the water's edge.

"Come back a little early, didn't you? Where's the other bucket?" he asked, looking into the boat.

When they'd told Sven about the bear, he sat on the beach and laughed. "That'll teach you to go messin' in somebody's private garden. Might teach a guy your size not to go tryin' to charge a bear, either. Good thing it was a black. Brown's nothin' to mess with." Sven shook his head. "I sure figured all the bears'd be up in the creek eatin' dead fish. Just goes to show there's nothin' pre-dictable here. 'Specially about them bears. How do you feel?" he asked, nodding toward Priscilla.

"Every time I come out here it's one adventure after another," she answered, "I would have just as soon skipped that one."

"You ever see a bear fish for salmon?" Sven asked.

"It's really funny," Orca said. "We watch them all the time. The black bears always look kind of silly. They go out into the middle of the stream and watch all the fish swimming between their legs. They have to try a lot of times before they catch one. They pounce. Then they start heading for shore with a fish. But they always stop and pretty soon they're looking down in the water until all those fish get to be too much for them. Then they drop the one they have and try to catch a new one. Sometimes they'll do it two or three times before they get to shore with one."

Sven added, "You can always tell a stream where black bears been feedin'. There's all these fish around with one bite taken out of 'em'. Looks like you guys saved at least a bucket of berries."

"Priscilla kept hers," Orca said, "I left the bucket and everything."

"We can split them if you'd like," Priscilla offered.

"Nah, we'll get plenty. You keep what you got. You get enough?"

"I have enough so I don't want to go back."

"I don't guess you would, would you? At least you got a story to tell when you get to town."

"I suppose a person shouldn't live in Alaska without a bear story to tell," she said, "but after that, I'm afraid I'd rather listen to other people's stories."

That evening after they'd preserved the blueberries in the ice house, eaten dinner and straightened the shack, Priscilla said, "Orca told me about a story of yours about blueberries. Would you tell it?"

There it was again, story on demand. "Plenty of time for telling stories in the winter," he said gruffly.

"Come on, Sven, I told her about it," Orca enticed.

"Please."

"Oh, all right. It's a long story, though. You better get settled," Sven said. Then he fell into his storytelling voice, speaking his unusually formal language:

CHAPTER 11

PRINCE WILLIAM AND THE BLUEBERRY QUEEN

A sound is a noise like waves crashing on a beach. A sound also can be a large, protected body of water, a place where waves don't crash against a beach. This is a story about the second kind of sound, only one so long ago and so far away, you can't hear it any more.

In its beginning, this sound was not protected. It presented a wide-open mouth to an expanse of northern ocean whose weather drove storm after storm over the water against the mountains that rimmed the sound. Dark clouds stopped by the mountains always hung over the sound and precipitated a constant shower of rain into the bays and coves. The mountains around the sound always stood dark, black with trees that were bent by the constant winds that failed to blow away the clouds that delivered the rain. No one ever saw the tops of those mountains because they were always hidden by the clouds. As a matter of fact no one ever saw much of the sound at all for it was a dark and cold forbidding place. How cold and how dark no one knew for even the bravest of mariners avoided the sound. The sailors who plied the northern waters stayed away from it, for it was said an evil giant inhabited the sound and those unfortunate ships

that entered seeking shelter from a storm were never heard from
again. Few did enter, for besides the stories of the giant, the sound
offered little in the way of shelter without some land mass to cover the
opening as a buffer to the weather.

To the east and west of this sound lay two small kingdoms. These
kingdoms existed peacefully with each other, but the sailors from
each competed in the ocean for the same fish and there were occasions when one king would send an angry reprimand to the other
over conflicts on the fishing grounds. With no shelter between the
kingdoms when the great northern storms blew, often the fishermen
from one kingdom would seek safe anchorage in the harbors of the
other. Although the harboring would be allowed, the outland mariners would be made to feel they were unwanted and their welcome
ended with the storm they were hiding from. There were too many
arguments over the fishing for the fishermen to be welcomed into the
other's port.

The kings, seeing the conflicts growing and fearing their subjects
would make more trouble, began sending emissaries back and forth
with suggestions for resolving the issue. Eventually, as they neared
agreement, the court of the eastern king made plans to journey to the
west to complete the accord and celebrate with a feast.

The eastern king took with him many of his advisors and in an
attempt to broaden the world of his son, William, took him as well. In
three ships they sailed for the western kingdom. It was an easy voyage for no storms blew and their passage was a safe one. As they
crossed the mouth of the dark sound, Prince William asked his father
about the forbidding wilderness. His father told him about the sound
and when he'd finished, as if to prove what the king had said, way
off deep within the sound they heard roars and loud splashes.

"They say the rain drives the giant insane," said old King
Hinchinbrook, "and he goes into a bay and rips massive boulders
from the cliffs and hurls them far out into the water or, sometimes,
back into the mountains."

Prince William listened intently to his father and to the sounds
from the sound and thought long about the dark place. But, as they

passed into the sunshine of the western kingdom and new sights and sounds, his thoughts of the dark world faded. The three ships entered the harbor of the capital of the western king and were welcomed with great fanfare for the western king had hopes as great as his eastern counterpart for an accord. At a state dinner that evening Prince William was introduced to the western king's daughter, the beautiful Princess Virginia. During the days that followed, while the two kings and their advisors met in endless conferences, the Princess Virginia became guide and escort to Prince William, showing him her western land while he, in turn, entertained her with stories of his eastern homeland. As days turned to weeks, their daily trips became less guided tours and more in the style of time spent together. As time passed their talk turned to subjects beyond the homelands, and they found themselves growing into a fondness that with their first kiss blossomed into love. Where at first the meetings had been just a courtesy, they now became an obsession and they plotted to see each other. Their plots worked, for seldom was either seen in public without the other. Though the princess always had to have her chaperone, still, the two found ways to sneak away for their precious moments alone in sunlit glades, holding hands walking in the forests and dreaming the dreams of young lovers.

But, while the friendship grew into love for the two youngsters, their fathers and their advisors were growing farther apart. Where an accord had seemed so close at the start, as each day passed, the two sides seemed further apart. By the end of the second fortnight the eastern king and his advisors decided no treaty could be reached and they had just as well prepare to return to their homeland. Plans were made and Prince William informed. When he heard the news, the young prince felt a deep sadness. With a fear in his heart, he ran to the garden beneath his beloved's window. She came to her balcony when he called and listened with tears in her eyes as he delivered the news of the coming parting. Also listening from another balcony, unseen by either of them, was the Princess Virginia's father King Montague. The message was double for Montague as he had been so busy with the talks he'd failed to notice the growing affection between his daughter and the eastern prince. With this also his first news of the eastern delegation's abrupt departure, he rushed to his daughter's room where he burst onto the balcony and pulled her back into her chamber.

"I will love your forever," Prince William called after the princess before her father could slam the balcony doors.

"We will be together," the princess shouted back despite her father's efforts to silence her.

A morose Prince William boarded his father's ship the next day for the long trip home. He stood in the stern watching as the castle and then the city and harbor and finally the kingdom, all of which were home to his beloved princess, disappeared in the wake and with them faded the vision of the beautiful Virginia. Through the long passage home he walked the decks alone, barely even taking notice of the dark sound that had piqued his curiosity on the outbound voyage. Inconsolable he returned to his homeland and nothing his parents or friends could do would drag him out of his sadness. He shared his secret with no one, and even the king's funniest jesters could not raise the hint of a smile from him.

The prince had made a mistake. He hadn't properly heard the princess's call as her father pulled her from the balcony. In the words, Prince William had only heard a plaintive call of love, but the Princess Virginia had called out a promise, and even before Prince William departed her city, she was making her plans to fulfill that promise. She first consulted with her chaperone who had been her governess in childhood. They had loved each other very much and the princess had come to depend on her as a friend. The governess was the one who suggested a plan and called for her fisherman husband. To them both Princess Virginia explained her predicament and pleaded with the old fisherman to take her in his boat to the eastern kingdom to be with Prince William. The two heard her tale and the husband knew of the fondness between the princess and his wife and how well he and his wife had been treated at the castle. Although fearing the king's wrath should he discover who had taken his daughter, the fisherman agreed to make the voyage and plans were made to leave on the early morning tide. There would be a great ball at the castle that night and the king could be expected to sleep well past noon the next day so they would have many hours behind them before anyone knew the princess was missing. She would make her appearance at the ball and then slip away in the darkness to the boat and await dawn and the tide.

This she was able to do easily and the little fishing boat with the princess on board slipped out of the harbor unnoticed and caught a fair wind to the east. The Princess Virginia did not look back as the prince had done, but stood in the bows facing the direction of the harbor she sought.

As they sailed the ocean, the fair breeze freshened, propelling the boat faster and faster. The breeze grew into a wind as black clouds marched toward them from the horizon. The fisherman knew the signs and watched the storm grow, but the princess stared only eastward toward the love she sought to regain. Blue sky turned to gray and gray turned to black. As the waves began splashing over the sides, wetting her clothing, the growing danger began to intrude against her all-consuming goal. The fisherman fought the storm but to little avail as huge waves began tossing the little boat, carrying it ever closer to the dark sound. As the blackness deepened, fear finally encroached into Virginia's thoughts.

The fisherman knew the tales about the sound well and feared the darkness as he fought to keep the boat on course, but one wave after another carried them closer and closer. Then they flew atop a wave through the mouth into the dark sound. In fear the princess turned to the man at the helm, but before she could utter a word the boat and the two of them were plucked from the waves by a huge hairy hand. High out of the water they rose until, quaking with fear, they looked into an immense face to be examined by eyes as large as the sun but as dark as the new moon. The giant studied his prizes for some time until he picked the princess from the boat and then flung the boat and the fisherman far out to sea. The quivering, fearful princess he held tightly in his hand while he looked her over curiously. He spoke no words, only grunts, and his foul breath engulfed the princess, making her choke. After an eternity he turned and strode, wading, deeper into the bay until he came to a cave which he crawled into. There he put the princess into a stout cage. For a time he teased her with a stick he thrust between the bars. Then he tired of his game and grabbed a bone that had some meat hanging from it. From the bone he tore a piece of raw meat and tossed it to the princess as he would to a dog.

The princess ducked away from the flying meat. She stood defiant, wavering between demanding anger and quivering fear. As her hours of entrapment grew into days, she brought her emotions under control. She attempted escape; she actually got out of the cage once but the giant caught her quickly and fixed the hole she'd made. She determined to keep her courage though her plight left her in desperation. No one knew she was gone from her home and if by now they had found out, no one knew where she was. The old fisherman was dead no doubt, and she was a prisoner not knowing what her fate might be. In front of the giant she maintained her dignity as a princess. But she knew better than to raise his anger. She couldn't know what the giant had planned for her, if there was a plan at all, but she assumed angering him would not help her, so she gave the appearance of accepting her fate and all the time schemed a way to escape.

After her first attempt to escape, the giant no longer trusted her alone. When he left to make his rounds of the sound he took her along, tied into his shirt pocket in a sack with only her head showing. And there, under the giant's beard where he could not see her, she rode as he walked through his dark realm. She saw and felt his rage when he faced into the rain and tried to brush or even claw the water from his eyes. His roar would deepen and he grasped huge boulders and hurled them against the mountainsides. When his rage would subside he'd move out of the bay where the rocks were loose and search for food, but little game showed in an area so full of hate and fear and anger. Now and then the giant would catch an unsuspecting deer or bear that ventured out of the forest, or maybe a porpoise or salmon that swam too close to land. When he did he immediately bit off the victim's head, laughing as he did, and then devoured the animal whole, saving only shreds and bones for the princess who refused to eat them despite her hunger. Instead she gave the giant a haughty face when he teased her with the meat. She was a princess, after all, and resolved to show courage and grace in the face of such despicable evil.

But when she was in the pocket out of sight the princess's bearing and defiance broke down and she wept uncontrollably at her fate. All the time the giant walked the princess wept the tears of terror and hopelessness, and her tears fell everywhere on the shores of the dark sound.

The Princess Virginia had not been forgotten. Once the western king learned his daughter was missing he immediately suspected the truth, that she had run or been spirited away to join the eastern prince. The king dispatched his most important emissarial potentate to the eastern court to demand the return of the princess and threatened the direst of consequences if she were not. But news of the princess preceded the potentate, for the fisherman whom the giant had cast into the water to die had regained his boat. Fearing reprisals from his own king for aiding the runaway princess, he had continued his voyage to the east until he fetched that capital. Wet and bedraggled, he had been cast before the king on the supposition he had been poaching fish in the eastern waters. He told his story to the king and had just finished when the western emissarial potentate was announced to the court. The emissary reiterated King Montague's demands and threats and then King Hinchinbrook asked the fisherman to repeat his story. The potentate listened, then demanded a search party and army be organized to rescue the princess. He also demanded the fisherman be handed into his custody for punishment at home. This Hinchinbrook refused to do, extending instead his personal protection to the fisherman.

The king issued a call for volunteers to join the rescue effort, refusing to send any of his subjects into the dark sound against their will. No one responded; no one would go into the dark sound unless they had to, because it meant certain death. The king directed the visiting potentate to return to his own country and attempt to raise a party there.

In the meantime, Prince William had sequestered himself with the old fisherman, barraging him with questions about the princess, the giant and the sound. When he learned all the fisherman knew, he went to the wharves, to the boats and to the inns and taverns where the nation's mariners spent their time. Of all he asked for information about the dark sound, but the western fisherman was the only man anyone knew of who had returned from that dark place and even the eldest of seamen could add only the slightest to what the prince already had learned. As he listened to the mariners, two realizations became apparent to the young prince. The first had nothing to do with the sailors. He knew now that the princess's words had been a promise and not an idle call. He now knew, also, that it had fallen to him to fulfill that promise and he would have to do it alone.

Not only would he have to do it alone, he would have to venture into uncharted dangerous waters where none had gone before, at least none who had lived. As he came to understand his quest, his questions turned to boats and he asked after the fastest, most maneuverable boat available. Upon the advice of several sailors, he found the perfect boat. Then he approached his father. He, as heir to the throne, had trained as an officer in the king's small navy and this his father took into account as he pondered his son's request.

On reaching his decision Hinchinbrook said, "This, my son, is something you must do and no ruling from a father can stop you. This I can see. Go with my blessing, but be not afraid to turn back, for no man would call another a coward who had turned back from the dark sound. You go just more than a boy. Acquit yourself well and come back a man."

With this the king ordered the palace stores opened to the prince and the stocking of William's small, fast craft began. The king's own chandlers prepared stores for the long voyage and packed them for stowage aboard the small boat.

The king's shipwrights worked on the boat, fixing what needed fixing, making a new suit of sails from black fabric, painting the hull and decks black and cleaning what needed cleaning. The black boat would hide in its own darkness from the giant's watchful eyes.

The king's astronomers worked with naval navigators to plan the times and places and courses the prince should use on this most dangerous of voyages. Even the magicians of the kingdom offered him potions and incantations, and though the prince thought little of them, he took everything that might give him an advantage over the immense power of the giant.

Finally the day came for the prince to set sail on his perilous voyage. The navigators went over the plans one more time and the chandlers took a final stock of their stores. All the weapons were placed aboard carefully, and with great fanfare the prince was ready to depart safe harbor to rescue the fair Princess Virginia.

As William began to cast off his lines, the old fisherman who had first taken the princess into the dark sound rushed down the wharf with his sea bag slung over his shoulder. Despite his age and the weight of the bag, he leaped nimbly aboard the prince's ship and said: "Name's Blinker, sir. You never asked. And you never asked me to go with you, but I took 'er in there and it's only right I should be goin' along to bring 'er out. If you'll 'ave me, sire."

The prince welcomed Blinker aboard and together they cast off the rest of the lines. Once they passed out of the harbor and had trimmed the sails for their course to the entrance of the sound, the prince fell back into his thoughts. The voyage was timed so they would arrive at the entrance just before nightfall and could enter and find a hiding place, they hoped, without detection before daylight could betray them. Now the full weight of his mission fell over the prince and he wondered how the princess fared in the hands of the giant, if she were still alive, even. His fear was not for himself, but for her.

For her part, the princess refused, at least outwardly, to yield to the terror of the evil giant. She met his evil with defiance and in those times when she was out of his sight she began making herself a weapon, just a pointed stick to be sure, but she kept sharpening it as she could against rocks and other sticks and then she'd hide it in her petticoats before the giant could see her. She knew not when she might use it or if it wasn't a wasteful project, but it gave her something to do and something she might be able to employ at the right moment. Still, at times her plight became overwhelming and silently, riding in the giant's pocket, she wept.

Prince William and Blinker reached the outer entrance to the dark sound just as the sun dove in behind the western mountains, leaving a dark, moonless night. Even the stars hid from view over this darkest of waters. With only the slightest of twilight left to guide them, they sailed the boat into a small anchorage and set the anchor. They were in the sound now and the plan was to begin exploring for the giant's hideaway at the first hint of dawn. If they hugged the shoreline and moved slowly, Prince William thought they could go a long way without being detected. While Blinker slept, the prince spent a restless night. He would lie down, toss, turn, get up and pace the decks, then go back to his bunk, but there would be no sleep for the prince this night.

At last a morning halo of light rose over the eastern mountains, ending the prince's long night. Prince William and Blinker hoisted their black sails and made for the entrance of their anchor cove.

All day they sailed through the sound, hugging the shoreline, watching for some sign of the evil giant and the princess. By late afternoon the prince was beginning to think all the talk about the giant was just talk, but he had to remember old Blinker had seen him. They were nearing the mouth of a large bay at the end of a long fjord when they realized they finally had come close to the giant. First they heard a low, rumbling roar. Then came gigantic splashes and waves came rolling out of the bay.

William and Blinker quickly sought shelter in a cove just outside the bay and there the prince went ashore. He climbed a short ridge over white granite rocks until he could see into the bay. About a quarter of a mile away he saw the giant, a horrible creature with shaggy hair sticking out from his head everywhere. A big, bulbous nose hung out over a mouth full of broken teeth. The giant's clothing hung in rags. He stood knee deep in the sea, digging rainwater out of his reddened eyes, and then he'd grab huge boulders in his rage and hurl them out into the bay water. Prince William marveled at the power of the giant, but refused to be intimidated and as he watched he began to form a plan to subdue the beast. Also as he watched, he began to discern the cause of the giant's rage, for the constant water in his eyes was bothering the prince, too. He pulled the visor of his black battle helmet down to shelter his eyes from the rain.

Prince William returned to the boat where he told Blinker what he had seen and the two worked late into the night making a plan for the next day.

The plan they made was a simple one. Prince William would circle the bay on foot until he was close to the giant. After a time, Blinker would sail the boat across the mouth of the bay to divert the giant's attention and when the time was right, Prince William would shoot the giant with an arrow tipped with a potion given to him by one of the king's sorcerers. The potion, he was told, would put a whole regiment to sleep and surely would be enough for one giant. Once the giant had fallen, William planned to tie him to the ground, then search for the princess and hope for escape before the giant could awaken and threaten them again.

All the preparations were made and again at first light the prince began moving. He had three hours to reach the giant, for in three hours' time Blinker was to sail the boat across the mouth of the bay to catch the giant's attention.

Prince William had seen the section of shore where the giant snatched his boulders and that was where he intended to go.

William scrambled and fought his way over rocks and through thick brambles working his way to the giant's lair. But he was taking too long and he knew it. Blinker would be sailing before he reached the spot he wanted. Fearing he would expose himself if he rushed, he could hurry no more than he was doing already. Still he moved as fast as he could through the bushes and over the boulders. He kept watching the giant and the bay mouth hoping Blinker would hold off, but, too soon, the prince saw the black bows of the boat emerge from behind the rocks guarding the bay. When Prince William saw this he took a chance and sprinted across a clearing to bring himself within firing range of the giant. In this momentary exposure his motion was spotted, not by the giant, but by the Princess Virginia. Riding in the giant's pocket, the princess saw William as he raced across the clearing. From then she kept a watch, following his progress as he scrambled toward them.

The giant saw the boat first and his reaction was to grab a boulder to fling at it. When he did, the prince was not yet in position to stop the giant from throwing and the first boulder almost swamped the boat.

Fortunately Blinker had the boat up to speed and sailed past the opening before the giant could reach for another boulder. As the giant turned to rip another rock from the shore, he spotted Prince William scrambling through the brush toward him. The prince had climbed to a ridge almost at the giant's eye level and was concentrating on where to place his feet on the uneven ground. He didn't even know the giant had spotted him. But the princess in the pocket sensed the direction the giant's body and head had moved and realized he was staring right at the prince. In desperation, not knowing how much good it would do, she pulled out her sharpened stick and drove it as deeply as she could through the shirt and into the skin of the giant's chest. The giant yelped, not so much in pain as in surprise, for the stab could have had little more effect than a bee's sting. Still, it diverted the giant's attention just long enough to give Prince William an instant to raise his bow and let an arrow fly. The giant's neck was bent as he searched for the source of the sting on his chest and the prince's arrow struck the exposed neck just under the giant's ear.

Now a second bee had stung the giant and he reached for the new pain, but even as he did, his hand and arm slowed as the potion worked through his body. He blinked, looked at his hand that wouldn't go to his neck, and then sat down dumbly, his eyes falling out of focus. As his eyes began to close he fell over backwards, crushing several boulders into pebbles as he did.

Prince William scampered down the slope in front of him, ran around the boulders and climbed up onto the giant's chest. There he found the Princess Virginia just crawling out of the giant's pocket.

They met, standing knee deep in the giant's chest hair, and embraced. As they did, the joy of their reunited love coursed through their veins as if beaten by a single heart and they became one. And, as they stood there on the giant's chest, the rain increased. Water beat against their faces and their clothing soaking both of them, though they hardly noticed. The rain pounded the boulders and the trees and the mountainsides. It drove harder until sheets washed down the mountains and gullies and valleys and through the bushes. But as the water rushed on, it drove the darkness before it. This sudden rush of water drove away the darkness and with it the anger and both washed away into the waters of the sound, spreading and weakening until there was no more anger left in the dark sound.

Once the rain had cleansed the sky and the earth, the sun broke through, lighting the sound as it had never been before. Where there had been gray in the sky, now there was blue. White peaks of mountains split by blue glaciers towered over bright green forests. The water took on a brilliant green reflected from the mountainsides and the ocean sent happy little white-crested riffles to splash against the beaches. The ground where the giant slept turned white from the granite pebbles and made almost a sand beach where the two reunited lovers now walked to the water line to greet Blinker, who had seen the giant fall and was bringing the boat toward shore.

Their path took them a short way through bushes and there they discovered a miracle in a small clearing. It was a place the giant had stood often and a place, as may be guessed, where the princess had shed many tears. Now, everywhere a tear had fallen, a blueberry grew. And, everywhere across the sound where the giant had carried the weeping princess, now a blueberry bush sprouted. The prince saw this and said, "You are indeed the Blueberry Princess. Be my Blueberry Queen and we will forge our lives together here and it will never again be known as the dark sound."

To this the princess said, "Yes, and if I am to be the Blueberry Queen, let this place be known as Prince William's Sound."

"Hoorah! Hoorah! Hoorah for the Blueberry Queen and Prince William's Sound!" cried Blinker, who had come upon them without their noticing. "Long live the good Prince William and the good Princess Virginia!

"'Twill be a fine place, sire," Blinker called. "Done right it could be safe harbor and solve the fishing dispute between our nations."

"Excellent, Blinker," the prince said. The princess added, "For your fine thinking, you shall be prime minister and chief potentate and your first task will be to work out the details. Also, we must send for your wife. She also shall have a position of great responsibility."

Said Prince William, "We shall have to find a way to shelter the mouth of the sound to make safe harbor."

"I've an idea, sire," Blinker said. "'Tis true the heavy rain washed away the anger." Blinker walked over and sat down on the giant's chest. He sat for some time until the giant began to stir from his sleep. Prince William prepared another arrow just in case some of the anger remained.

The giant began to show some alertness and as he did, Blinker smiled. The giant smiled. Blinker spoke a few words the prince and princess could not understand and the giant responded. Blinker came over to William and Virginia, winked, and said, "The anger is truly gone, washed away. No water in the eyes." Then the giant rose with Blinker on his shoulder and waded to the mouth of the sound. Before long Blinker had the giant piling huge rocks in the water and within a few hours, they'd built two islands that stopped the ocean swells and calmed the waters of the sound.

The prince and princess stood at the water's edge and watched and saw that their new realm would be a good and peaceful one. "We shall name the islands after our families. The one to the east will be Hinchinbrook and the one to the west Montague," they agreed.

Before they could go on to live happily ever after in Prince William's Sound, the prince turned to Virginia and said, "I love you, my Blueberry Queen."

While he'd been telling the story, Sven had watched Orca fall asleep. Priscilla listened to the end. "She must have been beautiful," she said.

"Who?" Sven asked.

"The woman, the woman who was the blueberry queen."

"Oh, yes she was," he said, "She spent all her time here. Loved the blueberries. She was always goin' to shore . . . " Sven stopped, realizing he'd told more than he desired. "Another story for another day," he said.

CHAPTER 12

GONE FISHIN'

A FEW DAYS LATER AS THEY STOOD on the beach watching the airplane circle toward its landing, Orca said, "You know what? You forgot the jigsaw puzzles."

"Yeah," Sven mimicked, "What about the jigsaw puzzles?"

Priscilla smiled back at him and laughed. She let her voice go gruff, "Plenty of time to do jigsaw puzzles in the winter."

Orca laughed at her imitation. Sven hesitated. "Aw, I don't sound like that." Then he laughed, too. "You can bring them out next time."

"I'm welcome, then?" Priscilla asked.

"Priscilla, you're welcome around here any time. Ain't that right, Orca?" he asked.

"You bet."

Priscilla smiled.

"You made it here for blueberry season. Won't be no bears chasin' you off the crab grounds. We'll be lookin' for you some-time over winter. Might look Corky up once the crabbin' starts."

"I'd like that. And, thank you both. It's such a relief from town to be out here. I'm kind of sorry to have to go back." She turned to Orca and on an impulse hugged him to her. "You take care of yourself and work at that schoolwork." She reached for Sven's hand and squeezed it. "There might be some news when I get back," she said. "I'm afraid these things move awfully slowly. It probably will take a long time. But, sometimes they work faster. Family court can be backed up. I'll check first thing in the morning."

"Thank you, ma'am." He forced a floppy package wrapped in damp white paper between them. "Thought you might like a salmon to take back," he said.

She stood for a moment looking at the limp weight in her hands. "Thank you. And good-bye to you both." She walked along the airplane's float stepping confidently where before she had walked tentatively.

Sven and Orca pushed the airplane away from shore and within minutes it was skimming across the water. The airplane lifted into the air, Priscilla waving from the window.

Before the sound faded completely, the *Salmania* roared into Miners Bay.

"We're never going to get any work done if people keep comin' to visit," Sven said, watching Corky's boat approach. Almost before the *Salmania* came to a complete stop, Corky had jumped over the side into his skiff and raced toward the beach.

"What's up?" Sven asked.

"Need to talk to you," Corky said. "I got a problem." He stepped onto the beach and walked to where Sven and Orca stood. "How's your season going?"

"Pretty poor right now," Sven said, "You people keep interruptin'. We never get any work done."

"It can't be that bad," Corky said.

"No, it's not. Matter of fact we're just about to the end of it. Ain't five fish a day come in this bay any more. We was just talkin' about startin' to pack 'er in and get ready to go south."

"We got maybe three weeks left," Corky said. "Fish are in from the ocean capes now and they're thinning out, but you run into a school now and again. That's why I'm here."

"Why?" Orca asked.

"I had to send a guy back," Corky said. "I'm short crew and I got, like I said, maybe three weeks to go. I was thinkin', you know, what we was talkin' about. Maybe Orca could come with me a couple weeks."

Orca's eyes widened as he understood the invitation and he looked imploringly at Sven. For his part, the old man had stopped with his mouth open. Here it was and he wasn't ready. Idle conversation had become reality. His mind raced through all the implications he could imagine. He tried to gather objections, find some reason why the boy had to stay with him.

When Sven had been silent too long, Corky turned to Orca, "What about you? You want to come?"

Orca hesitated. He knew it all depended on what Sven said. Inside him, the anticipation threatened to burst through. Sven saw the boy's eyes begging him for the right answer. Try as he might to find reasons to prevent Orca from leaving, his mind kept telling him to let the boy go.

Finally he mumbled, "We still got a lot of work to do."

"But you said you could do it," Orca challenged, "You said you got along fine before I got here."

"He should make a good share with me," Corky said. "Fishin' ain't as hot as it was a month ago, but we'll still make money."

"Can I, Sven, can I?"

"Hate to get too dependent on money," Sven said. He knew money wasn't the problem, nor the work either. What bothered Sven, and he wasn't about to admit it to Orca or Corky, was that this would be the first time the boy went away for any length of time, his first time away from home. After all the years, Sven came suddenly aware of how dependent he was on their life together. Now he could see the bond unraveling as Orca approached manhood and wanted to strike out on his own. He stood ready to take the first step and it raised a melancholy in Sven from deep inside. He worked his way through the thought process until he realized the moment had to come sometime. Better it should come with Corky. Sven exhaled a deep breath. "All right," he said.

"Better pack a kit," Sven told the boy, but he had to tell it to his back because Orca had taken off running up the beach toward their shack.

"Kid don't waste no time, does he?" Corky said.

"He'll put in a good day for you and if he don't, I want to know about it," Sven threatened.

"I ain't worried about it," Corky said, smiling. "Thanks."

"Well," Sven turned philosophical, "It'll be good for him. Get away from me for a while. See something else of the world."

"I'll take care of him," Corky assured Sven.

"I know you will," Sven said.

Orca returned dragging a duffel. "What do I have to do?"

"You get all the hard work," Corky laughed. "The crew's already worked together most of the summer so they got their jobs down pretty well. You'll start out stacking the seine when we bring it on board. Sloppy work, but it's just as important as anything else. It'll take you a while to figure it all out. You ain't ever worked a real seiner before so you've got a lot to learn about the gear and the hydraulics and such. 'Bout time you learned to handle a big boat, too. You can't be runnin' around in skiffs all your life. Might give you another chore, too."

"What's that?"

"We been eatin' pretty much the same cookin' all summer. I know you can do it and the guys are ready for a change."

"Let's go," Orca said, barely able to control his excitement.

"Hold on," Sven told him, "You don't have to be in such an all-fired hurry to get away."

They walked down the beach, Orca with his bag slung over his shoulder. They pushed the skiff until it floated and Corky started the engine. Sven and Orca stood at the tide line. The old man extended his hand to the boy and Orca took it. They stood for a moment locked in the handshake, Orca fighting the urge to pull away and join Corky in the skiff.

"Put in a good day's work," Sven said quietly. He had to lift his head so Orca wouldn't see the mist he felt rising in his eyes.

"I will," the excited boy promised.

"I'll finish up here and start haulin' stuff to Cabin Bay. When you're done, check in there first before you come here. I'll try to have us all moved by then."

"Okay," Orca said and then his voice dropped and he looked into the old man's eyes. "I'll do right, Sven."

"I know you will. Good luck."

Corky had waited patiently in the skiff, but now he hollered "Let's go." Orca swung his bag and then himself over the gunwale and Corky drove away toward the *Salmania.*

"Keep the round side down," Sven called without much enthusiasm. He watched them go, again fighting the mist in his eyes. He saw Corky and then Orca climb aboard and then Corky haul the skiff up onto the deck. The engine roared to life and someone, he couldn't see who, walked forward to haul the anchor. It had happened so fast. One minute they'd been happy talking, watching Priscilla leave and thinking about going back to work. The next, Orca had taken off on his own. For a man who'd lived much of his life solitary in his own pursuits, Sven suddenly felt very alone. He stayed on the beach while Corky took Orca out of the bay and disappeared around the headland. Only then did Sven turn and walk up the beach. His feet felt heavier with each step. Inside the shack he saw signs of the boy everywhere. Rather than straighten the room, Sven sat in a chair, lit his pipe and barely half an hour into his solitude missed the boy terribly.

Aboard the *Salmania* and under way, Corky introduced Orca to the two men who would be his crew mates. "Calvin, here, runs the skiff and does some of the engineer work." Orca shook his hand.

"This here's Georgie Fagshark . . . Orca," Corky introduced the other crewman.

Orca gripped a bony, long-fingered hand that clutched his and let go quickly. A thin smile creased the angular features of the older youth's face and then disappeared as quickly as the hand.

"He'll be workin' with you stackin' net."

Orca said, "Good to meet you." The response he heard sounded more like a grumble than anything else.

Orca went with Corky to the wheelhouse for the trip out of the bay and down Unakwik Inlet. As they crossed the moraine, Orca realized in his excitement he hadn't bothered to wave good-bye to Sven, but he forgot the oversight quickly as he embraced his new adventure. While they traveled south, Corky explained the various electronic instruments important to navigating and locating fish. Orca tried to absorb the meanings of all the dials and readouts, graphs and video displays Corky used. "It'll take you a while to learn it all," Corky said. "Take the manuals to bed with you and read them. You'll figure it out."

As they emerged from Unakwik into the open waters of the sound Corky pointed to the southwest. "Hey, look over there." Orca turned toward the direction Corky pointed and saw a pod of killer whales, their fins breaking water at about the point he and Sven had seen them on their trip north a few months earlier. He slipped out of the wheelhouse and descended a ladder to the work deck where Fagshark also watched the whales.

Noticing his new crewmate approach, Fagshark said, "Black-fish. Oughta blow 'em away right here."

Fagshark's epithet caught Orca by surprise. He'd never heard anyone express hatred so bitterly toward the whales.

Fagshark caught the alarm in Orca's eyes. "They ain't good for nothin'. Just killers. They take salmon and salmon's money. We had a fair season, but it coulda been better, them blackfish wasn't around. We oughta go over there and shoot 'em and be done with it." He spat into the water.

The whales paid no attention to the *Salmania* as it passed, but Orca watched them, quiet now in the face of his crewmate's words, inwardly panicking at the thought of anyone wanting to harm them.

From the wheel house above the deck, Corky had watched the two youths' conversation, unable to hear over the sound of the engine. He followed Orca's gaze toward the whales, knowing Orca's history and Fagshark's prejudice and wondering if he had recruited a problem.

Orca wondered, too. He didn't think Corky would let anything happen as far as Fagshark's threat was concerned, but he hoped the whales wouldn't give him a chance to follow through with it. He hoped the whales would just leave them alone and not interfere with their fishing. If they didn't come around, they wouldn't antagonize Fagshark and that would take care of it.

After their first encounter Corky kept Georgie and Orca busy enough so they didn't have time for anything but fishing and sleeping. Learning the ways of a seine boat filled whatever free time Orca might have had. He found his main job not difficult, but uncomfortable. Even on the hottest days he worked in his rain gear under the power block with water and jellyfish raining on him as he gathered netting when it came aboard. He coiled it carefully so it would go out properly on the next set. He watched all aspects of the boat's operations, learning as he worked.

Running the skiff, Calvin would attach to the seine and pull it off the back deck, towing it toward a point on shore. As he did, Corky turned the boat into the current. Once the net had left the *Salmania* and the skiff reached the shore, the two boats held it in position, a line of corks like that on Orca's and Sven's net connecting them. While they held the set, Fagshark stood on the stern with a long pole with a bell-shaped cup attached at the end. At intervals he jammed the cup into the water, making a loud popping noise. This served to frighten the fish away from the opening between the boat and the net and chased them more toward the center. When Corky figured they had fish in the net, he radioed Calvin to pull the skiff away from shore, circling, pulling the net back toward the larger boat. Once they closed the net, Calvin let it go and tied off to the side of the boat away from the net. Then they began collecting the purse line, slowly closing the bottom of the net. The seine ran through a power block hanging in the rigging overhead. Corky operated hydraulic power controls to begin turning the block and they started pulling the seine on board.

Orca and Georgie coiled the net when it reached the deck. Corky then pulled the purse line, a rope that ran through a series of rings hanging from the bottom of the net. Pulling it on board with a hydraulic deck winch, Corky closed the bottom of the net, trapping any fish inside. They pulled the net to the deck until just a small portion remained in the water. Fish confined to a smaller and smaller area bunched next to the boat. When they had a large haul, sometimes they had to use a smaller net called a brailer to pull a few fish at a time from the seine. Most of the time they could lift the bag of the seine on board and roll the fish into the hold.

Toward the end of the season when the runs dwindled, they made fewer sets and spent a good deal of time cruising the shoreline in search of schools. The sets produced smaller numbers of fish than the crew caught during the height of the run. Many fishermen already had quit for the season, but Corky was one of the diehards and fished until the last salmon. This all served to allow Orca to learn the process under less pressure than he might have encountered during the strongest part of the run. It also gave Corky plenty of time to explain seine fishing to the boy.

Despite the confines of the boat and the intense periods of working together on deck, Orca and Fagshark managed to avoid any further disagreements. When he wasn't working or cooking in the galley, Orca spent his free moments in the wheelhouse with Corky learning everything he could. Fagshark for his part spoke little, even to Corky, and repaired gear on the work deck or lay in his bunk during periods of inactivity.

As they found fewer and fewer fish, the crew grew restless. Except for Orca they'd worked hard through the whole summer and as their efforts became less and less productive they thought more and more about returning home. Orca, on the other hand, was just getting started and hated the slow periods as much as they did only for a different reason. He wanted to catch fish. To the tired crew his enthusiasm was not infectious.

As Corky and Orca listened to the boat's radio, it crackled with short, dejected messages about no fish here and no fish there and thoughts about "packing it in." In the code of the fishermen these messages came across sounding like the sea flowed with fish. Only the tone of the voices hinted at the real situation. The fishermen had a way of not drawing others to their successful spots and if they were doing well, their voices sent messages like, "Aw, we picked up a few," which when translated meant something like, "We can barely haul the net and the deck's awash." The messages Corky heard and occasionally broadcast said just the opposite: "No fish anywhere."

One day they made a lazy set and held it longer than usual. Corky sat at his radio, an eye on the seine stretched toward shore. Calvin held it to a rock while Fagshark popped from the stern. Orca stood on the bow, looking at the spruce-forested rocky slopes of Knight Island when he first heard a loud exhaling breath. He turned to see a fin cut the water in the distance, moving toward the *Salmania*. Several others joined the first and they moved closer but still the other crew members didn't spot them. Then, a whale surfaced next to the boat with a loud "whoosh," catching Fagshark

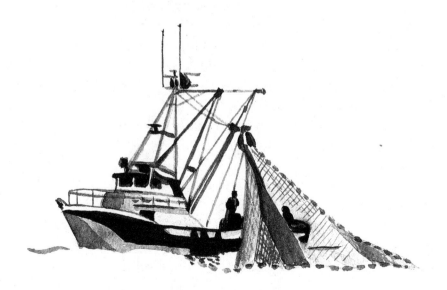

unaware. He jumped in surprise. The popper clattered to the deck
and Fagshark muttered the threatening oath "blackfish." He ran
into the cabin. The rest of the pod came up next to the boat. Orca
leaned over the side to watch them. In the wheel house, Corky
worried about his net, wondering if he should retrieve it. The
whales swam in half circles on the side away from the net.

Orca had become so engrossed in watching the whales that
Fagshark's appearance next to him caught him by surprise. What
startled him even more was the rifle in Fagshark's hands.

"You're not going to shoot at them?" he demanded, terrified.

"Shoot 'em all if I have to. All I can get," the older boy growled.
He raised the rifle and leveled it toward the nearest whale.

"Don't!" Orca's voice came out in nearly a scream. Then, recomposed and more threatening, he said, "Don't."

Fagshark ignored him and followed the whale with the muzzle
of the heavy rifle. The whale's white markings made it easy to see
just below the surface. Fagshark watched, waiting until the whale
rose to breathe. As the whale broke the surface, Fagshark's finger
tightened on the trigger. Orca shoved the rifle aside. A shot rang
off over the water. The report brought Corky running out of the
wheel house to find his crew scuffling on the deck.

Although overpowered by the bigger boy, Orca had managed
to roll on top and Corky grabbed him first, throwing him against
the cabin bulkhead. Fagshark scrambled to his feet, his eyes flashing belligerence, his fists raised. He looked menacingly at Orca
sitting by the bulkhead where he'd landed and then he turned on
Corky. The rifle lay on the deck.

"Just what's going on here?" Corky demanded. "Season's almost over and now you guys decide to start fighting."

"He tried to shoot a whale," Orca accused.

Corky turned to Fagshark, "True?"

"Yeah, I tried to shoot a thievin' blackfish. What's so bad about that?"

Truth be told, Corky really didn't know what was so bad about
it. From his years of fishing, he harbored the same feelings, perhaps not as intensely as Fagshark, but he disliked the whales for

the same reasons. Still, he knew Orca's history and if he thought about it, he'd never actually seen a whale pose any direct threat. What he did know was he couldn't have his crew fighting among themselves, particularly when a rifle was involved.

"I'll tell you what," he said to Fagshark with just the hint of a threat in his voice, "You go clean that rifle and put it away. I don't want to see it again."

"What are you gonna do about them blackfish? There ain't hardly any fish left," Fagshark demanded, full of belligerence. "I got a share, too, you know. Them blackfish chase the salmon away and nobody gets paid. We ain't makin' that much any more anyway. S'like we're workin' for free. Him, too, that whale lover. He's workin' against us. Hurtin' hisself, too."

"Put the rifle away," Corky ordered, "We'll just have to see about them whales."

Orca pulled himself to his feet and looked over the side, fearing what he might see. No blood discolored the green water and Orca felt relieved. The whales had disappeared and he wondered if the shot had chased them. He didn't want to show too much concern but he was worried. Fagshark's words about him working against them had stung deeply. Did Corky think that, too? For once he wished he'd never seen the whales. He wanted them to go away for good and let him fish. He walked to the stern and stood with Corky while Fagshark went below to clean the rifle and put it away.

"I won't let him shoot any whales," Corky promised, "but if they hang around, it might mean we'll have to move, or worse, I might have to take you back."

"I understand," Orca said, "thanks. I'll try to get along." He scanned the water, then turned back to Corky. "Maybe they're gone. Maybe the shot . . . "

Corky stood facing Orca, looking over his shoulder toward the water directly in front of the boat. While the boy spoke, Corky's eyes came wide open and he shouted, "Well, they ain't gone. Look at that!"

Orca spun to see a line of whales slashing through the water toward the net. Their backs rose out of the water, cutting wakes as they came. At intervals a whale would rise from deeper water, roll and knife back under. Their fins cut water as they bore down on the net.

"Holy cow!" Corky yelled. "We gotta close the seine or we'll lose it. Fagshark, get up here!" He raced for the wheelhouse where he turned the boat toward shore. At the same time he called Calvin in the skiff to bring his end back to the boat. Too late, the two men tried to pull the seine out of the way of the onrushing whales. The whole boat jerked sideways by the stern and the cork line disappeared into the water. The force of the impact caused Orca to stumble where he watched from the back deck.

"That's it," Corky hollered from the house, "They hit the net. They'll tear it to shreds." The corks still hadn't returned to the surface and the ocean boiled all along the line where they'd been.

Orca ran past Fagshark and up the ladder to join Corky in the wheel house. By this time Calvin had brought the skiff about half-way to the *Salmania*. Corky kept a running dialog with himself. "I don't know if we should close it or not. If there's a whale in there, it'd never hold. I don't want to pull it up backwards. I should tell Calvin to hold up. What if a whale's in there?" Calvin continued pulling toward the larger boat.

"Look over there," Orca said. He pointed to the pod of whales, now swimming quietly off the side of the *Salmania* away from the net.

"I wonder if that's all of 'em," Corky said. Then he made his decision. "We'll close and then hold the purse open a while. Any whale might swim out the bottom." He called Calvin to tell him to keep coming toward the boat.

Once the skiff had come alongside, the crew assumed their normal positions on the work deck. In a shorter time than usual, the machinery began to groan against the resisting weight in the water. The complaining lines and winches convinced Corky he'd caught ten tons of angry killer whale, but when they looked over the side all they could see were fish filling the inside of the cork circle. The boat listed precariously over the seine as the weight in the water pulling against the tall rigging threatened to tip it.

Operating the hydraulics, Corky kept the strain on the net as it rolled groaning through the power block over Orca's and Fagshark's heads. They coiled slowly, occasionally pulling one of the smaller fish out of the web. Some had hit so hard they passed halfway through. After they closed the purse, the weight of the fish in the net grew too heavy for the gear.

Corky retrieved his brailer net from its place in the rigging. He and Orca began dipping salmon from the seine and dropping them in the fish hold. All the while the whales swam around the boat. Fagshark cursed them under his breath, keeping a watchful eye on Corky.

Corky found it difficult to hold any anger for the whales. His expression alternated between jubilation and concern as he worked the brailer. As he brought more and more fish on board he wanted to cheer at the size of the catch. Then as the weight transferred from the water to the boat and he watched his freeboard shorten he began to worry about overloading. "We got more'n a deck load here," he said, "Must be over a hundred thousand pounds."

He and Orca continued to fill the hold and as they did, the boat settled deeper into the water and the slight swell lapped higher and higher along the sides. When the hold overflowed, they emptied the brailer on deck, but still enough fish remained in the seine to keep the boat heeled over the water. When the water reached the scuppers and washed across the deck, Corky began to worry. The scuppers were supposed to let water flow off the deck. Water sloshing across the deck moved the fish around and the crew found themselves walking a moving, slippery carpet.

"There's no way we're going to get all these fish on board," Corky said finally. "I've got to call a tender. I sure hope somebody's close."

On the radio, Corky interrupted fishermen telling each other how bad the day was. He called for a tender and waited for a response. The radio stayed quiet after he spoke, the rest of the fishermen waiting to hear about the catch to see if it might be worthwhile to move nearer the *Salmania* and make a set. For what seemed an eternity Corky waited, standing in the wheelhouse like a hiker on a side hill, one foot higher than the other compensating for the list the fish in the net caused. After what seemed an interminable silence while Corky tried to maintain his balance, a voice crackled out of the radio. He quickly gave his position and predicament and the tenderman said he'd be there within an hour. He didn't bother to disguise either where he was or the size of his catch as he normally would. Corky imagined he also heard the sound of dozens of fishing vessels roaring into life and heading toward him to join in the bonanza.

All they could do was wait. Corky descended the ladder to tell his crewmen. He found even Fagshark smiling. "Good thing we got 'em before them blackfish," he sneered toward Orca.

Corky smiled toward Orca, then turned to Fagshark, slipping in the mess on the deck. "You don't catch on too quick, do you?" Then, to Orca, "You made a believer out of me, or they did. Never seen anything like it."

Orca, sitting exhausted on the coaming around the fish hold, smiled weakly, relieved. He stood and waded across the deck through the water and fish to look over the side. Just as he did, one of the killer whales came up alongside, tilting its head sideways as if to look at the boy. The wet, dirty, exhausted boy somehow wanted to say thank you, but how could he? The whale submerged and moved off toward the rest of the pod.

Then they waited. Calvin used the skiff pulling on the *Salmania* to keep it steady in the current while Corky watched his freeboard and his list. He pointed to the red stripe around the hull marking the water line. Under the load, the stripe barely showed from beneath the surface. "Call that the money line," Corky told Orca. "Put that below the water and it means the boat's loaded, you're makin' money."

Corky kept scanning the horizon for the tender, wishing it next to the boat. Other fishing boats arrived first and began setting their nets, but they came up with very few fish. When the tender boat arrived at last, the captain maneuvered next to Corky's net. They tied off bow and stern, then the tendermen dropped a hose into Corky's seine and began pumping fish on board the larger vessel. When they had emptied the seine and the *Salmania* came upright again, the tendermen waited while Corky's crew retrieved the remainder of the net. Then they put the hose into the fish hold and pumped that dry, too. Orca and Fagshark chased fish around the deck and dumped them into the hold so the pump could reach them.

When the *Salmania* finally stood high in the water and level again, the tendermen gave Corky the report. "Two hundred and ten thousand pounds," they said. The jubilation on the *Salmania's* deck passed to those working on the tender. They had plugged the buyer's boat and once the pumping and weighing and transfer into the refrigerated holds had been completed, the tender headed north to the processing plant. They watched it disappear in the distance and then looked around to see most of the remaining fleet within a mile of them. Nets bobbed everywhere as the other fishermen attempted to catch what they thought was the last big school of fish.

The one set had invigorated the *Salmania's* crew as well. Where just a few hours earlier they'd figured the run had ended and were thinking of quitting, now they rushed to make another set and another, weaving in and around the other fishermen and nets. It was like they'd caught every last salmon in the ocean. Nets came up empty or with just a few fish, not even paying for the fuel it took to run the hydraulics. After four more sets and watching the others come up empty, they went to anchor, at least warm with the thought of a big payday.

For the next few days they followed the island's contours, scouting for fish, making a tentative set once in a while, but by that time the salmon had passed. Corky finally admitted the season was over and he told the crew as much. Aside, he said to Orca, "I've got an idea. What say we go get Sven and the two of you go to town with me? Be fun. You might find out what that Miss

Braithewaite's up to, too. I can send those guys back on a tender and we can stop and pick up Sven."

Orca fell silent. Corky had just made an offer he hadn't heard before. People who visited their cabin had suggested it now and again, but no one had ever made a definite invitation. Town. He'd heard about towns his whole life, but he'd never actually visited one. He'd read about them in his books, but in twelve years of life, Orca had never seen more than half a dozen people and maybe three buildings together at one time. Now Corky wanted to take him to town.

"You seem pretty quiet," Corky said.

"I've never been to town."

"Well, it's about time you went, then. We won't be there long enough for you to get into any trouble."

With that, Corky told his plan to Calvin and Fagshark who were only too willing to get off the boat and go spend their summer's earnings. Once the two crewmen boarded a tender for town, Corky turned the *Salmania* toward Cabin Bay and brought the engine up to speed.

CHAPTER 13

INNOCENTS ASHORE

A T THE SET NET SITE, Sven never became used to being alone. He immersed himself in the work of dismantling their fish camp, but he thought about the boy constantly, speaking to him aloud, but for only the trees and rocks to hear.

Each morning he looked up to find the termination dust had crept farther down the mountains overnight. That inspired his efforts. The size of their catch and the addition of Orca's school supplies and Priscilla's curtains along with their normal pile of gear forced Sven to make three trips between Miners Bay and Cabin Bay. When he finally reached their winter home with his last load, he began the chores preparing for the next season, mostly cruising the beaches looking for drift logs he could cut for firewood. He had reached the point of wondering when Orca would return when the *Salmania* turned into Cabin Bay and dropped anchor.

Following their reunion on the beach, Corky and Orca told Sven about the big set.

"I heard of that happenin' down in Canada," Sven said, "but never here. Those guys'll set right in front of the whales in this narrow strait and catch all the fish they're chasin'."

Then they told Sven about their vacation plans. The old man hesitated at first, as it seemed to Orca he did with everything lately. But the boy's enthusiasm eventually convinced him. They closed the cabin, boarded the *Salmania* and headed for town. The season had ended, the pressure to fish had been relieved, and they relaxed in the wheelhouse telling stories and answering Orca's questions about their destination.

Sven could only tell him what he remembered from years past, but Corky lived there and could embellish what Sven told the boy, and add stories of his own. So much had changed since Sven's last visit, he, too, in time came to look forward to a whole new experience. They traveled well into the early September night. Stars filled the clear northern sky as the boat broke the calm surface into sparkling riffles while the two men and the boy talked in the darkened cabin, their faces illuminated eerily by red lights of the engine gauges and the green of the navigation instruments.

Corky turned the *Salmania* around a point into a large bay, passing a flashing red light off to their starboard. "Entrance Island," Corky said. "There's the town."

Ahead, deep in the bay, more lights than Orca had ever seen sent shafts of yellow across the water toward them. They passed other boats, noted their direction by the running lights and their wakes that rolled the *Salmania*. Traffic increased as they approached the harbor despite the late hour. Other fishermen had joined them in the return to town. They passed tenders making their last runs to the processors. Pleasure boats ghosted past them going in the opposite direction, townspeople taking their days off to live in time counted by hours the life Orca and Sven enjoyed by the season and year. The *Salmania* cut water straight toward the lights while Orca stared silently through the front window.

"Won't be able to do much tonight," Corky said. "Everything's closed but maybe the Harborview. I'll bet that's where all the fishermen are, spendin' their summer's wages already. We can run up to the house and get some sleep. Give it a good shot in the morning. Be nice to take a shower, too."

Orca turned with a question in the expression on his face.

Corky caught it immediately. "Oh boy, have we got a lot of trainin' to do. It's a bath, only the water comes out of a pipe over your head and sprays on you."

"Is it hot?" Orca asked.

"Hot as you want it," Corky said.

"Where does the water come from?"

"You hire a guy," Sven said with a twinkle in his eye. "Guy comes and stands on the roof and he keeps a fire goin' under a big pot. When somebody wants a shower this guy dips water out of the pot and dumps it down into the pipes."

Corky started chuckling at the wheel and that broke Sven's serious expression into a laugh. Orca stared at the two of them, trying to envision how a man could spend his life standing on a roof waiting for someone inside the house to want a bath.

"I guess we better not do that," Sven said. "I'm sorry. You got enough to see without us confusing you. The city pipes water into all the houses and every house has a tank to heat water in. Sure would be funny, though, all them guys standin' on all them roofs with fires goin' and dumpin' water into them pipes every time somebody called for a shower."

"Make some jobs," Corky said, "Keep a lot of fishermen in groceries in the bad years. We're almost there now."

Corky slowed the boat and turned. They passed between two flashing lights, green on the left, red on the right, into a narrow jetty lined on both sides by piles of boulders higher than the boat. At the end of the jetty, they turned again and the harbor opened before them. An eerie yellow light illuminated the water and more boats than Orca had ever seen at one time floated nestled in orderly rows against the docks. Corky maneuvered the *Salmania* into an empty slot and Sven and Orca stepped off onto the dock. Sven showed the boy how to tie the boat to a dock cleat, his first lesson in town. "No anchors here," Sven said.

Corky shut down the *Salmania's* engine. "Made it," he said. "Cheated death one more time."

From somewhere up the dock Orca heard music and shouting and laughter.

"Sounds like the boys had a pretty good season," Corky said noticing Orca. "The Harborview's really jumpin'."

"What's the Harborview?" Orca asked.

"That's one place you ain't goin'," Sven said.

"It's a place guys go to let off steam after a week cooped up on a boat," Corky said. "No place for kids, 'specially one just come to town for the first time. Guess we got everything. My truck's at the top of the ramp. Let's go." He locked the door of the boat cabin. He saw Orca watch him turn the key. "Lotta guys lookin' for free gear," he said. "Don't suppose you ever seen a lock before. Ain't much stealin' around here, but no sense takin' the chance of somebody walkin' off with a radio or somethin'."

"That lock ain't goin' to stop them if they want it anyway," Sven said.

"Yeah, well, it keeps the honest people honest," Corky said.

Corky stepped off the boat and the three of them walked up the dock with Orca ogling everything they passed. At one point he almost walked off the dock into the water as he looked up into the rigging of a fishing boat bigger than any he'd seen visit Cabin Bay.

Sven grabbed him by the jacket and Corky said, "Ocean trawler."

They climbed the long ramp connecting the floating docks with shore. At the top, Orca saw spread before him more buildings and lights and people walking around even at that time of night than he'd imagined could be in one place. It was one thing to see photographs in his books and quite another to see the reality, even in a small town after midnight. Across a street from the harbor stood a row of buildings that included a grocery, a couple of restaurants, a hotel, a boat supplies store, an office building and a hardware supplier, most of them darkened for the night. In the middle of the row, its lights blazing and its sounds rising every time a door opened, stood the Harborview Tavern. Corky looked toward it for a longing minute. "Not tonight, I guess. Sounds like they're havin' fun, though."

Corky's pickup truck stood under the umbrella of an amber harbor light. He unlocked the door and started the engine. Another first for Orca. They drove slowly through town, at least slowly by automobile standards. Their speed still was faster than Orca had ever moved in his life. Twenty miles an hour was more than twice the speed of any boat he knew. Even at their slowest speeds, boats seldom came within a mile of each other. Now going faster than he'd ever gone, Orca rode in a truck that passed other vehicles within feet. Orca tensed every time Corky passed another car. They were going too fast and too close together for comfort as far as the boy from Cabin Bay was concerned, but he kept his silence. Only Sven, crowded next to him in the small cab of the pickup, could feel the boy's muscles tense each time they approached another vehicle. Sensing the boy's discomfort, Sven realized the traffic bothered him, too.

"There's where that Miss Braithewaite works," Corky said as they passed a building larger than most of the others around it. "Course she won't be there tomorrow, it bein' Saturday. We'll have to find her at home, I guess."

Corky turned the truck onto a side road where the buildings were spaced farther apart than they had been near the harbor. They passed several houses where, in the dim lights of the yards, Orca could make out piles of line and stacks of crab pots and bright buoys hanging from outbuildings. Some of them reminded him of their house in Cabin Bay.

"We call this fishermen's row," Corky said. "Lot of us live out here. My place is just down there." Shortly they turned into a driveway and passed between stacks of crab pots, their eight-foot square frames and heavy netting filtering what little light illuminated their passage. Corky stopped the truck and they crawled out. Corky went to the door of the small house and produced a key for yet another lock. They went inside and Orca looked around. "I'll light a lamp if I can find one," he said.

"No need," Corky said as he flicked a switch on the wall next to the doorway. The room immediately filled with light. Orca looked at the switch and then the bright fixture overhead.

"Electricity," Sven said, "pretty handy stuff." Orca knew about electricity; he'd seen and used it on the *Salmania*. He just wasn't expecting to see it in a house and he couldn't hear a generator.

"We best get cleaned up and get some sleep," Corky said. "I got a feeling tomorrow's going to be a long day. We got shopping to do and I suppose some exploring and who knows what all."

"We should go see Priscilla, too," Sven said.

"Let's see about that shower, huh?" Corky offered.

He showed Orca how to adjust the knobs to bring the dash of water to the right temperature. The boy removed his clothes and stepped under the cascade.

"It's kind of like a waterfall, only warm," Orca said as the water all but engulfed him. Corky handed him a bar of soap and then went with Sven to arrange bunks for his guests. One by one, they cleaned themselves and fell into beds. From his place on a couch under a window, Orca looked out at the night sky for a while, unable to fall asleep, imagining what was going to happen the next day. His mind didn't seem to want to relax as it raced through what he'd already seen and produced new visions of what was to come. For what seemed like hours, he flopped and rolled until at last his physical exhaustion overcame his mental activity and he dozed.

Corky rose first in the morning, or thought he was first because he saw no one else stirring. He shuffled into the kitchen and without looking around put a pot of water on the stove for coffee. Then he went to rouse the other two. He shook Sven into motion and went to the couch, but Orca wasn't there. He looked around the house, but found no boy. He peeked through the windows but still didn't see anybody until he stepped out onto the narrow porch. From there he spotted Orca out in the yard, sitting on a pile of line.

"I couldn't sleep," Orca said. "There's so much noise."

"The highway's right over there and trucks're runnin' most of the time," Corky said.

"It's not just that, listen."

At first Corky couldn't hear anything and then, slowly he began to realize what Orca was talking about, a sound unheard by those who lived with it constantly.

A buzz filled the air, not loud or sharp, but in the background as if it was part of the very air itself. It came from nowhere in particular and yet it came from everywhere, a collection of sounds, mixed and diffused. The city had begun awakening. A diesel-powered generator kept a steady percussion from somewhere in town. Trucks roared and bounced along the highway. A car started and idled in a driveway nearby and men talked in restaurants across town. Boat engines throbbed in the harbor and garbage trucks lurched down back alleys. Airplanes flew far overhead, leaving their engine noise behind to drift down over the town and mix with the cacophony. Now and then a car horn honked or a voice rose out of the morning. All of the sounds melded to form a low din like the constant rush of air.

"I hear it," Corky said. "I guess I never noticed it before. It's just part of everything."

"There's a smell, too," Orca said. There was, like the noise, a background odor, not the heavy smell of industry, but the combinations of engine exhausts and freshly cut grass, of the greasy mist blown by exhaust fans over the grills in restaurant kitchens where breakfast bacon fried. Pollen from the forest surrounding the town mixed with odors from fish holds being cleaned in the harbor and scents rising from the flower gardens in the town's parks. All of it mingled with the salty, seaweed air from the ocean and the crab pots in Corky's yard. The smell took the fisherman longer to sense as he tried to understand the boy's perceptions. "I never noticed that either," he said. "I guess it's all what you're used to.

"I got water on. Sven's in there makin' coffee. Don't know if I got any bull coffee or not," Corky said.

"That's all right," Orca said. "It's just soup, anyway."

Corky laughed. "He never fooled you for a minute, did he?"

"Maybe for a minute," Orca answered as he stood to follow Corky into the house.

"Thought we'd go out for breakfast, seein's you never been to a restaurant before."

"Sounds good to me," Orca brightened. The adventure had started.

The two men took cups of coffee with them in the truck and Corky drove them back to the waterfront where Sven and Corky introduced Orca to the wonders of eating out.

"You can have any of this?" he asked as he scanned his first menu.

"Sure can, and cooked pretty much the way you want it." Their only problem with the restaurant came when they tried to explain bull coffee to the waitress. Corky called "hello" to the people he knew and several of the other customers recognized Sven and Orca and came to the table to greet them. On hearing this was Orca's first trip to town, everyone offered an idea of what the boy should see and do and most of them offered to take him.

The waitress brought their breakfast, Orca having chosen a waffle covered with strawberries and whipped cream. They ate quietly, mostly listening to the others.

They politely declined the invitations, but added some of the suggestions to their plans. When they finished eating, Corky asked, "Well, where do we start?"

"First, let's get out of here," Orca said. Sven agreed.

They returned to the truck where Corky asked, "What do you think about restaurants?"

"I never had food like that before," Orca said, "but there were too many people in there."

Sven agreed again. "That's more people in that one room than we seen in maybe half a year all told."

"I guess there was," Corky said, "Never thought of it that way. Maybe we ought to stay out of places with crowds, least 'til you get used to it."

"Good idea," Sven nodded toward Orca.

"What do you want to do, then?" Corky asked.

"I think we best take care of business first," Sven said, "We worked up a shopping list for some stuff we need and we should let the boy here pick out some store-bought clothes. He needs boots for sure. Got to get some tools, too, and a prop. We need netting and twine. What say we do a little shopping first?"

"I want to see Priscilla, too," Orca added.

"Yup, we better find out where we are with that," Sven said.

"I got an idea for tonight," Corky said. "What say we go and see if we can't bail Smit out of that Old Salt's Home. You haven't seen him in a long time."

"He's here?" Sven asked.

"Yeah. I guess they about had to wrestle him down to get him in there."

"I can see that happenin'. He never struck me to be the retirin' type."

"He's the same guy, just older, now."

"Who is he?" Orca asked.

"Old-time sailor," Sven said. "I think he was old when I was a boy. Sailed with him a couple of times in my early years. Quite a character. I like the idea. Let's go see him, maybe take him out to dinner."

"Here we are," Corky said as he brought the pickup to a halt in a parking lot. The adjacent building held a sign over its display windows shouting "OUTFITTERS."

"Well, here we go," Sven said, reaching for the door handle, but Corky interrupted him.

"One thing," he said, "You ain't goin' too far without money. They don't give stuff away in there, you know. I parceled it out this morning. Course Orca here didn't fish most of the season, but we did have that one big set so he made a fair amount. Here's his share. Ought to keep you goin' awhile." Corky handed Orca a pile of green bills.

Orca's eyes widened. He'd never seen that amount of money before.

"Thanks, Corky. See you in a bit. Orca, let's go see if we can't put a dent in that," Sven said, indicating the boy's money.

"Meet you here in a hour, two hours, okay?"

"Sounds good."

Corky pulled away in his truck while Sven and Orca walked over to the store and pulled on the door. It was locked.

"I didn't even notice that," Sven said.

"What?"

"The sign there says they're closed," Sven said. "Says they'll be open in ten minutes. We can wait, I guess."

"How come they're closed now?" Orca asked. "There's people around and they are trying to sell things in there, aren't they?" He cupped his hands around his eyes and tried to peer through the display window.

"Yeah, that's true enough," Sven said, "but this here's one of the things you got to learn about town. Out where we live, we do things when we want to or when we need to, but it ain't that way in town. In town you got to do things on other people's time. Don't matter when you want to do something; it always depends on somebody else. Seems like everything you have to do in town you have to do it with somebody. And you always got to do it by their clocks, not yours. It's just like this: We're ready to buy stuff, that's our time, but they ain't ready to sell stuff. That's their time. So, you and me end up waitin' and wastin' our time so's we can do things on their time. Course there's a reason on their side, too. Why should they stay open all night just so's a couple of guys from out in the sound somewhere can come in and maybe buy a pair of socks? Costs them money to stay open. Them socks're probably be the only thing they'd sell all night and they got to pay help and heat the place and so on. They'd probably lose a lot of money just stayin' open to sell that pair of socks. Everybody does it, stays open and closes about the same times so you got everybody in town movin' around and doin' things on just about the same schedule. Then people like you and me come along and we operate on a different schedule and all of a sudden we got to use theirs. You give me my choice and I'd rather give up a lot of this, just so my time's my own. Don't care much for the tick of somebody else's clock."

They leaned against a railing in front of the store and watched the cars and trucks go by on the street.

"You didn't like how fast them cars went by us, did you?" Sven asked.

"It's awfully close and awfully fast," Orca said, "but it isn't just the cars, Sven. It's the people, too. Did you see the waitress in the restaurant? Everything she did was the same way. She walked fast and talked fast and wrote things down fast. It seemed like even when she was standing still she was doing it fast."

"That's part of it," Sven said. "They're in a hurry all the time and sometimes it don't make no sense. You hurry up and then you end up standin' and waitin' for someplace to open, waitin' and watchin' other people hurry other places. Don't seem to make a lot of sense sometimes."

Behind them the door lock clicked and they turned to see the store's door pushed open from the inside. "Guess they're ready for us now," Sven said and they turned to enter the store.

Before they could reach it, a woman pulling a child along with her pushed past them and hurried into the store.

Orca looked at Sven and the old man laughed, "They got to teach 'em young if they're gonna keep up. That little fella's growin' up on the run."

Once inside, their conversation stopped as rows and rows of dry goods opened before them. Orca wandered through aisles fingering the seemingly endless piles of shirts and pants stacked neatly on shelves along one wall. He looked over a display of boots and shoes that filled an entire corner by the front window. He twirled the swiveling racks of multicolored jackets and lifted hats to try them on his head. He stopped at a rack of neckties and asked Sven what they were.

Sven explained the need for neckwear in town. "Maybe I'll get one to wear tonight," Orca said. Sven rolled his eyes and looked at the ceiling while Orca moved to the next display.

When Orca had wandered through the store for about as long as Sven could stand it, the old man asked, "See anything you want?"

"We'd better get boots," he answered. "And some pants for working, and I saw a couple of shirts there. They have some neat knives, too."

"Let's get what we need first, then see what we got left over for what we want," Sven said. Then the idea of sizes confronted them. They'd ordered clothes from Corky or catalogs most of their lives, but the mountain of material in front of them coupled with Orca's recent growth confused them for a time. Orca tried to pick out a shirt. "Some of these have letters and some of the others have numbers. Those over there have two numbers. The pants have two numbers, too. The hats have letters, only some of them have numbers. All the boots have numbers, but the socks have letters, so how do you know which socks go with which boots?"

They picked out heavy rubber work boots and a clerk helped them find the proper sizes. They figured out the socks for themselves after the clerk took their boots to the cash register. Soon they wandered in the clothing aisles again. Slowly and when they could gain the bored clerk's attention, they chose new clothes, adding them to a pile they were building on a counter near the front of the store. Shirts went into the pile, heavy wool plaid ones, and pants, some wool, some denim. Sven picked out insulated coveralls for each of them, saying, "These'll make life a whole lot better in the winter." Then they returned to the shoes and added insulated winter boots to the pile.

Eventually they separated and lost track of each other as they moved about the store, occasionally taking something to the growing pile by the cash register. Orca saw Sven speaking with a clerk at a display of rifles. He had a rifle in his hands, feeling its heft and sighting at an imaginary deer. "Too much," he told the clerk. "More'n we can spend." He walked away from the display. When he'd disappeared, Orca asked the clerk if he could see the rifle. He looked at the price tag. "He sure could use this for deer hunting," Orca said, handing the rifle back to the clerk.

The next time Orca saw Sven he was looking at the mountain of purchases. When he spotted the boy, he said, "Maybe it's time to stop. Hey, what you got there?

Orca showed him a hat he'd found, a floppy kind of ivy league cap, but white, like the ones he'd seen halibut fishermen wear.

"That's about it, I think," he said. "We're already going to need a truckload of money to pay for it and another truck to get it out of here. Probably sink Corky's boat gettin' it out to the cabin, too." He took the cap out of Orca's hand, looked at it, and then slapped it onto the boy's head. "Okay, now let's see what the damages are."

The bored clerk took new interest as she began ringing up their purchases.

"Quite a machine, huh?" Sven asked Orca. "Adds up all the prices and even tells us how much change we get back. Don't expect much change after this." Orca watched the clerk punch keys. When their receipt flowed from the machine, Sven examined it for the total. He flinched and showed it to Orca. He handed his money to Sven who began counting bills for the clerk.

"Do we have enough left for that rifle?" Orca asked.

"Pipe dream," Sven said. "We still need to get gear and groceries." He looked at the pile of new clothes and then at the old ones he and Orca were wearing. "You got a place we could change?" he asked the clerk.

She showed them a tiny room in the back of the store and Sven and Orca crowded into it to put on a new suit of clothes for town. After giggling their way through changing in the confines of the dressing room, the man and the boy from Cabin Bay, Prince William Sound, emerged dressed and ready for the refinements of town, wearing brand new plaid shirts and stiff blue jeans, their own version of dress-up finery. Orca wore his fisherman's cap tipped at a jaunty angle.

"Well, if you don't look fine," Sven said, knocking Orca on the shoulder.

"You look pretty good yourself," Orca said. They gathered their bags and walked out into the sunlight.

"We got some time before Corky comes back. What say we get a couple of city haircuts and look fancy for Priscilla when she comes. There's a barber shop over there," Sven said.

"You mean they don't even cut their own hair here?" Orca asked.

"Nope. You pay people to do it for you. You think that's bad, you should see the places they got for women's hair. Takes 'em hours."

They walked to the barber shop but found another sign that read "Closed Saturdays."

"City time," Sven said, disgusted. "Now there's a store open you might like. Probably take just enough time to meet Corky."

The sign advertised something Orca knew well. "They have stores just for ice cream?" he asked.

"Sure do."

They went inside and Sven waited while Orca marveled through the variety of flavors. "Hard to decide," he said.

"Whyn't you try all of 'em," Sven kidded. "Way you eat ice cream, shouldn't take you more'n an hour or two." They each ordered huge ice cream cones with three flavors and went back to the parking lot to wait for Corky. They had just eaten down to the tops of the cones when the pickup pulled into the lot. Priscilla rode in the passenger's seat.

"Look who I found," Corky called, and then he saw the pile of parcels. "You guys leave anything in the store?"

Priscilla walked around the front of the truck.

"Don't you two look like something," she said, admiring their new clothes. "Welcome to town."

"Hi, Priscilla," Orca said, "We would have had haircuts, too, but they were closed. City time," the boy added, knowingly.

"What are you teaching him?" Priscilla asked Sven with a hint of disapproval. "I've been trying to reach you. You have a court hearing."

"We're glad to see you, too," Sven said. "When?"

"It's in just a few days. They issued the birth certificate. You passed your background check. Now all you have to do is convince the judge."

"We can do that," Sven said confidently.

"Well, I hope so. What else do you have planned?"

Sven thought for a minute and then said, "We got to get to a hardware store for one and we got to hit the Fisherman's Supply and maybe a sporting goods. Yeah, we want to pick up some new books and he's going to need some paper and pencils and that sort of stuff."

"We're going out to dinner and see Smit tonight," Orca said, still not quite sure who Smit was.

"If you're going to hit all those stores, we better get moving," Corky said. "They ain't gonna be open tomorrow."

Orca and Sven winked at each other. City time.

"Now, wait a minute, you two," Priscilla interrupted. "This may be all well and good, but I don't think he should spend all his time in stores following you men around. There's more to town than hardware. I want him to see something else, too. The museum for one."

"Okay, let's be goin' then," Sven said and they all jammed into the cab of the pickup. Corky edged out into traffic and soon they were caught in it with the rest of the townspeople. Now they hurried, too, just like everyone else, driving this way fast, driving that way fast, pushing through stores and trying to accomplish everything they needed to do and see everything there was to see in one mad rush of a day.

For a time, the town absorbed the man and boy from Cabin Bay into its rhythms and they flowed with the hastened pace, racing through stores, buying what they needed and some of what they didn't. Even their lunch they took on the run, driving through a line and past a window where they ordered meals and drinks and picked up a cheeseburger sandwich for Sven. They ate in the truck while they drove to the next stop. They found books, paper and pencils. They bought netting, shuttles and twine. They loaded food for Cabin Bay. The only time they slowed down came at the hardware store after Corky and Sven decided Orca should have tools of his own and they took their time choosing from the bins to fill the boy's brand-new tool box. They bought him some lures for snapper fishing, a pair of oars for the skiff and a new propeller for the outboard. They loaded it all into the back of Corky's pickup until the springs groaned and the truck could hold no more.

They stood staring into the back of the pickup. "You know," Corky said, "Alaskans don't need anything like those football stadiums. Biggest spectator sport in the state seems like just standin' starin' into the back of a pickup. That's our stadium."

"I still got to hit the machine shop for some hydraulic fittings," he added while they stood looking at the mass in the back of the truck. "I need some shackles and chain, too," Sven said."

"It's gettin' late, we got to keep going," Corky said.

"I think it's time to stop," Priscilla pleaded. "How about some quiet time, something slow?"

"If that don't beat all," Sven said, "I'm tellin' Orca here how fast everything goes in town and here you live in town and you're tellin' us to slow down. I don't guess I can just yet."

"I'm afraid I'm going to insist here," Priscilla said, "We still haven't done any of the things I wanted to do."

"How about if Sven and me go do the rest of the stuff and you and Orca go off and do whatever it is you want to do," Corky offered.

"That sounds fair," Priscilla agreed. "Let's do that and then we can meet somewhere for dinner, my treat."

"What about Orca? What do you want to do?" Sven asked, realizing they'd been making all the decisions for the boy without asking.

"I'm tired of stores, Sven. Let me go with Priscilla for a while."

"Sounds good to me," Sven said, "You mind if we bring Smit to dinner?"

"Not at all," Priscilla said, now along with Orca wondering who he was.

Corky asked, "Where do you want to go?"

"You can drop us at the museum," Priscilla said.

"What's a museum?" Orca asked.

He found out soon enough. While the two men went about their business, Priscilla took Orca on a slow walk through the town's small historical museum. Exhibits of photographs showed life in the earlier years of the sound and Orca learned more about the town he was visiting for the first time; how it had begun as a supply port for the gold rush farther north and later supported a smaller gold rush in the sound itself. He saw displayed pieces of machinery from the mines and old photographs from the early years of the fishing industry. In one of the photographs they identified a much younger Sven Kaartoonsen standing with a group of smiling fishermen admiring a huge halibut laid out on a dock. Priscilla wondered aloud if the photograph might help Sven in his talk with the judge. They examined displays showing life of the Native inhabitants of the sound along with stories of the early white explorers. Orca hesitated at one small display that included photos of shipwrecks and a list of wrecks and disasters in the waters of the sound. None of the sinkings coincided with his arrival on the beach at Cabin Bay and they passed on to the next exhibit.

When they had exhausted the museum, Priscilla said, "There's one more place. I'm sure we have time before we meet Sven and Corky and it's something you should at least be exposed to."

"What's that?"

"We have a small art gallery and I'd like you to see some good paintings."

"You mean like the pictures in books?"

"Yes, but better. These are pictures people have actually spent a lot of time painting and it's good for you to see them. You should know more than fishing and boats and Prince William Sound."

"All right," Orca said, "Let's go look at pictures."

They crossed the street and entered a small storefront. Inside, paintings lined the walls, all done by local artists. Priscilla walked slowly, explaining to Orca the different methods and materials used in the paintings and told him what she thought the artist was trying to convey.

"I like the ones with scenes and animals," he told her. "But, those ones with the lines and splashes . . . why do they do that?"

"It takes a while to understand them," she said, "The artist is usually trying to say something with the painting and with these, sometimes it takes a while to appreciate what that statement is."

"I think I'd stick to what's real, like that one," he said, pointing to a painting of a seal perched on a rock.

"That's one I wanted you to see. Do you like it?" Priscilla asked.

"Yes, it looks real, like a seal looks."

"Do you recognize it?"

Orca looked at her, puzzled.

"Remember the time we put the seal skeleton together and I took the skull?"

"The first jigsaw puzzle."

"The woman I gave it to is the one who painted this picture. She used the skull to make the shape of the head just right. I want to buy it for you if you like it."

"I like it the best of anything in here," Orca said. "I'm not sure how Sven would take it if I brought home a picture of a seal."

"Oh, he can learn to live with it," Priscilla said and then asked the gallery attendant to take the painting down and wrap if for them while they moved farther along the wall. When they had seen all the paintings, Priscilla paid and they walked outside.

Corky almost drove past them and the truck swerved to a stop at the curb almost losing the top of the load in the back. A driver behind him shook his fist as he passed.

"Get everything done?" Sven asked from the passenger window.

"As much as we could," Priscilla said, "There's never enough time, is there?"

"All the time in the world where we live," he answered. "What did you do?"

"We saw a picture of you at the museum," Orca said, "We went to the art gallery, too."

"Oh, that sounds like fun," Sven said, adding a fancy lilt to his voice and winking at Corky.

Corky grimaced and then laughed. "I always thought of you as a museum piece."

"You could help," Priscilla attempted to wither them. "Just because it's not your idea of a good time doesn't mean it isn't. I suppose I should have taken him to the Harborview or something like that."

"Or to tea," Corky kidded.

"All right," Priscilla threatened.

"I apologize," Sven said, "You're right."

"Me too," Corky agreed, "What's in the package?"

"It's a painting. Priscilla bought it for us," Orca said. "A friend of Priscilla's painted it. It's a seal. She used the skull from that seal we found on the beach."

"Oh, great," Sven said, "We going to hang a picture of a seal in our cabin? Maybe we could call it the fisherman's friend. How are we going to explain that one?"

"It's a good picture, Sven. Wait 'til you see it."

"Okay, okay."

Corky interrupted, "We'd better get going if we're going to eat. We still got to go get Smit."

"Maybe you could drop us and I'll get my car," Priscilla said, "and we'll meet you at the home."

"That sounds good," Corky said. "I know we all won't fit in the truck." He drove to Priscilla's home where she and Orca left the truck and stepped into her car. Orca ran his hands over the plush seat coverings, bounced once on the softer seat. When Priscilla started the car she put a tape into the player and Orca listened to music while they followed Corky to the Old Salt's Home.

Inside, the four of them walked down a hallway, checking nameplates next to each door. "Here it is," Corky called and pointed to the small sign that read "Maurice Hewlitt-Smith."

"Never knew that," Sven said. "I wonder if he knows they put his real name on the door." He knocked and opened the door after hearing a response from inside.

They entered the room to find Smit seated next to a window. The change in him shocked Sven. Where he'd known a robust sailing man in his prime, now he saw a thin, wrinkled, balding, sad-eyed old person with only a hint of his former self visible.

Smit brightened immediately when he realized who had come to visit. "Corky said he was bringin' a surprise. Couldn't of guessed it was you," he said. "Come over here by the window. Can see the ocean from here. All I got left of it."

Sven walked over and grabbed the older man's hands. "It sure is good to see you."

"You come to bail me out of here?" Smit asked.

"For a while anyway. You want to go eat a real meal? I can't believe they feed you very good in here."

Smit looked around Sven to the others. "Who're these folks?"

"You know Corky," Sven said, "This is our friend Priscilla Braithewaite."

"Fine lookin' woman," Smit said. "Fine."

Priscilla blushed. "I'm pleased to meet you," she said.

"Don't mind Smit," Sven told her. "Old habits die hard."

Ignoring him, Smit asked, "Who's this?"

"This here's Orca."

Smit gauged Orca as he might have judged the rigging of a clipper ship.

"So you got yourself a boy, Sven. Fine lookin' lad, too." Smit labored to rise from his chair, then he clamped his hands on Orca's shoulders. "You been to sea yet, boy?"

"I've been fishing with Corky."

"I ain't talkin' 'bout no pond like this here sound. You been on the big ocean?"

Orca shook his head.

"'Bout time then. I's eight when I first climbed a ratline. Shipped as a cabin boy. Sven, you wasn't much older first time you shipped with us."

Sven smiled and agreed, but sensing Orca's discomfort, said, "Let's get you dressed. We're goin' to dinner." He grasped the old sailor's shoulder for a moment, then turned and followed the others outside to wait for Smit to dress.

When the door opened, Smit stood there in bell bottoms and a striped jersey looking like he'd just walked off one of Her Majesty's Ships. Sven noticed the old twinkle had returned to his eye and though he needed a cane now, he still walked with the bow-legged roll of a big-water sailor.

Priscilla stifled a giggle at the sight of his costume. He stood shorter even than Orca but seemed to fill the hallway as they walked. Sven tried to draw him out with memories of their time together, but all Smit wanted to do was walk closer to Priscilla.

They helped him into Corky's truck and went to the restaurant. By the time they arrived, Smit had gained some momentum and while they perused their menus, Smit and Sven rattled on about this and that adventure, all but ignoring the others who listened enthralled with the experiences they were hearing about.

After they had ordered, Sven told Priscilla, "You like the stories. You should hear some of Smit's. He's got more stories than the library."

Priscilla smiled.

Smit asked Sven, "You remember that Adak Charlie?"

"Who?" Orca and Priscilla asked almost in unison.

"King of the king crabbers," Sven told them.

"Oh, boy," Corky said, now resigned to a story.

Through their dinner, barely stopping to eat, Smit fell into his tale. Unlike Sven, his syntax didn't change and the story flowed from conversation about menu choices into:

CHAPTER 14

THE LEGEND OF ADAK CHARLIE

We come off them square riggers in a hurry onct they shet down the whaling. We's comin' down the Bering Sea out of the Arctic when we heard, and the Skip, well, he says, What you want to do? and I says, well, I heard they was doin' some high-priced fishing right there in the Aleutian Chain. But, I also heard they was the roughest kinda sailors and I'd jest as soon head back for home. So the Skip, right predictable like he was, he says he's dumpin' me ashore at Adak and to go pack my kit. He says how we done so poorly my share don't come to passage to San Francisco, so he's tyin' her up right there and I could just go about takin' care of myself.

So, pretty soon there we was in Adak way out there so close we might as wella been in Siberia, which we might as well a been in anyways by the look of things. Just a little island out there, somethin' you could trip over if you wasn't watching, it was so small. Anyway, I bends my head into the horizontal rain and goes alookin' for some kinda ride. Weren't too many of them square riggers left no more and I didn't know what I was goin' to do. I jest went along hunchin' into that wind and rain proceeding one step forward and two steps back with my slicker a flappin' and that's when I run into Adak Charlie.

A course, nobody runs into Adak Charlie, he more runs over you. What I did was commence to crawl over this little hill until I realizes it's the big bulb toe of a bigger rubber boot and I looks up and there

was Charlie, well, at least there was Charlie's knees. Well, that man
stood tall as a mainmast and just as straight and he blocked out the
sun, at least he woulda blocked out the sun if there'd a been one. The
sun showed up so little out there most folks didn't really believe there
was one except now and again somebody'd recall seein' it one time
or the other. Anyway, I crawls into Charlie's lee and looks up. Sure
enough up there on toppa all that rubber, they's a face. I yells up
Howdy and he yells down Howdy and I says is there any work for a
honest sailor around here and he yells down he thinks they need
crew on his boat and I yells up what kinda boat is it and he yells
down BERING SEA CRABBER and I yells up Good-by and he yells
down Ain't man enough, huh? and I yells up, Yeah, but I ain't stupid
enough and right there he commences to look a little disturbed and I
decides this ain't the kind of man to be callin' stupid so I decides I
better ship with 'im or the whole situation could get a whole lot worse
right there in the wind and the rain and the mud.

So, me and Charlie heads toward the wharf and I'm runnin' along
in his lee while he's amblin' along and we gets to the ship and he
steps over the gunwale and I climbs the ladder and no sooner's we
aboard than I hear a engine start up somewheres and it scares me
right out of my sail trim. See, I'm a sailin' man. I ain't never been on
no steamer before and all that machinery whirlin' and growlin' kin
get to a man used to the quiet creakin' in the rigging. I'm lookin'
around for masts and canvas and the boat's moving and against the
wind and I'm wonderin' how that could be when Charlie, he points
to the focs'l and says, "Stow your gear."

Well, I walks down the companionway and runs into the roughest lookin' bunch a thugs ever turned a windlass. There was more
eyepatches than a herd of spotted dogs and more scars than one
doctor coulda ever sewed up in a lifetime of stitchin' and they looks
at me and I looks at them and to myself I curses the Skip real hard for
leavin' me to this and then one a these thugs points to a empty bunk
and grins so hard the scar that runs from his port-side ear to clear
under his chin turns so bright red he looks like he's smilin' twice.

We cleared port and heads out to sea and Twice-smilin', that was his name I swear by St. Elmo's fire, he says sleep some, but I ain't sleepin' with that bunch of criminals in attendance. I did lay down but I keeps one eye cocked, but I musta dozed some 'cause I hear this big CLANK and it wakes me up and I says what's that, and Twice-Smilin' says that's the first buoy and to hit the deck and then there's this other big clank and he says that's the other buoy and we goes up on deck and Twice-smilin' starts to showin' me the lines. I says I thought you picked little rubber buoys outta the water where the pots was and he says that's the way most of 'em do it but that was too slow for the likes of Adak Charlie and what he does is run with these two big magnets and when they come up on one of his steel buoys, them buoys jest fly outta the water and clangs into them mag- nets. "Saves a lotta time findin' 'em in the dark, too," Twice-smilin' says.

Well, we's standing there in rubber suits from head to toe and I says what's we supposed to do and Twice-smilin' starts explainin'. He says on most boats a guy stands there by this here little wheel pulley sort of a contraption, they call it a power block. Well, I ain't used to this power stuff and I got to ask just how many sailors it takes to power this thing and Twice-smilin', he shows me this know-it-all grin you save for a child, only twice, and he says it's the engine does all that powerin'. Anyway, he says one guy usually stands there and coils the line from the crab pot as it comes up through that block and one guy he runs the engine controls. I seen a guy in my mind with a whip floggin' them sailors to power that block, that's the kinda con- trols we use on the square-riggers. So, when the pot comes up over the side a couple other guys wrassle it around and separate the crabs and put in new bait and toss her overboard again. I asks Twice- smilin' what I'm supposed to do and he says, "Wrasslin'."

"Ya see, Smit," he says, "On this boat she's done a bit differnt."

Right then Adak Charlie himself comes walkin' out on deck. He looks at them two steel buoys aswingin' from them magnets and he walks to the middle of the deck and he spreads his feet and he says,

Let 'er rip. Two guys start them two pulleys and that line come flyin'
up at about forty knots and Charlie he takes one in his big right hand
and he starts to makin' a coil in front of him and he takes the other
line in his big left hand and he starts to make a coil behind him and
we commences to hauling them first two crab pots.

Twice-smilin' he takes me over to one a them coils and he says
we should just be watchin' them in case something goes galley west,
but he says with Charlie coilin' nothin' ever goes galley west and we
just watch that line go into those coils and the coils go higher and
higher and Charlie's hands is just a blur and he's singin' away at the
top of his lungs about great storms at sea and all I'm doin' is gettin'
wet from all that spray flying offa that line as it comes over the block.
Of course, nothing goes wrong and then there's the loud KEE-BANG!
and then another one so loud, sounded like the king's navy was
holdin' down on us with all their cannons blazin'.

"Pots," says Twice-smilin'. "Here we go."

We goes to one side and here's this big square contraption with
webbing all round it and Charlie he reaches over the side and throws
her up on deck and we tips her and dumps the crabs out. Twice-smilin'
says how on most boats you have to separate out the female crabs and
the small ones but on this boat we never get none o' them and sure
enough, every one a them crabs is a legal-sized male king crab, big
ones and Twice-smilin' he explains why. "Watch old Charlie there," he
says, "he always touches the bait with somethin' Charlie ain't tellin'
what it is but whatever it might be works. Guys get to jokin'," he says,
"and everybody figures it's the essence of Kiska Katie he's puttin' on
that bait and that bait draws them big males just like Katie herself
draws them crabbers to her place when they's ashore."

So, anyway, Twice-smilin' says, "We put them in the big crab
tank there," and I says, "It's full of WATER," and I goes lookin' for a
life jacket and Twice-smilin' he smiles twice and says it's supposed to
be full of water, but he ain't convincin' me and I'm ready to abandon
the sinking ship and he says it's to keep the crabs alive and I says
who ever heard of pumping water INTO a boat and he says again

it's OK, the boat's built that way and I says, all right, but I ain't convinced and I'm watchin' the freeboard from then on.

We goes on to dump them crabs into that water in the boat and Charlie he puts the bait into the pots, touches the bait and tosses 'em over the side and off we goes a runnin' until we hears them clangs again when two more a them steel buoys come flyin' out of the water and she starts all over again. I says to Twice-smilin' how this ain't near so bad as I'd heard and he gets to smiling real hard twice and looks at me real knowledgeable-like and he says wait 'til you see the mile-squares, and I says WHAT and he just walks off smilin' twice.

Well, we run like that day and night right into winter. Lost track of the days we just hummed along respondin' to them clangs and tossin' them crabs and working on the gear when there's time and I learned this and that and along the way I learnt these crab guys look the way they do from flingin' them pots and lines and crabs around all the time and gettin' banged up all the time and afore long I got a pretty good scar a formin' on my hand from the day the boat rolled when I was choppin' up bait and I'm startin' to look a little bit like the rest of them thugs, myself.

There was this day we was runnin' between strings of gear and everybody's sittin' around on deck on piles of line and we can hear the radio goin' and they come up on the weather report and we all liked to listen, even if it didn't make no matter, 'cause that Charlie, he didn't stop for nuthin, even a typhoon.

So, this guy gets through the weather report and starts to givin' what he calls notices to mariners and he says in this real official voice: "Two Aleutian islands are reported off station and missing," and he gives some latitude and longitude numbers from their last known position, and then he says, "Mariners are urged to exercise extreme caution when transiting the area." Then he says anyone seein' them islands should report them and that sets the whole crew to laughing. I'm wondering what's so funny about two missing islands and how they could be missing and Twice-smilin', who's laughing twice now, between giggles he says, "I seen 'em. Fer sure, Smit," he says,

"You seen 'em too." And I says, "Where'd I see 'em?" Then he gets to laughin' all the more and when he catches his breath, he says, "They're right up there in the wheel house," and that gets everybody to listing with laughter even more. When they finally got 'er down to where they can breathe and talk at the same time, Boarder, now he's a story, lets off with that high-pitched giggle of his and commences to tell me the story.

Now I been told not to pay much mind to Boarder 'cause he's a little off his trim, like maybe he don't have both oars in the water, and nobody knows if he's called Boarder because he's borderline crazy or because of the two-by-four he's usin' for a starboard side leg.

Well, he goes into this real authoritative-soundin' voice he could muster when he wanted to and he says, "You see, Smit, we came in from a long hard trip one time. We unloaded the crab and then everybody crawled off into town for the party. Adak Charlie, there, he went up onto a hill after a while and laid down for a nap. He's so big when he spread out his arms sprawled out there, his hands sort of slopped off the island and his hands landed palm up in the water. And he fell asleep that way. Unfortunately that was the day the government people came to chart that part of the country. They went flying over and drew everything they saw and when the charts came out, there were these two new islands. Of course, they weren't new to the people doing the charting because they'd never seen any of it before. Those islands are a perfect picture of Charlie's hands. Well, when Charlie woke up and went back to the ship, he took those two islands with him and they've been off station ever since."

"They help him a lot with coilin'," Twice-smilin' laughed twice and that set them all off to laughing again and Boarder finishes the story by sayin' the government people been out there every so often lookin' for the two islands and every so often they ask on the radio if anybody's seen 'em. That give us a laugh fer most of the day and we needed it 'cause it was that night we run into the big ones.

I was layin' in my bunk tryin' to get some sleep listenin' to them crabs a scritchy-scrawlin' around in that tank which didn't help none. Had a lot of trouble sleepin' on that boat and I had a lotta dreams about spiders, too.

Anyway, all of a sudden there comes one a them clangs again only, this one, it's different. For one thing, there's only one of them and for another it was louder than any I'd heard before. Twice-smilin' comes awake, too, and looks at me, only real serious, like he's frownin' twice and he says, "Mile-squares."

Well, all us thugs, yup I was one of 'em by this time, didn't have no eye patch, but I was gettin' pretty cut up, all us thugs comes a-boilin' up on deck and there's Charlie standin' there real serious, too, rubber all the way to the sky.

Boarder told me once how a Mr. Helly and a Mr. Hanson come all the way from Scandinavia somewheres to build that suit of rain gear for Charlie. They brought 400 acres, that's right acres, of cloth. Then they built a scaffolding around Charlie and twenty-seven tailors with block and tackle climbed that scaffold and built that suit of rain gear for Adak Charlie. Took 'em a month. His boots is another story.

Well, we's standin' on deck with Charlie and one of them thugs puts the line through both blocks and they crank 'em up and pretty soon line's comin' on board only slower and the boat's listin' way over to one side and Charlie's straining to take some of the weight off them blocks and I know somethin' heavy's coming up but all any-body says is "mile-squares."

Even Boarder come clumping up on that two-by-four and giggles the way he does sometimes real shrill and he says, "Now you'll see, Smit, mile-squares," and he giggles again and clumps off and I know he ain't rowin' straight.

When everybody got finally settled in and alls you can hear is the creakin' and groanin' of that line comin' through two blocks and Adak Charlie strainin', too, and singin' a slower song about a storm at sea, and the coil just keeps gettin' higher and higher, Twice-smilin' comes over and he says, "Smit, yer about to see somethin'. Seems," he says, "out here somewheres there's this king crab. At least we think there's just one and he's a big old crab. We seen a leg or a claw now and again where he's holdin' onto a pot tryin' to git at that essence of Kiska Katie and we had to wrassle a pot away from him more'n once. So, Charlie, he decides he's goin' to catch that crab and he went and made him up some pots just for that and he's going to be catching it one a these days. See, a crab that big couldn't get into one of our regular pots, so Charlie, he made up some pots and they're a mile square. I don't have to tell you, Smit, they're big and they're heavy and even Charlie there, he needs some help pushin' them around and we got a string of 'em out here and one a these days that big old crab's gonna be in one of 'em and that ought to be really somethin'."

Well, about this time the coil got up over even Charlie's head and he climbs up into the crow's nest still singing that song about that storm at sea and he's still coilin', and now and then a big grin comes 'cross his face when he looks over the side fer that pot and what might be in it.

The boat kept a-leanin' until the pot finally slams the boat's bottom and Charlie peers down from the crow's nest but he don't care for what he sees and we rigs all the winches and lines we can find and haul her up and it's loaded with crabs but there ain't none like Twice-smilin' was talkin' about. We can't put a pot that big on board so a couple of us thugs crawls down in it and starts to pitchin' them crabs up on deck.

That big old crab, he wasn't in that one and he ain't in the next one either, but he'd been around, 'cause the next one's got the web all tore out and the bait's all gone and all the rest of 'em on that string's just like it, tore to shreds and the bait gone like somethin' real big goin' real crazy after it and we're spendin' more time repairin' and sewin' pots than we're fishin'. In time we gets through them mile-squares and come back to the regular gear again and the hold's gettin' real full, which is fine with me cause there ain't so much room for water comin' aboard anymore. Never could get used to pumpin' water into a boat.

We finally got to the point where there wasn't no more room for crabs or water in that hold and I asks Twice-smilin' what happens now and he smiles twice and nods toward Charlie who's takin' off his boots. 'Twas then I noticed the little pipes comin' from the heel and toe and a couple of thugs hooks up some hoses to them pipes and all of a sudden we got two new crab tanks. We kept agoin' til we filled them boots, too, and then we turned 'er for Adak.

Charlie says it'll be a quick turnaround 'cause he wants to git back to them mile-squares and he has an idea.

I'll tell you it was a quick turnaround, all right. We got in late evenin' and we just worked right through unloadin' and we's pullin' out before first light. Charlie, he's gone most of the time, come back on the boat real sneaky, nobody really seen him come back, but there he was and he sets a course for them mile-squares out there in the big ocean. He never come outta the house, just serious runnin', but every so often we'd be hearing these high-pitched tones and we's all wondering just what's goin' on and where Charlie was when he was off the boat while we was unloadin' and what he mighta brought aboard.

Boarder, he giggles now and again and says he knows, but nobody'd listen to him anyway and Twice-smilin' says he thinks he knows but he ain't guessin' out loud and all we did was steam toward them pots.

We come to the first one and the buoy hit the magnet and Charlie commenced to coilin' with his big jaw set and the hairs in his beard stickin' out straight and singing a new song about a storm at sea. "Looks like Adak Charlie means business this time," Twice-smilin' says.

Charlie just keeps coilin' and again when the coil gets too high he goes up to the crow's nest and keeps on coilin' and when the pot's almost to the surface, he stops his song and lets out a bellow and the cabin door opens.

We's all lookin' to the door and out comes this woman and she's almost as big as Charlie himself and she's all gussied up with paint and perfume and when the wind spreads that aroma around it overpowers the smell of the herring bait; all them thugs come to a stop with their mouths open like a bunch of them Florida groupers, froze right there.

Twice-smilin' was standin' right next to me. "Kiska Katie," he says and that's all and she sashays over to the rail lookin' to that pot comin' up and it comes to the surface with them little crabs in it but not this big one Charlie's lookin' for. Well, we finally collected ourselves enough to get them crabs out and Charlie's gettin' ready to dump the pot over again but this time Katie herself puts the bait into the pot and blows a little kiss at it and Charlie sends 'er down, the pot that is, not Katie, and we heads for the next one.

It was on the next one that it all happened. Charlie coiled that pot up and Katie she watched and she put the new bait in it and, well, just as she was leanin' over to blow that kiss, this leg and then the claw come up over the far side of that pot and this giant crab come a clicking and raging out of the water after Katie. She screams and then she falls right into that pot and the crab come over the top a crackin' and a snappin' and all that weight on it was too much and she starts headin' for the bottom. About this time, Charlie sees what's goin' on and he's got to do somethin' and he dives right outta the crow's nest and right into that pot after the crab who was after Kiska Katie and him and the crab and Katie and the pot goes down and started pullin' the boat right along with them. Me and Boarder and Twice-smilin' jumps to it and lets the line fly so's the boat don't go down, too, and we looks over the side and all we see is water a boilin' and a bubblin' and a foamin' and every once in a while we see a big crab leg come up and go smashing down, or a big fist of Charlie's or a claw or somethin' and then more foamin' and boilin'. Then Katie come floatin' to the surface spitting and sputtering and sayin' a few unladylike words and we tosses her a line. But, instead of comin' to the boat, she takes that line and dives back down into the foam with it and the boilin' gets all the worse and then she come up again and swims for the boat. 'Bout this time we wasn't so sure we wanted her on board. With her in the water, the crab coulda cared less about the boat, but with her on deck he might be comin' after us, too. We brung her aboard anyway. Even thugs can't be completely fergettin' their upbringing. After all, she was a lady, at least fer them parts. So she joins us at the rail and says she got a line on the critter somewheres and now that she's outta the water and the current's carrying the essence away, it looks like the fight's calming down. Either the crab's lost interest or he's got the best of Charlie which nobody really believes, or Charlie got the best of the crab which everybody wants to believe and sure enough here comes Charlie to the surface and he's spittin' and cussin' almost as bad as

Katie, but the foamin's stopped and he crawls aboard, well, he's too big to just crawl aboard; we had to winch him up and then we gets him on deck and takes a good look. Well, Twice-smilin' takes to twice laughing and Boarder starts to giggling and everybody's laughing but me and Charlie and then he starts up. To look at him, he's got more pinholes in them rain clothes than a man can count. They were from all them spines on that crab and when Adak Charlie stands up every one of them holes starts spoutin' water so's he looks like he ought to be a statue in a fountain in a park somewheres. Here and there you could see where that crab got in a good slash at him, too. Charlie looks down at himself and allows how he's going to have to send for that Mr. Helly and Mr. Hanson again.

Anyway, they's all havin' a good laugh but me. I'm lookin' at what a crab can do to a man and I'm not so sure about this crabbin' anyway and I'm deciding right then I'm gettin' off this boat fer good next time she comes anywhere near land. About then, when I was decidin' that, the laughing kind of ebbs and they starts wonderin' about this here crab. Charlie says it's inside the pot and we got that line on it that Katie got a wrap with so he starts to pullin' the pot again and us thugs coiled on the Katie line. I really shouldn't say "we" cause I got as far away from that side of the boat as I could case that crab got a second wind or somethin' when he sees Katie and comes up snarlin'.

It took quite a strain on all the deck gear but they finally come up with the crab and the pot and the crab was sure enough subdued for good and they had to winch it on board, too, just like Charlie, and all in all it looks to be in a whole lot worse shape than Charlie did. There was no way we could figure the size of that crab. He took up the whole back deck, but a lot of him was still hangin' over the sides. Them legs was as big as spars on the clippers and the shell, well, they coulda held a concert in there. We tried to weigh the thing but he was so unconventional shaped, we couldn't ever get the lines on him right with the scale to haul it off the deck whole. We finally took to chopping up the legs in sections and tryin' to weigh them one at a time. We come up over a ton and then the scale broke, sproinged right over the side and we give 'er up. Charlie, he says save the shell and he gits this faraway look in his eyes and says how someday when he gets shut o' this business he just might haul her someplace sunny, settle down and make a swimmin' pool out of it. Katie, she hears this and looks at Charlie real misty like.

Then we, well, Charlie and all them thugs, agrees the one crab'll make one heck of a payday and they turns the boat for Adak.

I don't mind tellin' you that was the end of my career in the king crab fishery. When we got 'er back to Adak I jumped ship, I come off that boat runnin', lookin' for anything I could find to get outta there. I think I woulda rowed for Frisco if I coulda found a boat. While I was lookin' and moving down the road leanin' into that wind again, there he was, I run right into the Skip. He almost passed me up; he didn't recognize me at first.

"Smit," he hollers out when he finally figgers out just who the heck I am. "What happened to you?"

"I been crabbin', you Jack Tar," I says real mean like.

"You look like you been cut up by half the rum-runners in Shang-hai," he says. "You look criminal."

"Crabbin' did it to me," I says, "and I owe you."

"Gotta ship," the Skip says. I don't think he even knew I was threatening him. "A tramp, sailing south."

"Square-rigger?" I asks, forgettin' the threat for a minute myself.

"Yup."

"Got any fishin' gear aboard?" I asks.

"Not so much as a hook," he says.

"Good!" I says.

Then he gets this dirty smile of his and he says, "Git some if you want."

'Bout then I was ready to let him have it and he seen it comin' and he took a step back. He musta realized I was serious now, 'cause I never seen the Skip take a step back in his life. But I let him go. One punch wasn't going to make up fer what he did to me and right there I started to schemin' what was goin' to happen to the Skip for a payback.

So, like always, I shipped with him and we set our sails for the South Seas and that was that for my crabbin' days and I was pretty glad for it.

Still, you know, there's days at sea when a man's mind wanders and he gets to recalling this and that and there's even a day now and again in the doldrums and I'll get to thinkin' about that crew of thugs and Twice-smilin' and Boarder and who could ever forgit that Kiska Katie. But, mostly I recall that big man, that Adak Charlie, standin' there just as tall as a mainmast and just as straight and coilin' them lines clear to the sky with both hands and most of all singin' them songs about them storms at sea. Those times I gets to thinkin' real fondly about them poor souls in the Bering Sea and the time I spent there. Don't last long, though. I always come back to my senses.

CHAPTER 15

SMIT TELLS A RACY TALE

S OMEHOW, WITHOUT APPEARING TO MISS A BEAT
in his story, Smit had cleaned his plate by the time he finished. His audience had been silent throughout, eating quietly
and absorbing the tale from the Aleutians.

"They don't make 'em like that no more," Sven said.

"Sure don't," Corky agreed.

Priscilla and Orca remained quiet but a glance between them
questioned the truth of Smit's story.

"If I'm going to have to go with thugs, I'm not sure I want to
come out for crab season," she said.

That didn't stop Smit. "How 'bout some deee-sert?" he asked,
"Sweets for the sweet?" He winked at Priscilla. She ignored it and
signaled to the waiter.

When they had ordered, Sven asked Smit, "Is there anything
we can do for you? You look mighty out of place in that room."

"It sure ain't like the old days," Smit said. "Food's better though.
Now that you be askin'," he turned to Corky. "There is somethin'.
Might sound kinda funny."

"What is it?"

Smit hesitated. "Jest to humor a old man. I'd sure like to sleep
on a boat one more time. I get to feelin' real uncomfortable when
the world ain't movin' under me."

Sven looked at Corky.

Corky said, "We could put you up on the *Salmania* a night or two. Be in the harbor, but it's a boat."

"You'd sure make a old man happy. Square rigger?"

Corky laughed, thinking about all the modern fishing gear on his boat.

"Not quite," Sven said.

"Tell you what," Corky said. "Let's finish here and go down to the boat. I can make a pot of coffee and we can talk a little. I'll make you up a bunk. Come get you in the morning."

"Like I died and gone to heaven," Smit said.

They ate their desserts, then drove to the harbor and walked to the *Salmania*.

Corky led them onto the boat and into the cabin. He turned on lights, invited them to sit at the galley table while he started a pot of coffee. Orca walked forward while Smit ran his hands over the wood and fabric unfamiliar to him in his memories of the sailing ships.

"You must have had quite a life," Priscilla said. "Those sailing ships are so romantic."

"You see one a them ships under full sail, it'll take your breath," Smit said. "Course we never got to see that. We's always humpin' to keep 'em goin' lookin' out from the inside when you wasn't heavin' on a line or somethin'. Sometimes we'd pass by somebody, though, and then you see how pretty they are. We was pretty much the last of a breed, though. Ain't no square-rigger sailors around no more. This kid, Sven here, mighta been the last one go to sea on one, as a boy, you know."

"And the ports you must have visited," Priscilla asked, "Where did you go?"

"Seven seas, ma'am, seven seas. Sailed just about everywhere they was to sail, every ocean. Carried just about everything they sent in ships those days."

"They must have been long trips on a sailboat," she said.

"Ships, ma'am, ships and, oh, they was. We's at sea months to a time," Smit said. "Sometimes be gone a year or more. Course gone don't mean much 'cause the way we did it we's always home. Home was the ship. Didn't really have no other home to be gone from. Gone was like that time with Charlie."

"Yes," Priscilla said, "that time with Adak Charlie." She looked around for Orca, but the boy had disappeared.

"Home or not, we's always glad to make a landfall. See some hill come up over the horizon. Always glad to git offn the ship for a while, see what them towns was like. Never could stay long, though. Seems like somethin' always happened. We learned we was best off out to sea. I 'member the time . . . "

Corky put mugs of coffee on the table. He poured a cup of bull coffee, then looked for Orca. He went forward and then whispered back to the people in the galley. "Hey, take a look at this."

Sven and Priscilla peered into the forepeak to see Orca sound asleep on his bunk.

"Too long a day for the kid, I guess," Sven said.

"Jest as well," Smit said, "This story might not be the best for the ears of a youngster. Might even give you a start, honey," he said to Priscilla.

Priscilla straightened her back. She looked to Sven and Corky then back at Smit, "I'll be just fine, Mr. Smith, if you don't mind."

"All right then," Smit said:

THE TEACHER AND THE OLD SALT

We was berthed at one of them tight little towns in the Southeast, the kind that's all buildings crowded together with very little street to walk in, barely room for a square rigger sailor to swing his shoulders when he walks. Me and the Skip was walkin' through town, one behind the other, 'cause there wasn't room for two of us abeam each other. It'd been a long voyage, but we'd made it, now we'd shaped the ship. We was the last two off and jest feelin' good about walking about a town. We sort of skipped the waterfront places we usually went, and was just lookin' over the town. Course we had our eyes out for what sailors have their eyes out for. We was lookin' at land stuff and talkin' and wandering here and there.

It was a long passage this time and of course we was both a little lonely. In them towns they was used to us sailors, and once you get one street past the wharf, you wasn't' exactly welcomed with open arms. We knew all this, but we kept awalkin' and alookin' anyways. We'd jest about seen what there was to see without ever seein' what we wanted to see, and we's about to head back to the water when this woman come a bouncin' and a grinnin' down one a them hilly little side streets. She's just walkin' along, her skirts was a swingin' as she walked, and she smiles and says hello to everyone she come acrost, even us. I tipped my tam and says "Mornin'" but Skip, he didn't say nothin'. He just sorta watches a little awestruck as she swishes by us, smiling and sayin' good mornin' to the next folks down the street. The Skip, he turns and watches her go and makes a few steps there, tryin' to follow. I caught his drift, if you know what I mean, and I caught his arm, too, and I says, "Avast there, mate." He jest looked at me and I seen it in his eyes, and I says, "Oh, no, not her," and he jest looks at me like he sometimes looked at them beautiful sunsets out there on the big ocean and I says, "Loosen your mainsheets, man, she ain't one for the likes of us." But he'd already set his tack and shakes me off like I was so much water from a ragin' nor'easter and commences to walk off in that direction. I tries onct more to change his course toward a port where we was more likely welcome, but by this time he's got his sails set, and he's runnin' before the wind and they ain't goin' to be no heavin' to.

About then, when I seen the set of his jib, I give up. Might just as well try and stop one of them North Atlantic gales as turn the Skip to. I heads back to find the rest a the boys. I found 'em an' we did our usual carousing in places more suited to us. Tore up the waterfront a bit, we did, and 'fore the night was out I had to bail a couple of them outta the local brig, and so on.

Never did see the Skip 'til he's comin' outta his cabin the next afternoon when the rest of us is wanderin' the deck in the after-night haze of a bright sunny day. Now, we're talkin' here about one of the roughest old salts ever stood a watch. I seen him clean out a whole bar full of pirates in Singapore and I seen him carouse and brawl his way around the world. This is one tough Jack Tar, and here he comes outta his cabin dressed, well, clean, yeah, clean and well, it fits, pretty. That's what he looked, pretty. He's wearin' white pants and a clean shirt and one of them landlubberin' jackets, the kind shows a tie and darned if he ain't wearin' one a them, too. I never would of guessed he even packed one around with him. His hair is trimmed and combed and his beard is nearly gone he worked it over so severe and his hands is clean. They's so clean I'd be keelhauled if it don't look like he took some a the calluses off with a file or somethin'. He goes by and says, "Howdy," like nothin's different and then the wind shifts and the smell comes and if he don't smell like one of them fine Europeen women, I'm the squirreliest little ensign ever climbed a ratline.

"Goin' to tea," he says. Tea. That old salt never drank nothin' weaker than Barbados rum in his life and he looks so proper and now he's goin' to tea. Tea, and he's dressed like good king George or somethin' and I look at him and I says, "You caught up with 'er, huh?" And he winks and he says something' about he ain't lost his head, he's jest chasin' up a differnt tree after the same old fruit. And this bothers me 'cause I don't care for it much, takin' a bawdy old sailor's needs up to the nice folks of a town and I tells him so. He ain't buyin' none of it. Matter of fact he's barely listenin' atall. And there I am, my ownself, defendin' this woman's virtue who I don't even know, and against a friend and shipmate and that bothers me all the more. But I know that pretty slip of a innocent woman ain't ready for nothin' like the Skip and what he has in that mind of his. Nope. "Leave her alone," I says, "Stick with your own. There's plenty of 'em and they know the score. All you're gonna do is get yourself in trouble up there in that town and most likely cause it." He ain't havin' none of it. All he does is winks and then kinda rolls 'crost the deck and down the gangplank on them old bow legs of his and saunters up into the town headin' for tea.

Mind you, I wanted to follow and do somethin' to stop this. It could only end in tragedy fer somebody, but we was supposed to be settin' sail with the next mornin's tide and there was work to be done, and with the Skip gone, it was up to me to get it done. So, I went at it and pretty much forgot all about it until I realized it's gettin' on to eight bells and I ain't seen no Skip yet and I think, "Oh, no, I told him." That's when I went lookin' for him. Tried a couple of the pubs along the wharf, figured by then she'd trimmed his sails and he's fillin' up his empty with rum, but I found big nothin'. I checked the brig, by this time I figure he really done somethin' and she's called for help and they drug him off, but he ain't there neither. In the course of all this lookin', it come out a little from this person and that person who this woman probably is, and I finds out she lives in a little house up that street we see her comin' down that day. So, I goes there and sure enough, there's a light on and I steals up to the window for a peek and there's the Skip and there's the woman and they's pretty close, but not compromised far as I could see. But, I see this look on the Skip's face and I know this look. I seen it everytime he got past "Hello" with women in every port from St. Charles to Punta Arenas. And I thinks again, "Oh, no," and then they comes together in this kiss and I could see this wolf look on the Skip like "This lamb's about to go over." I steps back from the window, not wantin' to watch no more and leans against this building and waits.

I figure when she starts to screamin', I'm gonna break in there and get him away from her, and get him outta there afore the gendarmes come runnin' and maybe I can save both their hides. Well, in less time'n it takes a gale to blow up full, there was screams all right, if you wanted to call 'em that. But, they wasn't all that terror filled and they for sure wasn't for no help. And get this, she ain't the one screamin'. And it goes on and I'm hearin' all this and I'm wonderin' exactly how long this can go on, but it keeps goin' on and I'll be stripped with a cat-o-nine-tails if I didn't just fall asleep right there 'twixt the houses and 'twixt the screams while they was still makin' them noises and I remember thinkin' jest 'fore I fell off he was gonna kill 'er, mind you I knowed him, but by them sounds I couldn't really tell who was killin' who and like I said, I fell asleep right there in that alleyway.

Next I know I got this shaft of light in my face, the sun comin' up and comin' down this crack 'tween the houses jest hit me right. I wakes up and it takes a while 'til I realize where I'm berthed and then I comes stark awake like somethin' jest bumped the hull and then I look at the house and the noises has stopped and there's a light on and movement inside. I just stuck where I was and watched. Soon enough this woman come abouncin' out the door and down the steps just like we seen her the first time, and she says "Good mornin'" to a neighbor and she smiles, and he says, "Mornin' Ma'am," and what's she goin' to do with the school kids today, and she laughs and says somethin' I didn't hear and then she heads on down the street with this little dance in her step just like we seen her before. Now, I at least heard what went on in there that night, and here she comes a bouncin' along like the wind ain't even changed direction. I watched the door . . . and I watched the door . . . and I watched the door. I was just about to match the sail to the yardarm—wondered if maybe she killed him and stuffed him someplace—and I was about to go in there and then the door swings open. And there stood the Skip.

Well, you couldn't say he was exactly standin' there. Leanin' might even be a little too strong. 'Bout all you could say was he was more longitudinal than latitudinal and he looked to me with the kinda look in his eye that says, "I been shipwrecked and I been floatin' in this life raft for seventy-two days and I run outta food and water after twenty days and I'm sure glad to see you, 'cause I really need to be rescued." He had the rescue look in his eyes. Now, this ain't the roarin', brawlin' sea captain left the ship day before and come up to this place. I'm lookin' at a man thrashin' in deep water with all his seacocks open. He takes a step towards me and then another. No swagger in that step, now. He don't even look bowlegged, no sirree, more like legs of hardtack been soaked in water. It come over me slow, but I'm beginnin' to see the humor in all this. He says to me, real weak, "We oughta get back to the ship." I took a long look at him and then I asks how we gonna do that when he ain't got no wind in his sails, and he looks at me like he wants to look at me like he'd like to kill me, only he can't even muster up the look, and that was the point of too much. I took to laughin' and I got to laughin' so hard I had to sit down, and he's lookin' at me tryin' to be mad and all he can get up is that lifeboat look again, and that makes me laugh all the harder and pretty soon we're both sittin' there in the gutter both of us lost in our own little weaknesses and neither one of us can move.

Then I sensed the killer. See, I ain't never been one to luff a sail and I looks at him and I says, "I warned you. I told you leave her alone. Stick with your own kind. I told you all you'd get was trouble if you started mixin' it up with the nice folks of a town."

Now he come outta that lifeboat look and I could see a little fire buildin' in his eye so I figgered enough was enough. I helped him back to the ship, tough to do in them tight little streets, and I dumped him into his berth. That was the last we saw of him for a while. I had to take her outta the harbor and it wasn't 'til about the eighth watch out to sea he finally come up on deck. And then he made it the roughest trip ever on that ocean. He just give it to us for the whole voyage, drivin' everybody and the ship hard. It was enough to make me look for another berth once we hit the next port.

Over the years I sailed on different ships with different captains, I even run with the Skip again. I run with him and at times I'd run into him in some port or other and he's still the same old brawler. But I never again seen him venture off them waterfronts. Never seen him in a tie again. Never did muster up the courage to remind him why, either.

Smit finished his story and took a long sip from the coffee mug. None of the men at the table looked directly at Priscilla as they sat in the silent cabin.

"You certainly tell a colorful story," she said. She let them sit in their embarrassed silence for a moment longer and then she laughed. "You're really something," she said at last, "you're these rough, tough fishermen and all of a sudden this little woman from town has you all intimidated. Good for that schoolteacher. You're so full of yourselves you don't think anybody else can do anything." Then she let them off the hook. She asked for another cup of coffee and allowed the conversation to turn to other subjects.

"She was a fine seemin' woman," Smit said. "Sailed a lot of lonely seas and thought about her. I always thought, maybe we got back to that port, I might go look her up myself, you know. Take a bunch of flowers. That Skip, he even turned down a couple of cargoes to keep from goin' back there again."

"Maybe we better get back to my place," Corky said. "Been a long day. I'll make you up a bunk," he said to Smit.

Corky and Sven helped Smit while Priscilla sat in the galley refusing to clear the coffee cups, enjoying her moment of superiority.

When they had Smit settled, they roused Orca to grogginess and guided him to the truck. They said their good-nights to Priscilla, who took the white fisherman's cap from Orca's head, saying, "I've got an idea for this." At Corky's house they dumped Orca onto the couch and went to bed.

CHAPTER 16

GAINFUL EMPLOYMENT

THE NOISES OF TOWN DIDN'T BOTHER ORCA in his sleep that night, but in the morning he had disappeared again and Corky found him outside sitting on the pile of line in the yard.

"Not so much noise today," Orca said.

"Sunday. Not so many people moving around."

"It's still there, though."

"Yup, I guess it is. You had quite a day yesterday."

"I don't remember coming home."

"I believe that," Corky said. "We had to all but carry you. You get everything done yesterday?"

"Most of it," Orca said. "There was one thing. Sven was looking at this rifle at the Outfitters. I'd sure like to get it for him."

"Expensive?" Corky asked.

"More than we had, I think," Orca said. "That one he has at the cabin is just about shot. I know he wants that rifle."

"Hey, I bought some bull coffee yesterday. You want some?" Corky went inside the house and returned with two cups.

"I was thinking," he said, "There might be a way to make a little money. Maybe enough to buy that rifle."

"How?" Orca asked.

"I was over to the fish plant yesterday. The foreman there, McKenzie, said he's hurtin' for help. They got that last rush of fish after all the kids left and went back to school and he's still got to put it up. Maybe you could work a day or two over there cuttin' fish and pick up enough money to get that rifle."

"Do you think I could?" Orca's face brightened visibly.

"Don't see why not," Corky said.

"I'll have to ask Sven. He might not want to hang around town."

"He's got to hang around for that hearing anyway. He's usually only good for a day or two 'fore he wants to get back, but this time he's got to stay," Corky said. "Let me work on him a little. He might be happy just sittin' around and tradin' lies with Smit. You think he'd mind you workin' in a plant?"

"We can convince him. Don't tell him about the rifle, okay?" Orca asked.

"Not a chance," Corky agreed.

Sven surprised them when he agreed right away to Orca working at the processing plant. "Be good for him to work with other people," he said. "He'll get to know the buyers, too. Looks like he might be dealin' with them for a long time. Sure, let him go work a couple of days. We can get the boat loaded and pick up on some other stuff we never seem to have time to do. Maybe we can get this court thing settled with Priscilla, too."

After Orca had devoured another strawberry waffle at the restaurant, Sven walked down the dock to find Smit and Corky drove the boy around the harbor to the Skookum Alaska Fish Co. There they located McKenzie and offered Orca's services. "He can go to work right now," the foreman said, "Say, he ain't too young, is he?"

"He'll put in a man's day, I guarantee you," Corky said. "You've never seen anything like this boy around a fish."

"Good. We sure need the help. We'll put him sliming," McKenzie said. "Come on with me." They followed him into the plant. If the city noises had bothered Orca before, now he walked into a wall of it, pounding him at tympanic industrial levels. Machinery loud enough to hurt his ears forced them to shout. Stretching away from the garage-type doors, trays of stainless steel led in rows deep into the building. Workers dressed in rain gear stood next to the lines, here cutting the heads off fish, there removing the entrails. McKenzie led them to an area where several workers scraped slime off the fish bodies before they went on to cooking or freezing.

"That's what you'll be doing," he shouted to Orca. "I'll get you some rain gear, a knife." He winked at Corky.

After McKenzie had dressed him for the slime line, Orca stepped in and began cleaning fish as they came by, washed along by a steady stream of water. Corky watched him for a while, then left to find Sven and Smit.

Orca's hands flew over the fish, the motion turning automatic within minutes so he found he could work and look around at the rest of the plant at the same time. He noticed his fellow workers methodically performing their chores, then moving the fish along to the next station. He watched the machines that took the heads off and cleaned the insides. To his right, some of the fish went onto carts that a worker pushed into a freezer when they were full. Behind that, rows of cans moved along a conveyor to be filled with salmon, topped, sealed and cooked.

He paid little attention to the fish in front of him, his experienced hands finding and positioning the fish for him to scrape them. When he'd absorbed what he could see of the plant his thoughts drifted to his goal. He could see Sven holding the new rifle, cruising the beaches of Naked Island hunting for the venison they loved.

Then he heard someone shout "Hey, stop the line." As if responding to a symphony conductor's baton, all the noise around him ceased. Workers looked up from the trays. McKenzie came running. "What's going on? Why's the line stopping?"

"It's him."

Orca recognized the voice. Standing next to a fish tote where the slimed salmon fell off the conveyor stood Georgie Fagshark.

"He's messin' up the line," Fagshark told McKenzie. "Look at this." He dug into the tote and pulled out a fillet. McKenzie took it from him and held it up.

"Who's doing this?" McKenzie shouted, waving the fillet.

Orca looked down at the salmon in front of him and blanched. He had stopped with his knife halfway down the backbone of a fish, slicing the meat off the bone.

He turned to find McKenzie standing right at his shoulder, wishing he could hide the fish in front of him.

"You?" McKenzie asked.

"I, I wasn't thinking," Orca stammered, feeling the eyes of everyone in the plant burning into him. "It was just so automatic."

McKenzie examined the fillet closely. Fagshark stood at the end of the line smirking. "This is good," McKenzie said. "Better than the machines do. No bones. Most of the meat. No cuts." He walked back to the fish tote at the end of the line where he found almost a third of the fish in the bin had been filleted. "Must be fast, too," he said to Fagshark. Fagshark had started to look deflated.

McKenzie returned to Orca who stood in embarrassed silence.

"You did this, huh?"

Orca acknowledged that he was the culprit.

"You come on with me," McKenzie said. "Start the line back up," he shouted to Fagshark.

They walked away from the increasing whine of the machinery, outside to the dock.

"I'm sorry," Orca said. "I didn't realize I was doing it. I'll do better, I promise." He felt Sven's rifle slipping overboard.

"Don't apologize," McKenzie said. "That wasn't the place, but we can use a talent like that." He explained to Orca how most of the fish going through the plant went either into cans or to freezing in the round. Neither of those demanded the extra cutting required for fillets. "We just do a few fillets with the highest grade fish for restaurants and the like," he said. "We got a machine to do that, but it leaves a lot of meat on the bone. We lose a lot. Doing it by hand's better but it's slow. What I want to do is, I'll set you up a line and they'll high grade fish to you. Cut the fillets the way you been. We'll do a test. We'll run the machine, too. See how you do. That sound all right?"

Orca saw the rifle rising back into Sven's hands. "You mean it's all right? I'm not in trouble?"

"Trouble?" McKenzie said, "You just got a raise and a promotion and you only been here a couple hours." He led the smiling Orca to another line of stainless steel. He pointed to a row of sharpened fillet knives and told him to go to work. Where the fish came from the dock into the plant, workers sorting them began sending the highest quality fish sliding toward Orca where his deft fingers began slicing the fillets from the bones.

McKenzie watched him for a few minutes, then told another worker to set up the fillet machine. Because the machine stood behind him, Orca couldn't see or hear them preparing it. He did hear the added noise when they started the motor and began running fish through it. The operators adjusted settings until the machine hummed smoothly and began spitting out fillets of salmon.

Without telling Orca what he was doing, McKenzie ordered the others to empty the collection bins at the ends of the two lines and then he stood back to watch, checking the time. Orca and the machine started even against McKenzie's watch.

Not realizing he had entered a contest, Orca let his mind wander and his hands work automatically. He caught the fish sliding by, sliced the fillets and passed them along while he thought about his summer's adventures and the winter to come, particularly seeing Sven hunting with his new rifle.

Behind him one person fed fish into the fillet machine, another watched the machine, occasionally adjusting the controls, while a third separated the waste and the fillets and sent them sliding along their respective lines.

At the beginnings of the lines, a worker weighed the fish before he sent them along. At the ends of the lines the piles of fillets grew.

McKenzie told the operator to increase the speed of the machine. Fish moved through faster, but judging by the pile in the tote, Orca stayed ahead of his opponent. They increased the speed again, but still the machine couldn't keep up with the boy.

At the end of an hour, McKenzie shouted "All right!" The machine's whine decreased and Orca turned to see what the shout had been about. That was when he realized the fillet machine had been running. "You can stop now," McKenzie told him.

"Let's see how you did." Fagshark had walked over to see the results. First they weighed the fillets. Orca's product weighed 60 pounds more than the machine's. "There's the key," McKenzie said. "Let's see how much went in against how much came out." McKenzie's accountant took the numbers from the man who'd weighed the fish going in and figured the percentage of usable meat to waste. By this time, the plant's owner Boss Gregg, who'd heard about the contest and the remarkable boy in his plant, stood behind McKenzie watching in silence, chewing on his cigar.

When the accountant looked up he spoke in amazement. "That boy got more than 10 percent less waste than the machine."

Boss Gregg was digging into the bins. He held up a fillet from each. "Cuts are neater, too," he said. He looked disgustedly at the machine that had cost him more than a month's profit and walked away in a cloud of smoke. On his way, he kicked the machine's electrical plug out of the wall socket.

McKenzie clapped Orca on the back. "You got a job," he said, "we'll keep this line goin' for you. I'll give you a helper, keep your knives sharp, feed you fish. You're going to be famous. You beat the machine." He looked around, choosing Orca's assistant. His gaze fell to Fagshark, considered him for a moment, then decided the better of it and appointed another.

He sent Orca back to work, the boy happy to be at least partly removed from the noise of the machinery. His helper kept the fish flowing and arranged the fillets for freezing, at times stopping to sharpen a knife the boy discarded. Occasionally one of the other workers walked over to watch, many of them marveling at Orca's skills. McKenzie checked on him once in a while, but left him alone for the most part. With a whole plant to manage he didn't have a lot of time to spend on any one job.

Orca worked through the day until the plant had exhausted the incoming supply of fish. As one after another the processing lines wound down, McKenzie came over. He'd been keeping track of Orca's production. "Sure wish I had you all season," he said. "Corky wasn't kidding. You're the boy lives out there with Sven Kaartoonsen, aren't you?"

Orca admitted that he was. Suddenly he felt tired. He hadn't noticed through his shift, but now his hands and forearms ached and his muscles wanted to relax.

"We're pretty much to the end of it," McKenzie said. "Got only a couple more tenders comin' in. That might be a day, maybe two days' work. Some of these are going to be good late-run reds, the kind we want to fillet, so we can use you. Can you stay a couple of days?"

Orca said he thought so.

"Well, good," McKenzie said, "Corky's on his way to pick you up. See you tomorrow." He walked away. Orca walked to a sink and washed his hands, then went outside to wait.

In the truck riding back with Corky and Sven, the two men were incredulous. "They started a line just for you?" Corky demanded.

Orca nodded agreement.

"You beat a cutting machine?" Sven asked.

Again Orca nodded confirmation. The feats didn't seem all that extraordinary to him since he had nothing for comparison.

"I seen him cut fish," Sven said, "but I never thought he was that good."

"I never heard McKenzie talk about anybody in that plant," Corky said, "let alone praise somebody the way he bragged on you today. You'd think he fell in love or something."

Sven said, "I guess you'll go back tomorrow, then."

"He said there might be two more days is all," Orca said.

"That's when that hearing's supposed to be," Sven said. "I talked with Priscilla today. She sent you this." He handed Orca his white fisherman's cap. Near the brim she had embroidered the word "Orca" with red thread. At Corky's they ate dinner, then moved to his living room. Before Orca could finish a sentence, the exhaustion overtook him and he fell asleep. The trucks could have driven through the living room that night and he wouldn't have heard them.

The next he knew Corky was shaking him awake. "Wake up, bud, you're burning daylight. You're a working man now, got to keep the pace."

Orca rubbed his eyes, "Other people's time," he said. He stretched his arms and wiggled his fingers. "I feel stiff," he said.

"Comes with workin' a regular job," Corky said. He fed Orca a quick breakfast along with a cup of bull coffee and drove him to the plant.

"Looks like you're going to be busy," he said as they approached the building. "They're unloading that big tender there already."

Orca walked through the bustle on the dock where workers lifted fish from the tender's hold, weighed and separated them and moved totes into the plant for processing. He walked to his own processing line where his helper already had organized and begun stacking fish for cutting. Orca took a deep breath, picked up a knife, pulled a fresh fish to him and went to work. That day he saw very little of McKenzie. The foreman had become involved in a problem elsewhere in the plant:

CHAPTER 17

THE SKOOKUM ALASKA FISH CO.
AND MATERNITY WARD

"**T**ell me again, lady, you wanted it for what?" McKenzie listened into the telephone, his eyes, which had been wide and incredulous just a moment before when he'd first heard the request, relaxed now almost into mirth. When the caller finished repeating her request, he spoke louder to overcome the steady beeps of a forklift's safety alarm as it backed along the dock below his open window.

"That's what I thought you said. We're awfully busy right now. I don't know if we can get one free. Anyway I got to ask somebody. I can't let it go on my own. Can you wait a few minutes? I got to ask the boss."

More than that, he had to tell someone. Anyone. He laid the receiver on his desk, then as an afterthought he picked it up again and asked: "You want it in pink or blue?"

He walked to the window and scanned the dock. Below, several workers were in the process of unloading the tender. The big vacuum pump hummed as it sucked a steady flow of brine and salmon from the boat's hold and up into a receiving line, irrigating the long stainless steel slide where workers in rubber suits of yellow and olive drab separated the salmon according to species and quality and dropped them into white fiberglass bins for removal into the plant where they'd be cleaned and headed and blast frozen. The best of the fish they now sent to Orca's table. When each of these totes was full, the forklift picked them up and took them into the beginning of the slime line where more people and machines worked on the fish.

McKenzie searched the group on the dock for Boss Gregg. The way he did it was by looking for the one person not wearing rain gear, or in this case, slime gear. He located his target at the edge of the dock peering over into the boat's emptying fish hold and shouting at the skipper.

"Hey, Gregg, Gregg," he screamed over the noise on the dock. The head lifted and then the shoulders started turning, gaining leverage to bring the man's huge paunch into motion. Once all of him was turning he had to plant his feet to halt the momentum of all his weight. An object in motion . . . .

"Wha-a-at?" The boss answered and the noise or effort of talking seemed to bring the rest of him to a stop.

"We got a tote we could let go?"

"Who needs it?"

McKenzie hesitated. In an instant he wondered if maybe he shouldn't yell across the dock for everybody to hear. This was a private, intimate occurrence after all. But McKenzie only entertained the thought briefly. The whole idea was too good to waste on just one set of ears, one mind, one sense of humor.

"Lady wants to have a baby in it."

The fish pump stopped. The forklift's alarm ceased. Fish already sliding along the stainless trays skidded to a halt. Workers let go of whatever they were doing and turned toward the second-story window, faces uplifted, awaiting revelation. A glob of fish halfway up the suction hose fell back into the boat. The boat's crew tried peeking around pilings and through open spaces between the dock planks to see who was talking.

"McKenzie," the boss shouted into the silence, "I told you if I ever caught you giving artificial respiration to a whiskey bottle during work, I'd fire your raunchy behind."

All the heads turned back to McKenzie in the window.

"I'm serious," he shouted back. "Lady on the phone here wants a fish tote to have a baby in."

"McKenzie, I'm warning you."

All heads turned back to the boss, then to the window.

"A tote. She wants a tote. Something about having the baby in water. I'm serious."

The heads turned again.

"Tell 'er them totes ain't for fry. They're for adults, caught ones at that." The boss shook his head and started the process of turning his body back toward the fishing boat.

"I can't tell 'er that. She's serious. What am I gonna tell 'er? We got a tote somewheres?"

All of the boss except his belly stopped turning. That center part continued around, twisting the man so his head and feet faced one direction while his midsection tried to go the complete opposite. The abrupt change almost threw him off balance. Now the faces didn't know which way to look. Half watched McKenzie, at least a few expecting him to fall out the window in a dead stupor. The other half tried to stifle their laughter as they watched the plant owner try to regain his balance.

The boss managed to remain upright and get himself all facing in the same direction while at the same time producing half a cigar, still smoldering and stuffed it into his mouth. Through teeth clenched around the cigar he let McKenzie know he'd talk to the lady on the telephone. With that he headed toward the outdoor stairway to the second floor. Halfway up the stairs he turned to the dock workers, still immobilized by what they'd heard. "What's the matter with you? Get back to work. Ain't you never heard of no lady havin' a baby before?"

The pump slushed back into action. The forklift started backing with its raucous beeping. The workers began sorting fish again and Boss Gregg continued his slow journey up the staircase.

He burst into McKenzie's office full of righteous anger, but stopped when he saw the man cup his hand over the telephone's mouthpiece.

"Now what's this all about?"

McKenzie leaned forward, handing the receiver to his boss, his hand still covering the mouthpiece.

"Like I said, lady wants to have a baby in a fish tote. Talk to her yourself."

Boss Gregg took the proffered telephone.

"Hello. Yes. Uhhunh." He looked at McKenzie, his eyes widening just as the foreman's had a few minutes earlier. He cupped the mouthpiece. "She's serious.

"Look, lady, them totes are for our business and we need 'em. This is our busy season."

He fell silent, listening. McKenzie guessed what he was hearing now, just what he'd heard a few minutes before about water births and how the six-foot-cubed totes were the best thing anybody could think of.

"Suppose you'd want that thing clean, too." McKenzie heard the boss softening. The caller was very persuasive. "They had dead fish in 'em all summer and all we do is hose 'em out once in a while." Silence. Then, "A car wash?!!

"Look, them totes are expensive, too. You plannin' on returning it? Oh. In that case, then. Yeah, I guess. Well, work it out with McKenzie. We'll find one."

He looked at the foreman. "Whew, we oughta have that woman buyin' fish." He handed the phone back to McKenzie.

"Thanks, granpaw," the foreman said.

The boss flashed him a look of pure disgust. He headed for the door.

"Women today. I don't know. She wants to have the baby in water whyn't she go up some stream and spawn like one of them fish? Why does it have to be in one of my totes?" He closed the door roughly behind him and McKenzie turned to the telephone to arrange for the caller to pick up her tote. Once they had agreed to a plan he hung up and that was that. He went back to his work.

The boat at the dock being the last one expected for a few hours, McKenzie took advantage of the brief respite and headed for home and a good sleep, something he hadn't enjoyed in almost two months.

Two days and the lady would collect her tote and that episode would be closed, too.

The next morning, refreshed from his rest, McKenzie walked the dock toward the plant and his office. He passed a couple of the employes sitting on the dock's bull rail, but at his hello, they smirked and turned away. He reached the front of the building to find Boss Gregg standing facing the huge front doors looking up, or at least McKenzie guessed he was looking up because his head was enveloped in a cloud of smoke emanating from a cigar the boss was puffing as if he hoped to make enough heat to melt steel. McKenzie looked up the building. Across the top of the door frames their sign read "SKOOKUM ALASKA FISH CO." But now there was more. During the night someone very carefully had lettered underneath it, "AND MATERNITY WARD." McKenzie laughed through his nose, the sound coming out as quick, loud exhalations.

The boss noticed him then. "Get somebody to work on that now," was all he said. McKenzie nodded, still smiling. He found two workers and sent them up a ladder. With no boats scheduled at the dock they had a little time for maintenance and cleaning. It also gave time for diversion and creativity.

The next morning when McKenzie returned to work he found the boss again in a cloud of smoke, this time staring at the huge windowless side wall of the plant, the one that faced the town across the harbor. This time a fairly competent artist or maybe more than one had been at work. The wall sported a striking multi-colored rendition of the traditional stork in flight delivering a baby. Only, instead of the cloth sling the stork usually used, this one had a fish tote slung from its beak. A happy baby waved from inside the tote and a cartoon bubble leading from the baby's mouth showed a salmon marketing slogan: "Eat fish and love longer." Emblazoned on the side of the tote were the words, again, "Skookum Alaska Fish Co. and Maternity Ward." The painting wasn't small. The stork was at least ten feet long, easily visible across the harbor. McKenzie noticed a small group of people over there pointing and talking. He thought he heard a laugh across the water.

"Paint it out," Boss Gregg said, "and do something about this foolishness. I'll be glad when a boat gets here and everybody's too busy to fool around."

McKenzie called for a couple of workers, but even before they could find a ladder, another tender entered the harbor and headed for the processor's dock. That ended the painting. Everyone had to work, leaving the stork to his flight along the wall.

McKenzie climbed to his office and scribbled a hasty note which he pinned to the plant's employe bulletin board:

"Anyone caught defacing company property will be dismissed.— McKenzie, foreman."

He walked on to a small lunch room for a cup of coffee and by the time he made the return trip to his office someone already had written "Dr." in front of his name. An hour later when he passed for another cup, the "Dr." and "foreman" had been crossed out and "R.N." appeared after his name. By the time he went to lunch, all, including his name had been struck out and in place were the words, "The Head Nurse."

McKenzie scanned across the plant but with some fifty employes all looking the same in their rubber suits and at the moment all looking away from him, he knew he wasn't going to spot the culprit. "At least," he thought, "tomorrow she'll get the tote and all this will pass."

By quitting time he'd been promoted to "Dr." again, this time "chief of obstetrics."

Just before he left he asked two of the slimers to take a tote aside, one of the newer ones, and hose it out, then leave it upside down to drain.

"Is this the one?" he was asked.

"What one?"

"Come on, Mack, the one the lady's going to have the baby in?"

"Yeah, it's the one. But don't tell anyone. I don't want any funny business. Maybe you better cover it with something, too. And don't call me Mack."

With that Dr. McKenzie, O.B., R.N., left for the day, hoping the next would bring an end to his career in obstetrics and graffiti obliteration. "Oh, boy," he thought as he walked along the dock, "never did get that stork off the wall. 'Nother day won't hurt. At least nobody can paint anything else there."

In the morning, the "AND MATERNITY WARD" was back under the Skookum Alaska Fish Co. sign on the front again. Not only that, but somebody had put an "Emergency Room" sign over the main doors and under it someone had written, "We don't do CPR on dead fish." McKenzie ignored the "Delivery Room" sign over his office door and went inside, closed the door and hid himself in paper work at his desk. No sense even dealing with it anymore. Just ignore it. Let the lady take her tote, have her baby and in a week all would be forgotten. Then the phone rang. He answered to the introduction of Dr. Sam Rigger, head of the town's small clinic, who then demanded an explanation for the birthing center Skookum Alaska had opened. McKenzie explained and the doctor rang off laughing just as Boss Gregg walked through the doorway and the cloud of cigar smoke that preceded him.

"What's going on here?" he demanded. "I got a bunch of women down there wanting to know what we're doing to babies here."

"Small towns. I hope you told them," McKenzie said.

"I ain't at all sure they believed me," he answered. "How'd we ever get into this?"

"It'll be over in an hour or so. She'll be here and take the tote and we can get back to the fish business."

A knock came at the door.

"What?" they both snarled.

"She's here," a voice called meekly through the door.

"Finally," Boss Gregg said.

They walked down the indoor stairs, passing "Surgery" at the bottom of the steps, turned right at the "Pharmacy" and walked out past "Radiology" to a small foreign station wagon with a trailer attached to the rear bumper. McKenzie walked through the gathering of slimers and sorters to the driver's side window, introduced himself, then directed the driver to back through the doors to where the covered tote awaited.

Two workers hoisted it onto the trailer with the covering intact. The woman thanked McKenzie and he wished her well with the birth. She drove away weaving around the equipment and people on the dock, heading for the road around the harbor. Boss Gregg and McKenzie watched her go, then Boss turned and said, "At least it'll be a good Alaska way to be born. Well, we're done with it. Let's get back to work."

"We ain't quite done with it," McKenzie said. "Look."

The cover had blown off the tote on the trailer revealing yet another work by the midnight artist.

Along 300 miles of road, through several small towns and the largest city in the state, motorists were sure to see the fish tote with the rainbows colorfully emblazoned on the side, a stork with a tote hanging from its bill and a salmon waving from inside the tote. Underneath that, prominently lettered, Gregg and McKenzie read the words, "Another Skookum Alaska Fish Co. Birthing Center Tot Tote."

The back side of the tote carried another message:
"SKOOKUM ALASKA FISH CO. AND MATERNITY WARD TOTE YOUR TOT IN A SKOOKUM TOTE."

And underneath that:
"NOTHING BUT THE BEST FOR YOUR SMALL FRY"

"I'll sue somebody," Boss Gregg said, looking around for someone to blame. But all he saw were the faceless backs of identical yellow. Not even a shoulder movement gave away the hint of a giggle.

"I kind of like the pink bow on it," McKenzie said.

"Your office!" said Boss Gregg and he stomped off past X-ray and the nurses station and on up the stairs to obstetrics.

McKenzie followed and once they were in his office, he closed the door and both men slumped into chairs.

"It's done."

"In a week nobody'll remember what the signs were about and we can take 'em down," said the chief obstetrician. Boss Gregg agreed.

The phone rang.

McKenzie answered with "Skookum Alaska. Yes ma'am." He listened for a moment, then asked, "Can you wait one?"

He tendered the receiver toward his boss. "For you."

"Who is it?"

"Lady says she's a midwife."

CHAPTER 18

THE VOYAGE HOME

T HE PLANT FUNCTIONED DESPITE MacKenzie's distractions. By the time he'd finished dealing with his medical responsibilities, the work crew had disposed of the last fish from the last tender. Orca stayed at his table filleting salmon into the third day, one longer than MacKenzie had promised. The foreman began regaining control of the operation only to begin dismantling the salmon lines for the winter. Orca cleaned his own area, then joined the other workers cleaning and oiling machinery and scrubbing the plant.

When MacKenzie had reached a point where he thought he had things under his thumb again, he separated Orca from the crowd and took him to his office.

There he pointed to a chair for Orca, then handed the boy a bank check. Orca looked down at the paper in his hands, then at McKenzie questioning.

"It's your pay," he said. Then he realized Orca probably hadn't seen a check before. "It's as good as money. You take it to the bank and they exchange it for cash."

Not wanting to look foolish, Orca decided he'd wait to ask Sven what a bank was. He thanked McKenzie after reading the numbers. If this actually worked, he had enough money to buy Sven the rifle and a little left over.

"It's a little more than your actual wages," McKenzie said. "You did a fine job. Reason I wanted to talk to you in private is, we want you to come back for the whole season next year."

Orca considered the offer, weighing the check in his hands and the idea of a whole summer inside that plant with its noises and smells and in the town, as well.

"Thank you," Orca said, "but I think I like the fishing end of it better."

"I can understand that," McKenzie said. "Me and Boss Gregg both started out fishing. In the long run there's more money to be made here."

"I don't know."

"We could put you on a tender, too," he offered. "You don't have to be locked up inside the building."

"Can I think about it?"

"You can think about it all winter if you want," McKenzie said. "For that matter you can think about it a couple years. Point is we want you to come work for us. You did a terrific job. When you beat that machine, it set technology back ten years."

He stood up and reached to shake Orca's hand. Orca stood, too. "Thank you," he said.

The interview ended, Orca walked down the outside steps to find Priscilla waiting for him, standing next to her car in the parking lot. He called "Hello" and quickened his pace.

Inside the car, Orca showed her his check. "I got this," he said.

Priscilla looked at the amount. "You made a lot of money for just a few days' work," she said.

"They asked me to come back for the whole season next year."

"Do you want to do that? It might be interesting for you to spend the whole summer in town," she said.

"I don't think so. I told them I like the fishing part. Will you take me where I can change this into money?"

"All right," she said, "but we have to hurry. The reason I came to meet you is the judge has allowed us to have the hearing this afternoon. Sven and Corky should already be there. We only have about twenty minutes."

Priscilla drove him to the bank and showed him how to cash his check. Because he had no identification, the teller had to call McKenzie to confirm the transaction. Once she hung up the telephone, she counted Orca's money and handed it to him. Orca leafed through the bills. "Will you take me to the Outfitters?"

"Sure, what do you need to buy?"

Orca explained his purpose for going to work in the plant in the first place.

"I think you might be too young to buy a gun," Priscilla said, "I don't think they'll sell it to you. I don't want to be a part of that either, letting a twelve-year-old have a gun. I know you and Sven live on what you hunt, but something about it bothers me. I'd rather not get involved with it. I'm not against it, mind you, I know what it means to you. It's just I'm not going to be the one to help you get a gun."

This confused Orca. Where he lived, a gun served as a tool, just as much as a shovel or an ax or a net. And Sven needed a new one, as if he'd broken the handle on a hammer. They needed it to provide their food, and then, too, there were the bears. Obviously, Priscilla saw it differently.

"I guess I can ask Corky," he said.

"I'd feel better that way," she said. "Here we are. Are you worried?"

"A little. Do you think it will go all right?"

"I think so, but you never know. Something can always happen."

Priscilla drove the car into a parking lot next to the building Corky had pointed out a few days earlier as the place where she worked. She parked next to Corky's pickup and they walked toward Sven who stood at the entry pulling on his pipe, chatting quietly with Corky.

They entered the building where the officiality of the surroundings intimidated them into silence. Priscilla led them to the judge's chambers and tapped lightly on the door. A woman emerged to greet them and said the judge would be ready in a minute. They stood fidgeting in the hall, Orca twisting his fisherman's cap in his hands. When the judge's secretary invited them into the office, they walked politely across the thick carpet to the door the woman held open.

In the judge's chamber, a gray-haired man looked up from his desk to greet them. "Please be seated," he said. Without another word he lifted a manila file folder from the papers on his desk and opened it. He leafed through the documents inside, pausing to read individual pages until he looked over the file at the people sitting in front of the desk.

"You must be Orca," he said.

Orca nodded.

"Miss Braithewaite. Why are you here?"

Priscilla stood and explained to the judge how Orca had come to her attention, told about her investigation, and then pointed out the petition she had written that explained her involvement, her analysis and her recommendation. "You seem to have all of the paperwork in order," the judge said. "There's the birth certificate, a home study . . . " He stopped for a moment and flipped through the papers in the file. He removed the study Priscilla had prepared and scanned it. "The physical home appears to be a little rough."

Sven noticed the manicured fingernails on the judge's hands as they gripped Priscilla's petition. "A little rough," he thought. "How can this man sit at his polished desk with his polished hands and decide anybody's home was rough?" He held his silence.

"Do you feel the boy has proper shelter, enough room for himself?" the judge asked.

Sven opened his mouth to speak but Priscilla grabbed his shoulder sharply. "I have visited their home on several occasions, your honor, and while you may call the home rough and small, you have to understand the circumstance. These people have perhaps the smallest home imaginable, but in a sense they have the largest home as well. You see, they spend a good deal more time outdoors than in. In my visits, they only went inside to eat and sleep. If you look at it from that perspective, all of Prince William Sound is their home and to my mind you couldn't find a more beautiful one."

The judge's expression offered no clue as to how he took Priscilla's suggestion.

"I read your report," the judge said, "The way you describe the home life, it sounds more like a vacation paradise than a critical evaluation. Are you sure you don't want to move there, yourself?"

Priscilla blushed. "I tried to be as professionally objective as possible."

"I see the background investigation on Mr. Kaartoonsen is fairly sketchy," he said. "There's not very much on record. That could mean he's lived an exemplary life, or it could mean he's very good at hiding his past. What do you have to say?" he asked directly to Sven.

"Well, your honor, I was born to the North Sea . . . "

Corky covered the chuckle about to escape.

Priscilla interrupted. "You honor, in the interest of saving the court's time, you might not want to get Mr. Kaartoonsen started." Corky's chuckle escaped. The judge looked at him sternly, then his face cracked into a smile as well.

"Are you telling me this might be a long story?" he asked Priscilla.

"Believe me, your honor, these people don't know any short stories," she said. "All of the information available is in the report I submitted to the court, along with my own observations."

"All right, then," the judge said. He turned to Orca. "We're here to decide what's best for your interests."

The center of attention, Orca dropped his twisted cap. "Yes, sir."

"Have you anything to say?"

Orca glanced nervously at Sven whom he noticed was fidgeting with his pipe. "I want to stay with Sven," he blurted, surprising himself at how loud he sounded in the quiet chamber.

"I guess that's fairly succinct," the judge said. "Can anyone speak for them? I see by the file you have more references than anyone wants to read."

Priscilla introduced Corky.

"Keeping it short, Mr. Netsworth, can you tell me your experience with them?"

Corky told the judge the history of Sven and Orca as he knew it, adding the role he had played as supplier and friend. He produced his boat's log book from the time Sven had found Orca and showed the judge the entry describing the baby and Sven's story of Orca's arrival. He related the summer's experience fishing including the story of the whales. He concluded saying, "That boy don't belong anywhere else except where he is. He's a child, well, now a man, of the sound and if he's anybody's son, now, he's Sven's. It'd be criminal to send him anywhere else."

The judge hesitated, absorbing Corky's monologue. "You're not just trying to keep a crewman, are you?" he asked finally.

Corky laughed.

"You brought up this matter with the whales. That's quite a story, how you found him, I mean," the judge said, turning to Sven. "By the birth certificate here, I see you managed to convince somebody."

"It's the truth." Sven said.

"Be that as it may," the judge said, turning to Priscilla. "Your search turned up no trace of any family?"

"We did a thorough investigation," she said. "There isn't a trace."

The judge leaned toward them, a smile beginning to crease his face. "I know what you mean about the sound," he said. "I've got a boat, you know." Sven and Orca cast sideways glances at each other. They caught Corky looking around, too. "I might want to make an evaluation visit, myself. Maybe even find out where you catch all those halibut." Sven's face broadened, relieved, and he met the judge's smile.

"In the mouth, your honor," he said with a wink. "We catch them in the mouth."

"You're not going to give up a fishing hole even to a judge, huh?"

"You never know," Sven said.

"All right, then," the judge said, excusing them. "You will hear my decision shortly."

When they had returned to the hallway, Sven asked, "That's all there is?"

"It's all up to him, now.
You could have at least told
him where he could catch a
halibut," Priscilla said. "They'll
call to let us know."

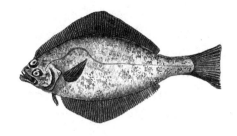

"Oh, I'll tell him," Sven
said, "maybe after the
decision."

"Well, what should we do now?" Corky asked.

"I guess it'd be best to go back to your place and wait for a
call," Sven said.

"I'll go with you," Priscilla offered.

"I'll go with Corky," Orca said, "Maybe Sven can ride with
Priscilla."

"All right," Sven said, "Don't know why, though. I never had a
ride in one of these fancy new cars."

They left in their separate automobiles. Once in the truck with
Corky, Orca explained his purpose. "Priscilla wouldn't let me buy
the rifle," Orca said.

"Different people got different views toward guns," Corky tried
to explain. "Out where you live you got to have one. It's just a
tool. But in towns, in the big cities guns mean a whole different
thing and there's a lot of people get hurt. It's hard to sort out. I
been around 'em all my life and never had to level one at a human
being yet. I don't know if I could if it did come up. But it's different in them cities. I got no problem with it. We'll go get the rifle
and put it on the boat. You can surprise Sven when we get to
Cabin Bay tomorrow."

"Thanks, Corky. I'm glad our life isn't so complicated," Orca
said. They drove to the Outfitters and Corky bought the rifle. Then
they took it to the *Salmania* where they stowed it among the rest
of the gear they planned to take to Cabin Bay the next morning.

From the harbor they drove to Corky's house. Priscilla's car
stood in the yard empty now. Sven and Priscilla came out to meet
them.

"Any word yet?" Corky called.

"Not yet," Sven said. "Say, how did your work go?"

"They paid me. And they want me to come back next year."

Sven frowned, but he had all winter to convince the boy otherwise, so he held his thoughts.

A ringing telephone intruded into their conversation, stifling it to dead silence. Corky ran inside, stood for a moment staring at the instrument, then lifted the receiver. By then the other three had joined him. Corky spoke a greeting, listened for a moment, then handed the receiver to Sven. "This is it," he whispered to Orca and Priscilla.

Sven listened intently. Then a smile began to spread until his face could barely contain it. "Yes, yes, thank you," he said into the telephone. He handed the receiver to Priscilla. "He wants to talk to you."

While Priscilla spoke on the phone, Sven shouted: "We're free and clear. You get to stay on the island."

At the words spoken out loud, the realization and then the joy passed through the four of them. Sven danced a little jig. Priscilla hung up the phone and hugged Orca. Corky shook everyone's hand.

"Got to keep up your school work, though," Sven said.

"Do I have to call you father?" Orca kidded.

"Sven'll be just fine," came the answer.

"Shall we go out to dinner to celebrate?" Priscilla asked.

"Yes, yes, yes," they all agreed.

"Should we go pick up Mr. Smith?" Priscilla asked. Corky and Sven traded glances.

"Leave 'im be." Sven said

Corky explained, "It took us the last two days to talk him off that boat. He wasn't gonna leave. Just kept on tellin' stories and sippin' coffee and then he'd fall asleep and we couldn't move him."

"Finally had to almost carry him up to that home," Sven said. "Let's not get him started again. We can see him next time."

Over dinner in conversation underlaid with joy and relief, they talked about their time in town, telling Priscilla about Orca's race with the fillet machine and the story of the fish tote. She'd seen the maternity sign and wondered what it had been about. Gradually their conversation turned to the future and Sven and Orca began laying their plans for the winter. As they planned they both realized how much they wanted to return to the sound and Cabin Bay. When they finished dinner they said their good-byes to Priscilla.

"I should be able to bring the adoption papers down to the boat before you leave," she said, and made arrangements to meet them in the harbor the next morning.

Back at Corky's, Orca again had difficulty falling asleep. Between anticipation of his trip, the memories of the town, the noises that intruded again and a street light he couldn't seem to escape, he tossed on the couch until well into the morning. Still Sven and Corky thought they were trying to raise the dead when they roused him.

They gathered the few belongings they'd brought to Corky's and headed for one last plate of strawberry waffles.

When they reached the *Salmania*, Priscilla already sat on the deck waiting for them. She had a manila envelope in her hands. In it she had the papers for Sven to sign, a copy of a birth certificate for Orca and some new materials from the school. Sven stood on the dock looking at the boat's water line. "You know," he said, "that money stripe, when it goes down, it's supposed to mean you're makin' money. Way we got this boat loaded, s'more like countin' how much you spent." Corky laughed and ascended to the wheelhouse.

While they talked and Corky warmed the boat's engine, Sven looked up the dock and said, "Oh, no. Corky, come here, look at this." Corky emerged from his wheelhouse to see Smit struggling along the walkway dragging a duffel bag.

When he looked up and saw them watching, he called, "Got my kit. Whar's she pointed? You got a berth for one more jack tar?"

In chorus they laughed.

"Now what're we gonna do?" Sven asked Corky.

"Aw, let's take 'im for a ride."

"He misses the sea something awful, doesn't he?" Priscilla asked.

"It's part of him just like your blood is part of you," Sven said, "Orca, go give him a hand."

Orca ran to take the sea bag from the struggling old sailor. Immediately Smit straightened and he sauntered toward the boat with his old sea strut. "You'll be needin' a mate for the trip back," he said to Corky.

"C'mon aboard," Corky said. "We'd best be settin' sail," he winked at Sven. Priscilla stepped off the boat. Orca began untying lines.

"We'll be lookin' for you," Sven told Priscilla.

"I should be out in about two months," she said, "When does crab season start?"

"That'll be about right," Sven called back.

Orca released the last line, touched Priscilla on the shoulder, then jumped aboard. He tipped his cap with the "Orca" stitched on it. "Thank you. For everything." Then Corky pulled the *Salmania* away from the dock.

Their trip to Cabin Bay passed uneventfully. Each of them fell into his own thoughts for the most part. Even Smit remained quiet as he sat in the wheel house examining all the instruments and watching the ocean and mountains. He seemed almost melancholy, his mind taking him over other horizons sailing square-riggers on other oceans. Only once did he speak. Looking toward Hinchinbrook Entrance over the deceptively calm water, he said, "She's a fair horizon." Corky understood the old sailor's lure toward the open horizon on the big ocean. Even the waters of the sound must have felt confining to a blue-water, square-rigged sailor. Where Smit saw the entrance between the two barrier islands as the opening into bigger oceans, the other three saw it as the one place that allowed the ocean and its storm waves into their mostly protected waters. Orca thought about the storms that sometimes blew into the sound through that entrance.

The crew in the wheelhouse fell back to their musing until Corky asked Orca what he'd thought of the town. Orca thought for a moment about the people and the noise and the odors. "You know, one thing I noticed. Everything is square and regular. The streets are square, they meet at right angles. The buildings are square. Everything's square."

"Nothin' square out here," Sven said as he looked out over the irregular shapes of the mountains and the bay mouths. Even that cabin's a little rounded, all the sinking and earthquakes been workin' on it."

In Cabin Bay they retrieved their dory and Sven and Orca lightered their supplies to shore. Orca beamed when he handed the brand-new rifle to Sven. "It's why I worked in that plant," he said. Sven took the rifle and held it gingerly, overwhelmed for a moment. The thought of the boy working so hard for it moved him more than the tangible weight in his hands.

Orca invited Smit to the cabin, but Corky stopped him. He could just see Smit starting to tell another story and then he'd be stuck there for a week. "We'd better head back," he said. "It's going to be dark as it is."

For his part Smit allowed how he'd rather be on the boat anyway, thank you.

Sven and Orca sat on their pile of goods to watch the *Salmania* disappear around the headland. When its sound faded into the stillness of their wilderness, Sven said, "It's good to be back, isn't it?"

"Yes," was all Orca answered.

In time they rose and began yet another round of hauling boxes and bags from the beach to their cabin.

CHAPTER 19

LEGENDS ARE BORN

AFTER A COUPLE OF DAYS, SVEN AND ORCA had found places to store all their new purchases. They had relaxed from the rigors of their visit to town into their normal routines on the island. They renewed their eternal search for firewood and watched the hills for signs of deer. Equipment worked hard during the summer had to be repaired and stored. Other tools they would need for the winter had to be brought out and inspected. They ate first from the fresh foods they had bought in town, knowing soon enough they'd be back to salmon and venison and preserves and canned goods.

As the equinox approached, storms mustered around deep lows in the Gulf of Alaska to march across Prince William Sound at three-day intervals. The morning after the winds from one storm had rattled their roofing, Sven looked at a pan full of water on the floor and said, "Them storms are comin' pretty regular now. I'd better fix that leak before winter comes and we can't get at it through the snow."

He placed a ladder against the eaves and climbed it with his bucket of tar to the wet tin roof. Indoors, Orca could hear Sven tromping along the roof while he worked at his school studies.

After a period of quiet while Orca was sure Sven had stopped to patch a spot, he heard a thump louder than a footstep. Then Sven yelled. The bucket clattered along the roof followed by something else, softer and heavier. Then he heard Sven yelling again, closer, and he ran outside. He found Sven lying in the mud on the downhill side of the cabin, writhing in pain, his back to the door. Orca ran to him, touched his shoulder and then saw where Sven held his leg, moaning. The leg had slipped through the ladder when Sven slid off the roof and Orca saw blood flowing around the leg bone where it protruded from his pants leg.

A picture from his primer flashed in his mind, a compound fracture. Sven's writhing slowed as shock came over him. Orca raced through what he could remember from his first-aid book. Don't move him. But he had to move him. He had to get Sven indoors and treat for shock. He took his knife and cut away the cloth of Sven's trousers. By the bleeding, Orca could tell Sven hadn't cut a major vein or artery. He found some cloth to cover the wound and attempted to stop what bleeding there was. From two-by-fours, Orca fashioned a traction splint for the leg. Then he worked through plans to move the old man indoors. Sven remained calm, his moaning ceased for the moment. Orca found a sheet of plywood. He laid it next to Sven and told him to hoist himself onto it if he could. Sven dragged himself to it inch by inch on his elbows, at the last using his hands to hoist the injured leg aboard, flinching from the pain the movement generated. Orca lifted the end at Sven's feet and started dragging the plywood around until Sven's feet pointed to the door. Then he lifted the end supporting Sven's head and dragged that around. Moving the plywood end around end, Orca gained a few feet each time and eventually dragged Sven on the plywood to the cabin door.

Orca panicked when he saw the plywood was too wide for the doorway. Again he asked Sven to move himself, this time inching himself backward off the plywood on his elbows and through the doorway into the house. Sven's eyelids tightened against the pain as he pulled himself along the floor. For a moment Orca

wondered how he would get Sven up to his bunk, then he ripped
the mattress off the bed. He helped Sven lift himself to the mattress, where the old man collapsed. The boy rolled a blanket that
he placed between Sven's legs and tied the legs together. Orca
covered him with blankets, tenderly placing two pillows under his
ankles to lift the legs slightly. He found gauze and replaced the
cloth he'd put around the wound. When he had Sven comfortable,
he watched his face for color.

"You're going to have to go for help," Sven grimaced through
tightened lips.

"I can't leave you like this," Orca said.

"You got to," Sven told him. "No way we can fix this ourselves.
You can make town three, four hours." The pain clamped his eyes
shut again.

"Let me think, Sven," he almost felt the pain visible in Sven's
face.

"You look to the weather, too," Sven said. "No use gettin' caught
and killed if there's a storm."

Orca stood and walked outside. To the southeast black clouds
boiled above the hill behind the cabin. He saw the dory floating
near shore and then thought his way through preparations for a
trip to town. If that was a new storm growing, could he beat it?
Mentally he put on his rain gear, he filled two extra gasoline tanks
for the outboard, he threw a little food into a waterproof bag and
he made the trip to town, wondering if he could find the way.
He'd only made the trip once, well, once out, once back. Then he
decided.

He found a short length of rope and a dowel and ran back to
Sven.

"Okay, Sven, I'll go. But you have to do some things. For one,
I don't want you to fall asleep if you can help it. Here's some stuff
to make a tourniquet. I'll set it up for you. If that bleeding gets any
worse, you use it." He looked at the wound. It appeared the bleeding had stopped for the time being. "You can't move that leg."

Through his teeth Sven asked, "How's the weather look?"

"Some clouds to the southeast, but no wind right now," the boy answered. "It just stormed yesterday. I should be able to beat the next one."

"Don't be afraid to turn around if you have to," Sven winced.

"I'll make it."

Orca physically performed the preparations he'd made earlier in his mind. When everything was ready, he filled the wood stove and damped it down so the fire would burn at least for eight hours. He put a pot of coffee and cup where Sven could reach it. "To stay awake," he told the old man, wondering if the coffee might create other problems. Whatever they were, they couldn't be as bad as bleeding to death which could happen if Sven fell asleep, twisted the bone and cut an artery.

Then he put on his rain gear, as an afterthought picked up a sleeping bag and ran to the dory.

"You keep the round side down," he heard Sven say as he went out the door. This time it came through more as an order than a salutation.

Orca wasted no time firing the outboard and for the second time in a month he left Cabin Bay for the town to the north. All the while, those clouds moved closer, drawing a dark gray curtain across the sky from the southeast.

Orca motored northward along the western shores first of Naked Island and then Peak and Storey. In the calm lee of the islands he couldn't tell what the weather might be once he cleared the land and exposed the boat to the broad expanse of water to the southeast. Protected by the islands he could only guess how far the storm had progressed and whether the first of the winds might already be ripping around the north end. Already he could see the tops of the trees on the higher parts of the islands bending slightly before the wind.

Between the Naked Island group and the next shelter to the north Orca would face a couple of decisions. He had to cross twelve miles of open water, one of the widest areas in the sound and one exposed to the North Pacific through Hinchinbrook, the primary entrance from the ocean. When southeasterlies blew, waves rolled from their source in the Gulf of Alaska through the entrance unabated for fifty miles before they crashed against the shore of the mainland along its northern shore. On a calm day he could go straight across the open water to the northeast, skirting the south side of Glacier Island and turning around its eastern end on the most direct route to town. If the seas turned rough, he would have to alter his course more to the northwest toward the western end of Glacier Island to reach a protected channel between the mainland and the island on its north side. If he did that, he'd have to contend with masses of icebergs generated by Columbia Glacier, the largest in the sound. The trip through the channel would take longer and the ice probably would slow his progress if he had to weave through it. That was the decision he hoped he'd have to make. The second would be the more difficult. The weather could prevent his passage altogether and force him to return to Cabin Bay. Once he cleared the northern shore of Storey Island, the farthest north of their three islands, he knew he'd have maybe half an hour before he had to make his decision, or the waves made the decision for him. He thought about Sven lying on that mattress on the cabin floor and knew it would take an awful storm to make him turn around.

As Orca passed the western point of Storey Island and moved north past that sheltering land, he began to feel a gentle chop tickling the sides of the dory. A slight breeze, he thought mostly caused by his own speed, chilled his skin where his clothing left his hands and cheeks exposed. Pushing to the north, he tried to read the signs, estimating the forces he could expect to encounter. He knew what he was seeing at that time could only grow more intense, but visions of Sven writhing in the mud with the bone protruding from his pants leg obscured the almost instinctive caution he'd developed over his years learning the sound and its ways. He scanned the water ahead looking for telltale white. Where he could see horizon he tried to judge if waves distorted what should have been a straight line. To that point he saw no white-

caps, even to the east and around to the south as far as he could
see before the islands blocked his line of vision. The dark sky and
mountains obscured the horizon. He saw Sven on the mattress. As
he moved farther north, that merry chop started slapping the boat
harder and Orca felt the skiff begin to move on the waves. Still, he
didn't have to slow down, yet, and he skimmed across the waves,
the blindness caused by his mission making the weather look less
threatening. Orca committed to the crossing. He would not go
back to Cabin Bay.

The chop grew into short waves that began to roll the boat.
Where the wind at first had merely chilled him slightly, he began
to feel it tugging at the loose ends of his clothing. Where at first
he'd felt wind only in his face from the forward motion of the
boat, now, gradually, the southeasterly from behind him grew
stronger until it blew faster than the boat was going and pushed
against his back. The waves and the winds increased so gradually
Orca barely noticed the changes as his mind raced with the boat
toward town and what he would do when he reached it.

From behind him the building waves changed again. Where
he had been riding a wind chop, once he passed out of the lee of
the islands, ocean swells began to lift and drop the boat in long
sweeps of hills and valleys. The wind chop remained, still skitter-
ing along the tops of the swells and along the troughs to slap the
boat. Orca ran over the long swells easily, driving up the slopes of
their backsides and riding down the fronts to surf into the troughs,
at first giving up none of his speed, still lost in his thoughts.

Then he pitched over the top of a wave just as another crashed
across the bow, pushing it sideways. Startled out of his reverie, he
found himself diving down the front of a wave, the bow aiming
straight into the water. Behind him the top of the wave curled into
snarling white foam. Orca pulled the tiller slightly, trying to turn
off the wave. He managed to turn enough to slide down the wave
mostly on his starboard quarter. When he reached the bottom he
turned beam to and raced along the trough, the wave curling and
breaking right behind the boat. He asked the outboard for all the

power it had as he tried to will the boat out from under the curl. Flying along the trough, he watched the top until he reached a lower part of the wave that had not yet begun to break and turned off it to climb the next one, this time careful to let it slide underneath. Now the storm had his full attention. Whatever was going to happen in town would. He still had ten miles of ocean to cross.

A gust of wind spattered the first heavy raindrops against his back. He had no doubts now that he had to try for the western end of Glacier Island. The eastern route would put the waves on his beam and that he couldn't do. Heading for the channel at the west end, he could run before the waves, take them on the stern, and even surf them if they allowed.

By then, some of the waves curled higher than the dory, and from the troughs Orca had to look up at their crests. They came closer together and steeper; the first gentle swells he'd felt were turning into a higher, nasty storm chop. As he felt the waves his actions became almost automatic, like with the fish cutting, responding to the movement of the boat. He almost slipped back into his thoughts, then he missed a wave and it crashed against the bow, driving cold spray into his face. He licked the salt from

his lips and scrubbed water from his eyelids. The cold slap in the face drove his fears for Sven deeper inside him and his concentration enveloped the greater, more immediate task.

He tightened his grip on the steering tiller and squinted ahead. Rain slammed harder against his back and again and again he felt the waves pound the side of the boat, driving more spray into his eyes. He blinked constantly and wiped his eyes with his free hand to clear his vision.

When he wasn't wiping his eyes, that free hand clutched the gunwale for leverage against the waves each time one picked up the little boat and hurled it forward. The waves grew to such a size he had to alter his speed constantly, slowing as a wave lifted him so he could let it slide underneath rather than drive over the crest into a another precipitous slide down the leading edge. The point of land, Iceberg Point on Glacier Island, the destination behind which lay the haven of the channel, had seemed so close just minutes earlier, but as he slowed the boat and altered his course to maneuver around each wave, the land receded into the distance.

Just those few miles became an impassable mountain range, close enough to see the point, but so far, far away. He drove toward the point when the waves allowed, but just as often he had to turn away from it as the incessant swells lifted and dropped him at their will. His zig-zag course across the waves would add miles to the distance. He knew, too, as the waves moved into shallower water close to the point, the rising slope of the bottom would force a ground swell, increasing their size and making them all the more dangerous. Despite that, he was committed. He probably couldn't have turned around. He had only one way to go, one place for shelter. He had to make the point and the calm channel beyond it.

So, he drove on across the waves and as he did, the wind blew harder, whipping his clothing, plastering it against his body. The waves built to a size where if he looked down from the crests into the troughs he felt the twinges of vertigo. He shivered and tried to shake off the shivering as he felt a fear growing inside him like an icicle forming in his abdomen. The ice spread through his body into his legs and feet and toes, his arms and hands and fingers. The icicle reached his brain and for the first time he realized he'd put himself into a position where he had to fight for his life and, alone, he had become the master by whose hand he would live or die.

The dory pitched crazily on the crest of a wave until it passed underneath and Orca slid seemingly backward into the trough behind it. He gripped the tiller, preparing for the next wave to lift the boat to begin the cycle again. Every nerve ending, alerted by the icy fear, tingled as his concentration closed around his goal as tightly as his fingers closed around the tiller. With the fear came a feeling of alertness he'd never felt before. All of his existence merged into one entity. Nothing existed for him but the storm, yet everything existed. There were mountains, and whales, Sven, and town. He was aware of them all somehow. They formed parts of an entire existence for Orca with the wind and the water, the boat and himself and the point of land that was his destination. Each reality merged with the next, individual, yet part of one contiguous flow with Sven and the mountains, the whales and the town. Every sense went on alert, every muscle reacted with the common movement. Nothing beyond the motion existed, yet he was aware of each minute detail, the crest of each wave, the one unpainted board in the bow of the boat, each raindrop that hit his shoulder, the bottle of bull coffee rolling in the bilge, Sven on the mattress in Cabin Bay and the mountains hidden in the distant clouds to the north. Next to the boat he knew a storm petrel floated on the wind facing into it, flying backward and keeping pace with him.

A life force circulated through him from the water as if all of nature were one fluid motion. It rose from the waves into the very boards of the boat and through his legs as muscles instinctively flexed at each pitch, straining to keep the boy upright. He could feel each muscle tense, yet he felt no control of it at all. The energy generated by the storm surged through him from his legs to the hand that reflexively steered the boat and to the other that clutched the gunwale for leverage. He heard each wave as it approached from behind, snicking and popping toward him. His legs tensed automatically for the lift and when it came, his arm easily steered the boat for the wave, riding it to a height from which he could see across the water to Iceberg Point, then reacted for the sickening drop into the valley of the trough. He felt every tiny nuance of movement in the water; he picked out individual trees standing on the point; he knew each board in the boat intimately. Through his hand he sensed the pulse each time the spark plug in the motor fired and each turn of the propeller. He saw the gulls fighting the wind overhead and the storm petrel still next to the boat.

His mind relaxed and he saw with his eyes only the goal, the point, the refuge, while every sense reached beyond his conscious command for every possible stimulus.

As he pushed on alone in his cosmos, gray from the sky merged with gray of the water into one indiscernible palette. That gray conspired with rain and spray to obscure his vision. At each rise to the top of the wave he could make out the point in the dim of the distance until, to his horror, the dory twisted at the top of a wave and he realized he could no longer see the trees. He squirmed around, looking to all points of the compass, but Iceberg Point had disappeared into that mist of unending gray. He looked behind for some trace of his wake which might give him an indication of the way he'd been going, but the wake had been swallowed into the foaming water. Orca panicked. He did not know which way to go. All he had to do was head north. He knew he'd make a landfall somehow in that direction, but the sky and water had merged into that curtain of gray broken only by the white, cresting wave tops and obscuring anything else that might have given him an indication of his proper course. He slowed the boat. He set his course only by the direction of the waves, hoping he had headed the right way. Even that, he knew, could have been deceiving. Some of the waves came from quite a different direction almost directly opposed to those out of the southeast. Orca strained his eyes for some glimpse of anything that might guide him.

Then about halfway up the slope of a wave in front of him he saw a killer whale. Its full length appeared before him, the white of its belly showing aqua green through the lens of water. The whale exhaled a breath and swam for a moment along the surface, lifted on the same plane as Orca. In the middle of the wave, the whale turned away from the boat, pushing straight into the wall of water seemingly aiming toward the same point as Orca. At the sight of the whale, the boy sensed a recognition of something beyond the animal itself. The whale and the motion of the boat on the waves merged into a recollection of dim memory. He understood he had somehow reached a place he had been before, but it was a place he could not identify beyond that sense of the familiar. Then, realizing that recognition, though not its source, he felt a new confidence as if another hand guided his on the tiller. The boy turned the boat to follow and for a moment felt escorted through the storm by a greater force. The whale surfaced twice more at intervals of about a minute, then disappeared into the waves.

Orca felt no threat. A serenity passed through him in his total absorption of the storm. The icicle melted away. The awareness his fear had raised took away all sense of time and distance, he knew only the incessant motion of the water while hours became minutes and then days and then hours again. For a time he lost the urgency he had felt attempting to reach his goal. Orca looked up from the circle of riffles where the whale had disappeared on its last dive and directly in line with the boat, the trees on Iceberg Point appeared dark through the mist. He could see the white of breakers as they pounded rocks below the trees. The deceiving perception of distances across water convinced him he was almost there, but that eventually frustrated him. Then that too became part of his serenity. Each minute, it seemed by inches, he moved closer and closer to the point and shelter. Through the next few miles, though he had no conscious thought of his manipulation of the tiller or the boat, he made no more mistakes with the waves. The storm had become Orca's entire way of life and he made his peace with the elements. They could harm him no more and he knew it.

So deep was his immersion in the storm, when the last of the ground swells threw him surfing into the channel behind Glacier Island, the calm water came as a surprise. As he drifted in water barely disturbed by a riffle, he realized he'd passed through the storm and his mind began a slow re-entry into the life he had left at the moment the storm took over his full consciousness. His hands shook and he shivered once as the effects of adrenaline gradually dissipated. Then he experienced a feeling he could identify only as regret. He found himself missing the storm as he might miss a comfortable home when he was away. For that short period the storm had been his entire life and now he had to go through a change again to yet another one similar to his old one, but changed forever by the experience. He began to notice the ache in his muscles and realized how tightly he clutched the tiller as if he still were fighting the waves. He had to uncurl his fingers one at a time and stretch them into functioning again. As the energy passed from him and his muscles relaxed, he stared blankly up the channel ahead, distractedly looking for icebergs.

He let the boat drift for a while until he regained some control. He drank from his jug of bull coffee and nibbled at a strip of smoked salmon. Once he'd relaxed and recomposed, and the realities of his circumstance came to the fore, he changed the fuel tanks on the outboard, restowed all the gear that had broken loose during the storm, bailed the water from the bilge, and then headed east along the channel. In calm water, he saw Sven again on the floor of the cabin and that vision cleared his thoughts. He knew his battle with the storm hadn't ended quite yet. After he passed the eastern end of Glacier Island, he'd be exposed again, but he also knew, or at least hoped, the waves wouldn't be as strong as they had been and once he turned north toward town they'd begin to diminish.

Orca raced down the channel as fast as the dory would go, watching carefully and dodging icebergs as he went. In time he felt the temperature turn cooler as he ran into the wall of colder air flowing off the glacier. He crossed in front of Columbia Bay, thankful he had only a few bits of ice in the water here and there to negotiate the dory around. As he approached the east end of the channel and the last comforting protection of the island, he felt the first of the swells begin to lift the dory again. For a while, at least, he didn't have to slow the boat and drove across the smooth swells quickly. These waves were just the residuals, waves that had radiated past the point where the land had broken them and released most of their violent energy.

The waves continued to grow until he had to slow the boat to meet them. At first they came right at his bow, then as he passed out of the lee of the island they came more on the beam. He found he had to tack to keep the boat steady, turning into the big ones, then turning off them to the northeast, inching toward his goal. If he went straight for Point Freemantle they would have pounded the side of the boat just as they would have when he left Naked Island. His tacking forced him far out into the center of the arm. To the north he could see where the arm narrowed between mountains and he knew that was where he had to go, but much of his progress took him east and southeast. He recalled the serenity he'd felt in his first round with the storm and tried to regain it, but this time it wouldn't come and each wave became a monumental yet tedious task. He began to lose patience with the storm. When he'd progressed almost four miles across the arm he judged the direction of the waves against the direction he had to go and turned north. With the waves behind him again he could surf, let each wave take the boat and propel it forward.

He picked a wave and then raced the motor until he had the boat caught at the top of the leading edge. Once he felt the wave's surge against the boat, he throttled back and let the wave propel him along with it. By maintaining the boat's speed the same as the waves' speed he could ride them until their strength diminished and dropped him into the trough behind. Surfing, he managed to ride individual waves for minutes at a time.

The waves pushed him northward toward that narrow passage through the mountains and as he progressed farther up the arm they began to diminish as he came more into the lee of mountains to the east. The wind gave him no such relief. It curled around those mountains and came howling out of long, narrow bays that cut deeply into the eastern shore of the arm. The screaming gusts of the easterlies took the breath from his lungs and drove rain into his cheeks so hard it hurt. Still he pushed forward, the fear gone and the cause of his trip returning to his mind. He checked landmarks off the mental list he'd made recalling the trips with Corky.

Even as the rain cut into his face, he increased his speed when the waves allowed until he passed the last of the bays to his right and entered the narrow passage into the port. By the time he recognized the light at Entrance Island the water had flattened into calm and the wind had dropped to a breeze. He gave the outboard all the throttle it would take and turned the boat toward where he thought the town was. In the dusk without the evening's lights to guide him he could only guess a general direction and he sped across the water to the northeast. Eventually he spotted the red and green lights marking the harbor entrance. He turned between the lights and throttled the motor back, idling his way into the harbor, pleased with himself that he'd weathered the storm and found the harbor, but that sense of accomplishment faded quickly into his anxiety for Sven.

He found a spot of open water along the main dock and bumped the dory against it. He went to tie the boat, but he had no lines. He and Sven never tied to a dock and they didn't carry any dock lines. He rummaged through the gear in the boat until he found the anchor and threw that onto the dock, wrapping the line around a cleat. Then he lay back in the boat for a moment, letting the rain splatter on his face, collecting his thoughts under the halo of the amber dock lights as they winked on to greet the night.

He heard footsteps.

"Hey, ain't you the kid from Naked Island? Orca."

Orca recognized the speaker. "Yeah, hi, Billy." The man had crewed on a crab boat that visited Cabin Bay once in a while.

"What're you doin' here?"

"I've got to find Corky. Sven's hurt."

"I seen him go up the dock to the Harborview just a couple minutes ago," Billy said. "Everybody's been down here today checkin' lines in the storm. C'mon, let's find him."

Orca jumped out of the skiff rejuvenated. He and Billy ran along the dock and up the gangway to shore. They crossed the street toward the lights of the tavern. He burst through the door, then stopped as a wave of dim light, heat and smoke hit him in the face. Low conversation and laughter broke over him. He rubbed his eyes to clear them and peer into the dimness of the room, searching for Corky.

A figure disentangled from a group of men at the far end of a long bar and the familiar face opened into a greeting: "Well, look what the storm blew in."

Orca stood just inside the doorway, feeling dull as the intensity of the storm wore off into the unfamiliarity of the new surroundings. Water dripped off his clothing to the floor.

By the time Corky reached him, he knew something was wrong. "It's Sven. What is it?"

Orca blurted: "His leg. He fell off the roof. It's broken. Compound."

"Let's go," Corky said and dragged Orca out of the tavern. They went to Corky's truck and he drove through the wet streets as fast as he dared.

"I sure hope they can fly in this weather," Corky said.

"Fly? I thought we'd have to take the *Salmania*," Orca said.

"They got a helicopter. They got one for the hospital and the Coast Guard's got one. You think that storm's lettin' up?"

"I don't know, I think so. It was better when I was coming up the arm. But it would be better there anyway."

"Feels like it's layin' down."

"Let's hope."

Corky slid to a stop in the hospital parking lot. They ran past a sign that read "Emergency Room," and through a door into a bright hallway. At the sight of the sign Orca flashed to a memory of the fish plant.

A man in white hospital clothes met them. "Can I help you?"

"We got a guy hurt, out in the sound. Boy says he's hurt bad."

The man looked at Orca. "He has a compound fracture of his upper leg." Orca told him.

"Where is he?"

"Naked Island. He's got a place in Cabin Bay," Corky answered.

"Let me see what I can do," the man said and he left them to walk into an office. They watched him pick up a telephone, dial and then speak into it. After just a few sentences he replaced the receiver and returned to Corky and Orca in the hall.

"They're going to try it. They'll bring the helicopter here to pick you up. Only one of you can go, though. There's just room for a medical technician, the patient and one passenger."

Corky looked at Orca. He could see the fatigue and the anxiety in the boy's face. "You better let me go," he said.

Orca wanted to argue. He wanted to rescue Sven. All he managed to say was, "What will I do? I don't want to wait here."

The roar of the helicopter overwhelmed their conversation as it landed on the circled "X" in the parking lot.

Another man in a white hospital suit joined them, introducing himself as Randy during their run outside. In the darkness behind the helicopter pad they could see automobile headlights approaching. While they waited for the rotors to spin to a stop, the car slid to a halt next to Corky's truck and Priscilla emerged to come running toward them.

"How did she know?" Orca asked Corky.

"Hard to tell," he said focusing on the helicopter.

"What happened?" Priscilla gasped, running up to them breathlessly. "Somebody called from that Harborview."

"Sven broke his leg. Boy came all the way in the storm," Corky said. "We're goin' to get him right now."

The pilot descended from the helicopter, opened a cargo compartment, then walked toward Corky and the medical tech carrying immersion suits. "Hope they fit," he said. "You get them on, we're on our way. Weather's lifting but it still might be touch and go."

The two men struggled into the full-body reddish suits, like the one the pilot wore. Once clothed and looking like orange Thanksgiving parade balloons, they hobbled to the helicopter and climbed aboard.

Priscilla held Orca's shoulder with her hand while they watched the machine lift off the ground and disappear into the darkness. When the night had absorbed the sound as well, she said, "We might as well go to my house and wait."

"Can't we wait here?"

"They said it would be a least a couple of hours. Why don't you come along?"

Orca turned and followed her docilely to her car. He felt deflated. Everything had passed out of his hands and he could do no more until they found Sven. He sat in the car quietly while she drove the few blocks to her home.

As they walked to the front door she said, "We'll be able to hear the helicopter from here." She made Orca remove his dripping rain gear outside the door, then let him indoors. He walked into a living room like he'd never seen before. After he discarded his boots she pointed to an upholstered chair and he sat down among flowers. "I'll make you a bowl of soup," she said and left him in her living room.

After a few minutes in the kitchen she returned with a bowl, but Orca had fallen sound asleep in the chair. She left him undisturbed to sit by the window closest to the hospital and wait.

On his mattress in Cabin Bay, Sven dozed fitfully despite Orca's admonition. He never fell asleep because each time he drifted his leg moved and sent a shock of pain through his body. As night drew over the cabin he wished Orca had left a light near his bed. He could see one on the table just a few feet away, but it might as well have been in Unakwik. He resigned himself to the darkness, dozing and wondering how the boy had fared on his trip.

The sound of the helicopter gradually grew to fill Cabin Bay and then the cabin itself. He saw his windows illuminated by its landing lights as the rotors beat the air overhead. Then he knew Orca had made it through the storm. He wasn't ready for the orange monsters who came through the door and he jumped when he saw them. That sent a pain shooting up his leg and he groaned.

"He's alive," Randy, the paramedic, said.

"Take more'n a broken leg to kill this guy," Corky added. "You all right?"

Sven muttered, "Yeah."

"Well, the cavalry's here," Corky said. "We'll have you goin' in no time."

Corky went to the table and lighted the lamp while Randy examined Sven's wound under the beam of a flashlight. He spoke more to Corky than to Sven. "It's a bad break," he said, "but they did the best they could. He'll be all right. I wonder how that boy got him indoors."

With Corky watching over his shoulder, Randy stabilized Sven's wound, wrapping it to prevent any movement while they transported him to the hospital. When he'd finished, the three of them gently lifted Sven to a stretcher and carried him out to the helicopter.

Beginning to feel the effects of medicine Randy had given him for the pain, Sven said, "Never thought I'd go as baggage."

When they had placed Sven aboard, Corky returned to the cabin. He made sure the fire had gone out, checked the windows and then doused the lamp. He closed the door and climbed into his seat in the helicopter. He could look down into Sven's face where he lay next to Corky's seat. With his pain eased and his wound stabilized, Sven slept, his snoring covered only by the helicopter engine as the machine rose into the air.

Priscilla heard the helicopter approach. She touched Orca's shoulder and the boy opened his eyes. Remembering where he was and what he was doing took a minute. When he realized his situation, he heard the helicopter. "Let's go," he said.

Priscilla drove like Corky to the hospital and they arrived in time to watch the helicopter land. Corky and Randy descended first and they walked swiftly to the back where they opened a cargo hatch. They pulled the stretcher out and began carrying it to the emergency room door. Two attendants pushing a gurney met them halfway and they moved Sven to the cart and rolled him the rest of the way. The old man slept through it all. Orca watched Sven's face as the gurney passed. To him Sven looked peaceful compared with the last time he'd seen him.

"Are you the boy?" Randy had sneaked behind Orca.

"That's him," Corky said.

"I can't believe the job you did. You might have saved his life. You might want to look at medicine when you grow up."

Orca blushed. Corky slapped him on the shoulder. Priscilla smiled at him.

"What will happen now?" he asked.

"He's going to have to have a little operation to set the leg. It looks like he had some muscle damage. We'll have to look at nerve damage. Judging by the way he looked and his attitude, I think he's going to be all right. It's going to take a while and he'll be out. You might as well go home and come back in the morning."

Priscilla touched his shoulder and tried to nudge him toward her car. He shook the hand off and said, "I'll wait here."

"You're sure he's going to be all right?" Corky asked Randy.

"Yes."

"I think I'll go home and get some sleep, then. You want to come with me?" he asked Orca.

The boy refused.

"Okay, then, I'll see you at first light. I'll bring some bull coffee."

"Good night, Corky," Priscilla said. "If he's going to stay, I think I will, too."

They followed the gurney into the hospital while Corky walked to his truck.

Randy indicated chairs and a couch in a waiting area and then went after Sven deeper into the hospital.

When Priscilla awakened from where she had dozed on the waiting room couch she couldn't find Orca. She sat up, pushed back a loose strand of hair and then went searching. From a nurse she learned Sven had come out of his operation and been taken into a room. She found the room number the nurse had told her, opened the door and entered. Sven slept in a field of white, his leg raised and suspended from the traction contraption. On the floor next to the bed, Orca slept on his side, his head cradled in the bend of his elbow.

Corky walked in behind her. "Ain't that a sight," he said.

Behind them in the hall they heard a commotion. They recognized the high pitched man's voice. "We crammed ten times that many in the foc'sl of a 50-foot ship," Smit hollered at a nurse who told him Sven already had more visitors than he was allowed.

"I'll have you keelhauled," he said. "Luff your sail."

Corky walked toward them, whispered something to the nurse and she stepped aside to let Smit swagger down the hall to Sven's room.

The noise had awakened Orca, who by this time stood bending over Sven. The old man's eyes had opened. "Doctor said you saved my life, maybe," Sven said.

Orca smiled. The rest of them gathered around the bed asking how Sven felt, if he needed anything, telling their parts in the adventure.

Sven listened to it all, smiling, glad to be away from the mattress in the dark house in Cabin Bay. His soft, graying blondish hair spreading across the field of white of the hospital bed, complemented by his benevolent smile, made him look almost beatific.

He studied the faces of the friends gathered around the bed and then spoke to Orca. "You put in quite a summer," he said.

"Sure did," Corky agreed. The others nodded.

"You fought off that sea lion. You saved me from the drink that once," Sven recalled.

"Those whales and the fishin'," Corky reminded them.

"He stood up to that bear," Priscilla said.

"He beat that cuttin' machine at the plant," Smit added.

"You made the run through that storm," Sven said.

"Course in the retellin' they'll get better."

"Yeah, it'll be a big shark or a whale he fought in the boat."

"Sure, and it'll be a whole boat fulla people he saved 'stead of just you."

"That bear'll be a grizzly and he'll wrestle it to the ground, probably kill it."

"He'll probably cross the whole Pacific in that storm."

"And it'll be a whole factory he beat cuttin' fish."

"Best one'll be he probably rode a whale to drive those fish into the net swingin' a popper like a lasso."

"See what you started now," Sven said, looking up from his pillow with a smile. "You better watch yourself."

"Why?" Orca asked.

"You're not careful," Sven said, "It ain't gonna be long, the boys on the boats are going to be starting to tell some of them stories about you."

Tim Jones

Tim Jones operated boats in Alaska's Prince William Sound professionally and for pleasure for almost 20 years. This is his sixth book; the first novel. Portions of *Keep the Round Side Down* were published previously in *Soundings,* a literary journal produced by Prince William Sound Community College.

Susan Ogle

Illustrator Susan Ogle lives and works in Cordova, Alaska. Before moving there in 1987, she and her husband spent ten years paddling their kayak in Prince William Sound. They guided guests on trips for part of the time, but their true mission was exploration and discovery. They moved to Cordova to become full-time Sound residents. Owners of a small bookstore named Orca Books on Main Street, they promote reading, art, and environmental causes. Susan paints every afternoon, usually large oils of the flora and fauna of the area, but she is sometimes tempted to illustrate a story she loves.